Born in Northe… of the
best and most … Having
worked as an … industrial
PR and journal… since
1975, turning o… consistently enter-
taining work.

By the same author

The Two-Timers
Palace of Eternity
One Million Tomorrows
Other Days, Other Eyes
Tomorrow Lies in Ambush
Orbitsville
Night Walk
A Wreath of Stars
Cosmic Kaleidoscope
Medusa's Children
Who Goes There?
Ship of Strangers
Vertigo
Dagger of the Mind
The Ceres Solution

BOB SHAW

A Better Mantrap

Nine science fiction and fantasy stories

PANTHER
Granada Publishing

Panther Books
Granada Publishing Ltd
8 Grafton Street, London W1X 3LA

Published by Panther Books 1984

First published in Great Britain by
Victor Gollancz Ltd 1982

ISBN 0-586-05706-4

Printed and bound in Great Britain by
Collins, Glasgow

Set in Times

To Harry Harrison
for hotdogs in Copenhagen

Contents

Conversion

When you love a woman you can forgive her for doing almost anything – but there has to be a limit.

And Sharly went way beyond that limit at 3.17 on the afternoon of June 12.

I know the exact moment it happened because the whole thing was recorded, though at a distance, by Arnie Archbold. He was making his scheduled round of Level Eight, pacing himself so as to be near the coffee machine when it came to break time, and was so wrapped up in visions of burying his nose in a hot foaming beaker that at first he wasn't even aware of Sharly on the gallery above him. His recorder picked her out, though.

All members of Icewell Security, myself included, wear wide-angle buttonhole machines which serve roughly the same purpose as flight recorders on aircraft – if one of us gets himself totalled the investigation team can run a tape through afterwards and settle back in comfort and decide what went wrong. To be fair, the recorders often provide valuable retrospective evidence concerning accidents and equipment failures, and I guess I should have been grateful that there was no doubt, none whatsoever, about what Sharly did. I was off the island on a five-day course at the time it happened, but the tape showed everything . . .

She came out of the Field Analysis suite on Level Nine and walked slowly in the direction of Structure Telemetry on the south side of the well. Nothing in her gait or manner suggested she was under any kind of stress. That was something to which I could testify because we had been lovers for some months and, although she was wearing a loose-fitting heatsaver, I could visualize the fine lazy action of every muscle in her body. She even, and it hurt me every time I watched it on playback, performed one of her most characteristic tricks with her hair – pushing the curls upwards slightly from the nape of her neck with one hand as though they were little springs upon which she was carrying out a compression test. I had seen Sharly do that a hundred times in reality, always when she was relaxed and pleased with herself and feeling good about life, and that made what came next all the more shocking.

About ten paces from the door to Structure Telemetry she came to an abrupt halt and clapped her hands to her temples. She rocked backwards and forwards for a few seconds, then turned towards the centre of the well. The blow-ups from Archbold's tape gave us a good look at her face in that crucial moment, and I pray never again to see anything so close to *The Scream*. Her eyes and mouth were circular black wounds, deep, incurable. She advanced to the gallery's safety rail, went up the four bars as though they were steps of a ladder, and walked off the top one into space.

Cold, empty, unforgiving, lethal space.

The sudden movement attracted Archbold's attention and dragged him around, with the result that all who studied his recorder tape got a clear view of Sharly's body plunging down into the well. There were lights down there, but they only had the effect of deepening the blackness in between, and her writhing figure disappeared into a complicated nether world of pipe runs, valves, ice bulwarks and pools of oil and oil-scummed seawater. She made no sound on the way down and the final impact was lost amid the massive heartbeats of the primary pump.

That's all there was to it.

Charlotte Railton had been part of the world scene as a

warm, intelligent, humorous person for twenty-six years, and suddenly – for no reason that I could fathom – she was gone. They didn't even manage to find her remains. The investigators who arrived next day by copter concluded that the body had been drawn into one of the main drainage outlets and expelled into the sea. They only stayed a day-and-a-half before heading back to Port Heiden and I received a distinct impression that if Sharly hadn't been a Grade One Engineer they would have taken off much sooner.

I resented that a lot. In fact, resentment was the driving force that got me through the following weeks. I felt other emotions, of course – grief, despair, anger, self-pity – but I was able to keep them in check by concentrating on my sense of outrage over all that had happened. One playback of Archbold's tape was enough to satisfy everybody concerned that they were dealing with a straightforward suicide, and from that point on the case was virtually closed. My testimony that Sharly had not been a suicidal type and had, in any case, been in excellent spirits immediately prior to her death was politely noted and dismissed as not being relevant. The evidence of the tape was all that mattered, and even I had to acknowledge it.

That was what helped crystallize my resentment against Sharly herself. Widows and widowers often feel anger – even though it is rarely expressed – towards their departed spouses for having spoiled everything by dying, and I came to know exactly what goes on in their minds. At times I actually hated Sharly for the pain she had caused me, then a reaction would set in and guilt would be added to all my other emotional burdens, and to help me squeeze out from under I would get out of bed, put on my uniform, sling the carbine on my shoulder and go patrolling the chill dark reaches of Icewell 37. I don't know what I was hoping to find. I wanted to blame *something* for

Sharly's death, but the rational part of my mind told me there was no chance of encountering a convenient and suitable external agent. There was no malign ghost of Level Nine, and even had there been it was unlikely that it could have been exorcized by a spray of high-velocity bullets.

The well is a creepy and fear-making place, though, especially at night. It is an artificial island constructed from ice, and it's hard for a non-scientist like me to accept that the localized coldness which makes it possible is imported from interstellar space.

Sharly knew as much about the telecongruency warp as anybody and she used to waste hours trying to make me understand how the focal point of the warp generator actually existed in two places at once – one of them here in the middle of the Bering Sea, and the other at some unknown location between the stars where the temperature was close to absolute zero. The position of the alpha-locus, the Earth-based focal point, could be accurately controlled and it was automatically drifted all over the island to keep the ice structure hard and strong, but nobody had any idea of the spatial location of the zeta-locus. Apparently it could have been just about anywhere in the universe. I never really got used to the idea of dangling a kind of cosmic fishing line in a distant part of space, but the notion held no fears for Sharly. It buoyed her up.

'This is only the beginning,' she had assured me once. 'The telecongruency warp is a powerful tool, but right now we're only debasing it. Using it as a heat sink to create ice castles in the ocean is easily the cheapest and best way yet of building deep-sea oil wells, but that's only playing with the concept. What we have to do is gain *control*. We ought to be able to reverse the potentials, make it a two-way thing. We should be able to pinpoint the zeta-locus anywhere we want it – and when that happens we'll be able to grow food or gather diamonds or pick flowers on any planet in the galaxy.'

When she talked that way I used to get jealous because the disks of misty white light appearing in her eyes were exactly the same as when we were making love and it was going well, but I had sense enough to keep my mouth shut about how I felt. Most people were surprised over a woman of her background taking up with a sergeant in Icewell Security, and as I couldn't quite believe it myself sometimes I knew not to strain my luck. And in the end it was Sharly's luck that ran out, not mine. She would never have the chance to pick those alien blossoms and I desperately wanted to know why.

I even, and this shows how obsessive my thinking became, considered murder. Post-hypnotic suggestion was one method I dreamed up – it seemed to me that somebody could have implanted a command for Sharly to walk off that gallery railing. Then there were exotic drugs which could suddenly trigger a self-destructive urge, and sonic beams which might scramble the brain and produce instant madness. Far-out ideas like those clamoured through my mind for hours on end, accompanied by equally bizarre notions about possible motives, so I was in a pretty abnormal psychological state during those nights when I was up there prowling on the high levels with the carbine nudging me in the back like a secretive accomplice. And I guess that's why I sensed there was something badly wrong as soon as Lieutenant Oliver came through on my personal radio.

'Sergeant Hillman,' he said in an irritated voice when I had identified myself and reported my position, 'what are you *doing* there? According to the roster you went off duty six hours ago.'

'I know that, sir, but I couldn't sleep tonight,' I told

him, raising my wrist set to my mouth. 'I decided to do an extra shift.'

'You decided to . . .' Oliver sounded incredulous now, as well as irritated. Obviously the idea of a man choosing to walk the galleries at three in the morning when he could have been wrapped up warm in bed was hard for him to ingest. 'Did you, by any chance, arrange to do Sergeant Dresch a favour and take over his shift for him?'

'No, sir.'

'Then why can't I raise Dresch or anybody else in the duty room?'

'Don't know, sir. He was there okay less than an hour ago when . . .' I stopped speaking as it dawned on me that it had been quite a long time since I had heard the elevator shuttling between any of the lower levels. Maddern and Katzen were the two men assigned to do the inspection rounds that night and neither was the type to use the stairs when there was any other option. I went to the rail and looked down into the well. The galleries below formed concentric circles, all of them beaded with lamps, surrounding the dimly-seen shapes of the wellhead equipment. A freezing mist drifted over everything, giving the most distant lamps the appearance of illuminated balls of lime-coloured candy-floss. The primary pump was beating steadily down there, transferring oil to the outer tanks, and I could hear the faint sound of ocean waves coming through the ice walls, but there was no sign of any human activity. There was no waving of flashlights or bellowing of supposed witticisms – two favourite pursuits of men on night inspection.

I eased the sling of the carbine off my shoulder and raised my eyes to scan the one gallery remaining above me. Saboteurs often came in over the top when they were mounting an all-out showpiece attack on a well, but I could see nothing up there apart from a circle of unblinking lights and a few stars barely piercing the greenish haze. Not comforted, I allowed the rifle to slide into my right hand.

'What are you doing, Sergeant? Are you still there?' Oliver was calling from Field Control, more than half-a-kilometre away at the opposite end of the island, and he was sounding increasingly annoyed. He didn't seem unduly alarmed at that stage, but I was the one who had been living on nerves for three weeks. I was the one who was keyed up to see spectres of death in every swirl of mist.

'I've been looking around,' I said, keeping my voice low. 'It all seems quiet.'

'It *is* quiet – that's what this is all about. See if you can raise Dresch on your ops band.'

I pressed the priority-call button on my wrist set and got no reply. 'He isn't answering.'

'*Damn!* You'd better get yourself down to the duty room and see what he's playing at. Tell him to contact me immediately. And Hillman?'

'Yes, sir?'

'Tell him he'd better have one hell of a good excuse for this.'

'Right!' I spoke crisply to conceal my deep uneasiness about the situation. The fact that it was three in the morning had something to do with it – three in the morning was a bad time, specially for somebody in my frame of mind – but, also, it was not beyond the bounds of possibility that Icewell 37 was under some form of attack. A mental scenario unfolded before me. International terrorist group . . . approach by submersible . . . take out guards by knife, silenced gun or gas . . . plant bombs . . . I could walk into anything down there, anything at all.

Even the thing that killed Sharly Railton.

The thought heaved itself into the full light of my

consciousness like some leviathan breaking the surface of a prehistoric swamp, bringing about an instantaneous and profound change in my outlook. It happens that way sometimes. You can be alone in spooky circumstances, alone but perfectly at ease, then a change takes place. Not in your surroundings, but inside you. An unseen hand is laid on your shoulder and an unheard voice whispers a few words of warning, and suddenly you're scared. And what makes it even more terrifying is that the silent voice is the voice of a friend. It is rueful, reproachful, concerned. Not only had you let your guard down, you had forgotten why we all need a guard in the first place – and that was oh so foolish . . .

'This is crazy,' I said, half-aloud, my gaze travelling on a circuit of Level Nine. The regularly spaced lights reflected off the back-drop of ice and from the prefabricated huts that housed an auxiliary power unit and some structural telemetry equipment. I knew that both huts were securely locked, and I had just come down from a tour of Level Ten, so the next logical step was to check out the gallery below and gradually work down to the duty room on Level Three. The elevator was only a short distance away, but it was a noisy, open-cage affair – a good way of advertising my exact movements to all and sundry.

I bolted a cartridge into the breech of the rifle, slipped the safety off and walked quietly to the nearest stair. The tower-like structure of the stairwell vibrated underfoot, and I cursed as I imagined it broadcasting messages about my position. I went down the four zig-zagging flights that took me to Level Eight, then did a cautious circuit of the entire gallery. Everything was as it should have been, and it was the same story on Level Seven and the two below that. Icewell 37 appeared to be running itself with its usual efficiency and there was no real need for human beings to fuss around the place at all – which was the principal reason for the rather hefty consumption of strong liquor on the night shift.

Now that I thought of it, Bert Dresch had been somewhat red of face and pink of eye when I saw him an hour earlier. It was possible that he was out cold in the office – it had happened before – and that Maddern, Katzen and the others were labouring to get him fit enough to answer his calls. The idea perked me up considerably and I was in a more relaxed mood when I began the circuit of Level Four. I even considered leaning over the rail and bellowing a few choice obscenities in the general direction of the duty room, which was basically a square hole cut into the ice on a level with the gallery below.

That was when I began to find small pieces of Dave Maddern.

I didn't even know what they were at first.

I was about a third of the way around Level Four when I saw that the metal floor of the gallery was badly cluttered up for a distance of about ten paces, as if somebody had spilled a couple of sacks of coal and had just let the pieces lie. Drawing closer, I saw that the fragments were deep red in colour, although it was difficult to be too certain in the artificial light. I disturbed several of them with my feet and found they were as hard as glass, and my next thought was that there had been an accident with some deep-frozen melons. Then I began to notice the whiteness of bone and a few seconds later saw three-quarters of Dave's face lying on the metal deck, like a discarded fright mask.

The shock seemed to clear my perceptions, for in that instant I became aware of other kinds of fragments lying around. There were irregular pieces of clothing – not with ragged edges, but as cleanly snapped as candy. There even were pieces of Dave's carbine, his helmet and his boots mingling with the glittering, dark-hued shards of what had been his flesh and internal organs.

'Oh, man,' I whispered. 'Oh, *man*!'

Suddenly fastidious about what my feet might accidentally touch, I tiptoed through the human debris, going faster and faster until I reached the uncontaminated part of the gallery at a near-run. The only conventional way of utterly destroying a man, as Dave Maddern had been destroyed, would have been to immerse him in a vat of liquid oxygen and then go to work on the frozen body with a sledge hammer – but there was another possibility.

All icewell personnel were assured that it was impossible for the alpha-locus to wander from its prescribed path. A computer and triplex controls kept it moving in a regular and pre-ordained pattern through the island, continuously reinforcing the ice structure with the unthinkable coldness of space, – but since when had men been able to build perfect machines? What if accidents sometimes did happen? We were busy sucking the last drops of oil from the Earth's crust, using new techniques that had been born of a desperate need, and no government in the world would draw back on account of a few operational mishaps. It would be perfectly natural to conceal the fact that every now and then there was a glitch in the telecongruency warp system, that every now and then the controls wavered and sent an invisible killer cruising through icewell living quarters. The bleak focus of interstellar cold would only have to brush through a man once to turn him into a crystalline statue.

I wasn't thinking as clearly as that while I ran for the stair that led down to the duty room. Shock, revulsion and fear had numbed my brain to the extent that I could scarcely nail down a coherent thought, and to make matters worse silent voices were screaming at me, hurling confused questions. *Is this what you've been looking for?*

What have you really explained about Dave Maddern? Was Sharly, in some way that you don't yet understand, driven over that rail? All right, you've frozen Maddern to death – but who or what broke him up like so much peanut brittle? And why?

I clattered down on to Level Three and sprinted a short distance along the gallery to the bright rectangle of the duty-room window, but slid to a halt just before reaching it, all instincts of self-preservation newly alerted.

The place was *cold*.

Icewells, by their very nature, are chilly places and our part of the world never warmed up, even in the middle of summer, but this was a different sort of coldness. It was hostile, totally inimical, far more so than the polar wind, and I sensed – even before looking into the room – that it was a bad omen.

Perhaps there had been three men in the room, perhaps as many as half-a-dozen. I wasn't able to say for sure, because the entire floor area was covered with a gruesome organic rubble, the redness of which was slowly beginning to disappear under a coating of rime frost. The furniture in the room was quite untouched, but its occupants had been pulverized, degraded, robbed of every last vestige of their humanity. Had it not been for the previous experience with Maddern I wouldn't even have recognized them for what they were.

And, reacting according to a classic human pattern, I had two virtually simultaneous thoughts: *Thank God that didn't happen to me,* and, *How can I make sure it doesn't ever happen to me?*

There was no room behind my eyes for anything but those two linked expressions of self-interest. I turned towards the elevator, determined to ride it up to Level Ten and the starlit surface of the island, and it was then that I saw the thing with many legs.

It was huge – easily the size of a car – black and nightmarish, and it was rushing towards me with hideous, soul-withering speed. There was no time to think, only to react, and so I did the most natural thing in the world.

I grabbed the gallery rail and vaulted over it into space.

For a second or so I fully expected to die – just as Sharly had done – but the remarkable thing was that I didn't mind. I had avoided being taken by the black obscenity and in that first airborne instant nothing else mattered – then I hit a large-diameter pipe and caromed off it into a latticed stanchion with a force that came near to breaking my ribs. My carbine flailed away into the dimness as I tried to throw my arms around the stanchion, but I had gained too much impetus for that to work and I continued falling, slithering, bouncing, impacting with steel, with lagged pipes, and finally with sloping buttresses of ice. Seemingly a long, long time after clearing the rail at Level Three I found myself lying on my side in a shallow pool of water. The surface below me was cold soft mud, and I knew I was almost right down on the seabed. All the complex structures and machinery associated with the wellhead towered up somewhere above me in a spatial confusion of shadows and areas of wan, misty light.

I lay without moving for an indeterminate period, not so much recovering from the fall as trying to construct a new version of reality in which there was a place for the horror I had glimpsed before jumping. I have been told many times since that I didn't actually see anything on Level Three. The theory is that human beings are naturally programmed, that we are incapable of perceiving any phenomenon which lies beyond the in-built limitations of our world-picture. I had faced a manifestation which inspired me with the ultimate dread, and I therefore had endowed it with the attributes of dread, which in my case happened to be a multiplicity of legs. All that might account for my impression that the thing, although black in colour, was transparent to some degree, like a badly done special effect in a movie, but I'm not sure if I really can accept all that stuff about the limits of perception. The people who are so positive about it have no idea what it was like to be there at the time, and I *knew* I had seen something big and black and with a lot of legs.

The trouble was that I wasn't certain of anything else. A kind of detachment had stolen over me as I lay there in the bilges of the icewell – waiting for my breath to return and for my body to give some evidence, one way or the other, about its general condition – and I was able to think more rationally than one might have expected. But I couldn't fit the pieces together. A number of my friends had died in a particularly horrendous manner, but to me the cause had seemed highly technical – I had predicted something like an intermittent fault in a computerized control system – and what had showed up was the worst possible embodiment of ancient nightmares and superstitions. Coincidence? Not likely. Impossible was more like it, but what sort of creature could or would turn its victims into ice and crunch them into a bloody slush? And where in God's name had it come from? There had to be something missing somewhere, a connection I had failed to make.

Still numb with sensory overload, I raised myself to a sitting position and tried to make a decision about what to do next. I wanted to get away from the well and reach Field Control at the other end of the island, and there were only two possible routes – through the service tunnel at Level Nine or along the surface from Level Ten. Both alternatives involved passing through the region of the well where the black thing stalked the galleries, and I had a powerful aversion to doing that. I put my wrist set to my mouth and tried calling up Lieutenant Oliver. There was no reply. Either the radio was broken, or the nightmare creature had roved further afield.

Perhaps I was the only person left alive on the entire island . . .

Repressing violent spasms of shivering, I looked around in the cavernous dimness and tried to establish exactly where I was. Faint reflections marked numerous dark pools, and there was no way of telling which might be drain tunnels through which waste liquids were pressure-pumped into the sea. This part of the well was a Stygian no-man's-land, visited very infrequently by maintenance inspectors, and to get out of it I would have to locate a ladder and climb it to the first gallery. I decided the most likely place would be near the automatic pumping station which was steadily pounding somewhere off to my left, rippling the reflected lights.

Turning in that direction, I lurched to my feet and immediately became aware of a pale object a few paces away. My eyes still hadn't adjusted properly to the darkness, but the object seemed to have human proportions. It was slumped against a discarded wooden box in much the same attitude as a rag doll would have assumed. I stared at it, trying not to cringe, as a terrible idea wormed into my mind followed by an equally terrible dawning of recognition.

Sharly!

I had found Sharly's body.

Extraordinary situations, I have learned, elicit extraordinary human responses. I was already far too shocked by what had been happening to react to the ghastly discovery in a normal manner – instead I felt a pang of rage, resentment and hatred towards the so-called investigators from Icewell Exec who had been so careless, so anxious to get back to their warm offices on the mainland, that they had allowed a thing like this to happen. Had they done their job properly, Sharly would have been found three weeks earlier and given a decent burial. She wouldn't have been left to bloat and rot down here in the oil well's stinking black sump.

I think it was with some notion of determining the full extent of the investigators' crime that I approached Sharly's body and knelt down before it. My gaze hunted over the human wreckage, recording the sickening distortions of the broken legs, the multiple seepages of blood through her clothing, the lacerations which had disfigured that beautiful face . . .

Oddly, though, *very* oddly, Sharly's head was upright, not touching the wooden box, apparently supported by a firm neck.

Stricken, bemused by new visions of horror, I slowly put out my hand and touched her cheek. The blackly contused eyelids snapped open.

'Hello, Jack,' she burbled. 'I've been waiting for you.'

I screamed. Throwing myself backwards from her, I screamed as only a person who has been totally betrayed by reality knows how. There are some things that simply never should happen to a person, and one of them had happened to me and my entire being protested about it until the moment when screaming was no longer enough. Eventually I had to look at Sharly again and try to cope with the situation.

'Don't be afraid of me, Jack,' she said in a voice which seemed to force its way through a larynx filled with water. 'I can't harm you.'

'You . . . are . . . dead,' I accused, raising myself to a sprinter's crouch in readiness for the flight which might become necessary at any second.

She smiled, and to this day I wish she hadn't. 'How can I be dead if I'm talking to you? Come on, Jack – take me out of here.' She extended her arms, begging for my help.

For a moment I wavered. I *wanted* Sharly to be miraculously alive, and I was in no condition to think rationally. Perhaps she had survived the fall – just as I had done. Perhaps she had somehow managed to cling on to life down here in spite of her awful injuries and the cold and the wet. Then I noticed that the effort of speaking, of expelling air, had caused black fluids to spill down her chin. I backed off a little further, shaking my head.

She must have been able to interpret the reaction because she lowered her arms and the ghastly caricature of a smile left her face. 'I wanted to die,' she said. 'I tried to die, but it was no use. I may have to live a very long time . . . but I don't want it to be down here, Jack . . . not like this. You've got to help me.'

'I . . . I don't understand.' That was true – and most of all I couldn't understand what was keeping me from running. Perhaps it was just that my mind had reached its saturation point as far as horror and fear were concerned, enabling me to hold my ground and carry on something like a normal conversation.

'Perhaps you understand better than you realize . . .' Her throaty, bubbling voice was almost lost in the sound of the primary pump. 'I was supposed to be the great warp engineer, but your instincts were better than mine, Jack. You said it was like . . . dangling a fishing line in a distant part of the universe. I laughed at that because I knew how empty space actually is . . . but we caught something . . . then it caught me.'

I nodded because it seemed the only thing to do. A black multi-legged nightmare was roaming the icewell above me, presumably in search of new victims, and I was crouching in the throbbing darkness at the bottom of the well beside the undead corpse of the woman I had loved. And all I could do was nod my head.

'Zeta-loci are highly visible objects as they drift about the galaxy . . . to certain kinds of senses, that is . . . I was being pursued . . . wrong word – a virus does not pursue its host . . . tried to escape through the zeta-locus, but found I was trapped . . . chose the most suitable instrument of change, but there was resistance . . .'

The hissing beat of the pump was obliterating many words, words whose import was totally bizarre, but I was oddly – almost telepathically – in tune with what was being said to me. My understanding was only partial, but it came quickly because I was preconditioned. I had believed all along that Sharly's was not an ordinary suicide. She had been possessed by a disembodied life form that the icewell's warp had somehow dredged from out of space, and rather than submit to it she had walked off the top rail of Level Nine. The tragedy was that her bravery had been in vain. The life force that had locked itself on and into her was so powerful and tenacious that it could compel a ruined body to go on living. Sharly was now Sharly-Plus, and her main preoccupations were those of an alien being . . .

'I can't walk on these legs, Jack,' she was saying in her laboured gargling voice. 'The bones are smashed . . . no longer work as levers . . . but the arms are all right . . . and you could get me to Field Control, Jack. You remember how I used to talk about reciprocity . . . the need for a two-way exchange . . . I know how to do it now . . . you can make it possible for me to escape . . . '

'You're too late,' I said harshly, marvelling at my ability to think and speak. 'The thing you're running from – it's already here.'

'But that's impossible!' Her head turned jerkily. 'I would have *known* . . . my senses can't be so . . .'

'I jumped from Level Three to get away from it. They're all dead up there.'

'So that's why you're here . . . I thought I had finally managed to get through to you . . .' Her eyelids closed, wavered and opened. 'But you couldn't have escaped from a Taker so easily . . . Did you see it?'

'I saw it, all right.' The memory made my present situation almost bearable. 'Black thing. Legs.'

'How big?'

'It was the width of the gallery.'

'That means it's still trying to emerge . . . still tied to the alpha-locus . . .' Her eyelids flickered again, interrupting her blind white stare like signal lamp shutters. 'Jack, you're going to carry me to Field Control . . .'

I still think there must have been some element of mental control involved, in spite of all she told me about the nature of the Takers and what it would mean to this planet if one of them were to be set free here. Otherwise, I don't know how I could have borne to pick her up. She stank, my once-beloved Sharly did, and she was *cold* and the lower half of her body felt like pieces of miscellaneous junk in a plastic sack. Perhaps the worst thing of all was the way she slid her arm around my neck. The movement felt so natural it reminded me that Sharly wasn't truly dead, that her own original personality was trapped in the decaying shell, being used by an alien creature which had no right to be on Earth. For an instant I almost squeezed her, to try communicating across the gulf that separated us, but commonsense reasserted itself just in time.

'The alpha-locus is programmed to pass through each region of the ice structure once in every two hours,' came the throaty voice in my ear as I stood up with a dead weight in my arms. 'It is now at the far end of the island and dropping to the lowest level. That means it will be back here at the well in less than five minutes, bringing the Taker with it. It will pass very close to this point, and the Taker will have emerged more fully by then, so it will appear to be much larger. We must reach Level Five or higher within the next four minutes.' The engineering analysis of our situation made use of Sharly's knowledge, but there was a clinical quality in the phrasing which told me it was Sharly-Plus who was speaking. And she was informing me that I had to move quickly or die.

Guided by the sound of the pump, I lurched in that direction with my burden. The surface underfoot was hidden in a slurry of mud, oil and water, and was made more treacherous by the presence of industrial detritus – pieces of cable, submerged metal bars and slimed sections of timber. I kept falling to my knees and each time that happened it was harder to stand up again. Only numbness and shock kept me from realizing the extent of the punishment I had taken during the hurtling descent from Level Three. By the time I located the ladder which slanted up to the first gallery I had serious doubts about my ability to climb it, but the thing I was carrying gave assistance, reaching for higher rungs with eager hands and pulling upwards with unnatural strength. There was no mistaking the urgency which galvanized those limbs and fingers. Sharly-Plus and I had one thing in common – we were both deathly afraid of the Taker and wanted to get as far away from it as was possible in the time available.

I had no check on how quickly our time was running out, but it seemed to me that four minutes had passed when I reached the elevator and found that the passenger cage was somewhere high above, lost in the alternating circles of light and dark. There was a dead silence after I thumbed the call button. For a panicky moment I thought the power was off, then the steel lattice enclosing the elevator shaft began to thrum. I instinctively glanced at

Sharly, got my first good look at her face in adequate lighting and turned away with my eyes closed.

Standing there in the self-imposed darkness I could almost sense the alpha-locus racing back through the length of the island and carrying with it the night-black antithesis of life I had glimpsed earlier, still trapped and squirming, but grown much bigger now, more capable of destroying me without even being aware of my existence. A Taker, from what I had learned, was less of a malevolent being than an unconscious agent of entropy. It seemed to be a kind of materialized force which reacted blindly against organization in matter or energy, but the outcome was just the same as if it were a hate-crazed animal which had scented my blood and was coming to claw me apart. Every nerve in my body was telling me that I ought to be running for my life, and all I could do was stand there on the first gallery and pray for the elevator to arrive. It seemed to me that the air was growing noticeably colder.

When the cage finally clanged to a halt in front of me I grabbed for the sliding door, but Sharly was already dragging it open. The air *was* colder now, filled with a premonitory chill. Sick with fear, I stumbled into the cage and pressed the button for Level Ten. There was another silence, the machinery playing cruel pranks again, then the cage began its painfully slow climb. I counted the numbers painted at each level. Two. Three. Four.

It was when the cage was passing Level Five that the Taker went by not far beneath us. I didn't see anything this time, but a convulsion went through the upper part of Sharly's body and I felt the temperature in the cage momentarily dip to sub-Arctic levels. For a few seconds I was unable to breathe. I stood perfectly still and wished miserably that I could be somewhere warm and safe and very far away from Icewell 37.

'The alpha-locus is programmed to describe an ascending helix around the well shaft,' Sharly husked. 'Multiple passes may be required in some areas – I can't say without the hourly report on wave and tide action – but the entire operation is unlikely to take more than thirty minutes. When it is completed the locus will make a scan-pattern return on the surface of the island, terminating at Field Control. We must get there well ahead of it. Do you understand?'

I nodded, not trusting myself to speak. Field Control was actually a converted trawler housing all the essential telecongruency warp generating and control equipment. Two years earlier, working by satnav, it had taken up station near the drilling site and had built around itself a rectangular island of ice. The well and the embedded ship were at opposite ends of the artificial island, and I would have to travel the length of it with Sharly. That in itself wasn't much of a problem, because there were Moke transports for communal use both on the surface and in the Level Nine connecting tunnel. My main worry was about what would happen at the far end. There was no way, especially in the time available, of explaining the facts to a man like Lieutenant Oliver, yet I couldn't see how I was going to get Sharly-Plus into the warp control room unobserved.

I was still trying to think constructively about the matter when the cage reached Level Ten and jolted to a halt. We were in a small machinery house situated on the topmost gallery of the well. When I opened the door I was very conscious of being on the surface. A strong, ocean-tanged breeze hustled noisily through the various superstructures, and the clustered lights of Field Control were visible at the far end of the island. The air was clear in comparison to the chilly mists that drifted far down in the icewell, and the moon was riding high overhead, looking serene and remote. Everything was deceptively normal.

'We must hurry,' Sharly said in her rattling whisper. 'There is very little time.'

Trying to avoid looking directly at her, I turned my head and saw there were three open-sided Mokes parked only a few paces away. I went to the nearest and placed the undead body in the rear seat, wincing at the pain which needled through my side as I bent forward. With a considerable effort of will, I tucked one of the shattered legs inside the line of the vehicle and made to climb into the driving seat.

'Where are you going, Hillman?' a man's voice called. 'What do you think you're doing?'

Lieutenant Oliver came striding towards me from the shadow of a crane shed, a borrowed carbine in hand. His oval face was pink with anger and exposure, and the overlong sandy moustache he had grown to make himself look more mature was bending this way and that in the wind. The winter-weight coat he had put on seemed several sizes too large, giving him something of the appearance of an extra in a low-budget movie, but I'd had run-ins with him before and knew him to be an ambitious man who jealously guarded his career prospects.

'I've got to get down to Field Control right away,' I said. 'There's no time to explain now.'

'*Sergeant!* Am I hearing you right?'

'You'd better,' I replied heavily, 'because I'm only going to say it once. Dresch and all the others who were on duty tonight are dead, torn apart. The thing that did the killing is still down there, around the lower levels, and there's only one way to get rid of it.'

Oliver's eyes narrowed. 'Are you telling me there's a bear or something loose on this well?'

'Not an ordinary animal.' I hesitated, aware of how

ridiculous I was going to sound, but with no alternative but to press on with the story. 'It's some kind of alien thing the warp has sucked in from space. It killed Dresch and the others, and . . . Look, I've got to go.' I reached for the Moke's ignition key.

'Don't move!' Oliver stepped in front of the vehicle. 'I think you're drunk, Hillman. Falling-down drunk, by the look of you, and I'll bet Dresch is worse.' He raised his wrist communicator to his lips. 'Pilgrim and Dubois! Forget about checking out the galleries – go straight to the duty room. Pilgrim? Answer me, Pilgrim.'

'If you've sent them down the well, they're dead. I can't explain any more now, but you'd better grab yourself a power boat and get the hell off the island, and that's the truth.' I switched on the Moke's engine and in the same instant Oliver snapped his rifle up to point at my chest.

'Switch off and get out of the vehicle,' he ordered, moving around to my side.

I clenched and unclenched my fingers on the wheel, afraid of getting myself shot, but even more alarmed about this fresh delay in reaching Field Control. Vital seconds were flitting past – and the Taker was on its way.

'I'm warning you, Hillman,' Oliver said, drawing level with me, reaching a position from which he could get an unimpeded shot. 'If you don't switch off that eng . . .' His voice faded out as he saw what lay on the Moke's rear seat.

'It's Charlotte Railton's body,' I heard myself explain. 'I found it down in the bilges.'

'And you carried it up here! What's the matter with you, Hillman?' Oliver moved closer to the inert body, apparently repelled and fascinated. 'Nobody in his right mind *carries* a thing like . . .'

Somehow I knew what was coming next and was completely prepared for it. Oliver wasn't. When Sharly snatched the rifle out of his hands he made a sound that was both a whimper and a moan, and which was drowned in the snarl of the Moke's exhaust as I gunned the engine. The wheels spun for a moment on the plastic mesh which covered the working areas of the island, then we were accelerating down the vee-shaped perspective of lights which terminated in Field Control. I watched the mirror to see if Oliver would come after us in one of the remaining vehicles, but he simply stood there until I lost sight of him.

The ramp to the old trawler's main deck usually had a guard on it, but I could see from quite a long way off that it was deserted, and it occurred to me that reaching the actual warp control room might be easier than I had anticipated. Oliver could have taken all available security men to the well with him, and as it was week-end there was a good chance that all the engineering staff had flown off to Alaska. If one or two had stayed behind, I had Oliver's carbine with which to keep them in line while Sharly-Plus did whatever it was she needed to do.

I have to admit that I had no real understanding of what her plans were. Even if I had been able to hear her properly down in the bottom of the well, even had I been in any condition for absorbing abstruse ideas, I still wouldn't have been able to understand. Sharly alone had always been able to think and talk rings around me – and now she was Sharly-Plus. There was another mind there, an alien mind accustomed to dealing with alien concepts, and in company with it my Sharly had travelled far beyond the bounds of contemporary human knowledge.

All I knew for sure was that the Taker was squirming through into my part of the continuum, and the only way to stop it was to get the dismaying object that was Sharly's body into the field control room without any delay. I broadsided the Moke up to the base of the ramp on locked wheels, jumped out and gathered the body up in my arms. Again it slid one arm around my neck, but I was too far gone to notice much. I struggled up the ramp, crossed an area of deck and opened a door in the superstructure and got inside. The companionways in the trawler were narrow, certainly not designed for the carrying of awkward loads, but I caromed my way along them, bursting doors open with my shoulder until we were in the rebuilt part of the ship, the area which housed the warp controls. In contrast to the spartan conditions elsewhere, this was a region of thick carpet and indirect lighting, with one large window giving a longitudinal view of the island.

'Over there,' Sharly burbled in my ear, pointing at a long console before which were three swivel chairs. I lowered her into the nearest chair, only then becoming aware of a disturbing new facet of the situation. Until that moment I had been under the impression that my plunge from Level Three had left me with nothing but a selection of bruises and perhaps a fractured rib, but all at once there came the queasy suspicion that something inside me was ruptured and leaking. I had always purposely avoided medical knowledge and so was unable to make any kind of diagnosis, but there was a definite wrongness at the centre of my being, and its effects seemed to be spreading. Holding a stanchion for support, I examined my surroundings and found them curiously distant and unreal. Horizontal surfaces appeared to slope, and solid objects tended to shimmy.

This must be what it's like to faint, I thought, bemused. *Or perhaps this is the way you die!*

There followed a period of blurry confusion. I clung to the stanchion, internally preoccupied, and was only dimly aware of what Sharly-Plus was doing. It meant nothing to me that she was moving herself from chair to chair by the strength of her arms, or that she was using the same physical power to strip cover plates from equipment banks and doors from cabinets. Other forces were at work too, because I know I saw drawers slide in and out by themselves, saw looms of wiring change shape like live creatures, heard the crackle of high-voltage current, smelt the ozone and the hot metal. I was in the presence of things far beyond my understanding. For a time Sharly-Plus was superhuman, perhaps supernatural, and she was imposing her unearthly will on artefacts of this Earth, changing their relationships and functions, moulding them to suit her own purpose. Stray currents of psychokinetic energy rippled the carpet, sent papers skywards like flocks of startled birds, tugged at my clothing. The very air hummed and crooned and was disturbed by strange flitting shadows. All I could do was stand there and try to endure.

The lull, the onset of silence, took me by surprise.

Fighting for a clearer picture of what was going on, I noted that Sharly-Plus, her head flung back at an unnatural angle, had ceased her labours and was staring at the window. I looked in the same direction and, in spite of all that had happened within and around me, I quailed.

The night-time scene was basically a familiar one – multiple rows of lights, flanking the helicopter pad and the STOL runway, converged on the accretion of greenish illuminated rectangles and points of brilliance which marked the head of the well shaft. The moon was too high to be visible from inside the control centre, but it sketched in a silver-grey background of ocean and cloud-vaulted sky pierced by stars.

And against that background something was moving. Something incredibly huge, and black, and with too many legs.

'Breakthrough . . . too soon,' Sharly-Plus breathed. She reached towards a tilted and displaced keyboard on the console and began to tap instructions into it at high speed. At the far end of the island the Taker loomed high above the cranes and machinery houses, its legs slowly windmilling across the sky, quivering, questing . . .

'Get away from here, Jack,' Sharly-Plus said, or it may even have been Sharly, for in that moment her voice was almost human. 'Take a boat and go fast.'

I gaped at her back, nodded without speaking, then pushed myself away from the stanchion and ran, partially doubled over, for the ship's entrance ramp. Whatever it was that was damaged inside me reacted by producing spasms of pain, nausea and weakness, and by the time I reached the bottom of the ramp I was sobbing aloud with every breath. It was only thirty yards to the jetty, but the crossing seemed to take a long time and all the while, at one corner of my vision, the night was hideously turbulent and alive.

I have no clear memory of reaching a boat, nor of starting the engine and casting off and heading out to sea. But in spite of being semi-conscious at the time, I can recall vividly what it was like when Sharly turned Icewell 37 into a miniature sun. I lay there, shielded by the gunwale, drowning in the sudden awesome wash of noontime brilliance.

It lasted less than three seconds, but when it was over the icewell and everything connected with it – including the Taker and the mortal remains of Sharly Railton – had vanished in a mile-high column of fire and steam. Clouds of vapour were rolling upwards to the stratosphere, and circular waves were racing towards the ocean's distant shores with their message that a battle had been fought and won.

I lowered my head and wept till I lost consciousness.

* * *

They'll never believe me!

The words of the old song kept mingling and merging with my own thoughts, interfering with all attempts at lucidity. I lay in that hospital bed for the best part of a day, fighting off the drugs that had cushioned my nervous system during the excision of the spleen, and my principal concern was that nobody would give my story credence. It was the kind of inversion of priorities which is typical of the semi-lucid state. I imagined myself to be in the situation which crops up so often in children's fiction, the one in which all evidence of a fantastic adventure is maddeningly lost and the protagonist, if he speaks at all, meets knowing smiles of disbelief.

But I had forgotten about my buttonhole recorder.

It had continued working through the entire episode, and its tape became one of the single most valued artefacts in history, even though the evidence was imperfect in many ways. The Taker, for example, registered only as a vague area of darkness – with no sign of the legs which I had seen so distinctly; and the scene in Field Control was obliterated here and there because I had been clinging to the stanchion. However, the scientific and technical teams got most of what they wanted from it. They were able to see something of what Sharly-Plus had done to the warp control complex, to deduce others, and to make inspired guesses about much of the rest.

That was three years ago, and they believe that before another three have passed the first of the new breed of power stations will be operational. It will employ much the same equipment as an icewell, but with the big difference that the zeta-locus, instead of wandering blindly in space, will be positioned exactly where we want it. Instead of serving as a heat sink for the construction of ice islands, it will be used to import unlimited energy from the vicinity of the sun.

Visionaries, and there are quite a few of them in the scientific community, say it won't be too long until we achieve the reciprocity that Sharly used to talk about, that an advanced form of the telecongruency warp is going to give us instantaneous travel to the stars. As Sharly once put it, 'We'll be able to grow food or gather diamonds or pick flowers on any planet in the galaxy.'

I guess that's the sort of memorial she would have chosen for herself.

Crossing the Line

When Hewitt picked the dog up he got the impression it was slightly heavier than a real animal, but that might have been because it was still inert, a dead weight in his hands. He ran his fingers through the wiry hair, noting as he did so that the markings of a Lakeland terrier had been perfectly simulated. There was no doubt that the dog was very well made, but there was a lingering question in his mind as to whether it was worth a month's salary. He turned the compact body upside down and gave it a tentative shake.

'It won't rattle,' Burt Pacer said, from behind the commissary counter. 'Fluid solenoid construction throughout. Just like real muscles.'

'I can tell it's a good machine, Burt.' Hewitt frowned into the dog's immobile face. 'It's just the money.'

Pacer smiled sympathetically. 'We're a long way from Earth.'

Hewitt nodded, wondering if the comment was meant to explain the cost of the little robot or to justify the extravagance of buying it. There were other things he and Liz could do with the money, and for weeks he had been stoutly rejecting the idea of getting a dog for Billy. The trouble with domestic budgets, however, was that they were sometimes required to accommodate items whose true value could not be reckoned in cash. Yesterday evening, for instance, Hewitt had stood at the rear window of his house and had watched his eight-year-old son scamper to the far end of the mowed plot which was their back garden. There had been nothing to stop Billy running on through the longer grass of the plain beyond, but the boy had come to a halt and had stood there, reluctant to advance into alien territories. The sight of the small figure – utterly alone, upright, probably thinking of friends he had left behind on Earth – had filled Hewitt with sadness. With the emotion had come uncertainty about the ambitions which had led him to subject his family to the rigours of the Ferrari Transfer, and he had reacted by deciding to enquire about a dog first thing in the morning. The memory of how he had felt at that moment resolved the conflict in Hewitt's mind.

'Okay,' he said. 'You talked me into it.'

'Right.' Pacer took Hewitt's citizenship card and showed it to the computer terminal along with the dog's specification tag. He worked with an airy casualness which was intended to remind people that he was a qualified electronics man and only helped out at the commissary on a voluntary basis, for the good of the colony.

His official ownership of the dog, now confirmed, prompted Hewitt to start activating it. He probed at the back of its skull with his fingertips, searching for the subcutaneous push-button which was mentioned in the instruction leaflet.

'What are you doing?' Pacer said with some show of concern.

'Trying to turn it on.'

'I thought it was for your boy.'

Hewitt was mildly surprised. 'What's that got to do with it?'

'It's best if the prime owner is the one who activates the dog,' Pacer said. 'His should be the first face it sees.'

'Is this a joke?'

'No joke, Sam. All our dogs are the same. We programme in a canine personality which causes each dog to fixate on one special owner.'

'I don't know if I like the sound of that,' Hewitt said slowly.

'Oh, it'll be friendly to everyone else in the family, but it's important to have that one special relationship with the owner – that's what the whole boy-and-his-dog thing is all about.' Pacer had forgotten to be nonchalant, and a note of evangelical zeal was creeping into his voice.

'I just wanted to make sure it works,' Hewitt said defensively. 'I was going to switch it off again.'

'You can't do that, Sam.'

'What? Why not?'

'The brain is too sensitive and complex for that sort of treatment. It *can* be wiped clean, of course, but it has to be done progressively, using special equipment.'

'What have I bought here?' Hewitt set the rodog down in a swath of sunlight which lay across the counter. The individual hairs of its coat gleamed brown and black and white. 'It sounds like it's going to be as much trouble as a real dog.'

'A piece of clockwork wouldn't be much use to your boy,' Pacer commented, folding his thin freckled arms. 'Besides, there's the security aspect – the way the dog is made, no stranger can come along and steal it and blank out its memory of the proper owners.'

'I must be mad,' Hewitt said as Pacer fitted the dog into its carrying case. 'I can't afford to pay eight hundred monits for a supertoy.'

'You can always bring it back.' Pacer closed up the plastic case and slid it across the counter. 'If young Billy gets tired of it, or maybe you get another transfer, bring it in and I'll give you a fifty percent refund.'

'Can you do that?'

'No trouble. We can wipe the brain clean and sell the dog to somebody else. There's a big demand for this sort of product on Mesonia.'

'I may take you up on that,' Hewitt said. He lifted the case and went out into the bright mid-morning ambience of the street. This part of the colony had been in existence for eighty years and the maturing shrubs and ornamental trees outside the buildings created a sense of homeliness and permanence. Feeling the warmth of the spring air, Hewitt was glad he had decided to walk to the commissary building. He was tall for a colonist and he enjoyed the exercise of striding along the busy street in the direction of the southern residential development where he lived.

His route home took him past the arrivals and induction centre, which was a pyramidal structure whose architecture reinforced the dual-space properties of the pyramid-shaped receiving chamber at its heart. The number of vehicles parked outside it suggested to Hewitt that the null-space transmission conditions were favourable and that new colonists were being brought through. He could imagine them stepping out of the chamber, naked and hungry, stunned with the realization that they – in one instant – had left Earth and all its ways forty light years behind them. The Ferrari Transfer was psychologically brutal, as well as being fantastically expensive, but it was the only practicable form of interstellar travel that mankind had ever devised.

At least, Hewitt thought, inhaling the scented air, *the newcomers are getting a good day for it.*

As he walked up the long slope his views of the surrounding terrain became more extensive and he could see, stretching away to the west, the manufacturing areas which were supplied from the mineral-rich hills beyond. He was always impressed and stirred by the visible evidence of how the original cadre of pioneers, equipped with only a few basic machines, had managed to create a viable settlement on an alien planet. That was where the real challenge and excitement of colonization lay – in being in the first hundred, stepping out of the chamber on to virgin soil, living rough and working hard to pave the way for others. It was also where the big money lay. Tax-free quadruple pay for the first four years, with nothing much to spend it on, and – at the end of that time – prestige and a plushy engineering consultancy. As an expert on extraterrestrial soil mechanics, Hewitt was doing well on Mesonia – on a raw planet it was vital to know how much or how little in the way of foundations each costly new structure required. But he had arrived seven years behind the trail-blazers, when the bloom was off the cosmic grape, and his only chance of rapid advancement lay in the possibility that he might be selected for a later outward thrust.

Hewitt neared the end of the main road and turned in to the side avenue in which his single-storey house was the last one before the sea of grass began. Billy was sitting on the front step, alone as usual. The Company encouraged settlers with young families, for the simple reason that a child's body had less mass than an adult's and therefore could be transmitted far more cheaply. It was an economical way of getting future colonists into space. Few people who underwent the Ferrari Transfer liked bringing children with them, however, and the colony tended to be a lonely place for a boy of eight. Billy, ever watchful, saw Hewitt as he turned the corner and came running to meet him.

'Hi, Dad!' Billy fell into step beside Hewitt and took his hand. 'What's in the case?'

'Guess.' Hewitt had not said anything about going to look at a dog because his common sense might have reasserted itself in time to prevent the purchase.

'Well,' Billy said soberly, taking measured paces, 'it can't be a dog.'

'Can't it?'

'*Dad!*' Billy looked up at him, his round face an absurd caricature of delight, and Hewitt experienced a pang of pure happiness. He handed the case to his son and almost laughed aloud with pleasure as Billy darted ahead and disappeared around the corner of the white-painted house. Hewitt followed at an unhurried pace and was met at the kitchen door by Liz, who was wearing a silver spark-suit which emphasized the blackness of her hair. The Saturday-morning aroma of coffee wafted around her through the open door.

'Thanks, Sam,' Liz said, pressing her cheek against his lips. 'I know we can't really afford it, but it'll be so good for Billy.'

'It's all right.' He drew her against him. 'We'll just economize on toothpicks and string and things like that for a while.'

'You're crazy,' she said warmly. 'Come in and have some coffee.'

'Okay, but I'll show Billy how to get the dog going first.' Hewitt paused as he heard his son talking to someone in the living room. 'Who's in there?'

Liz looked apologetic. 'Carl's here.'

'Aw, *Christ*! This is supposed to be my day off.'

'I know, darling, but I can't very well send him away when he calls at the door.'

Hewitt closed his eyes for a moment, then went through to the living room, suppressing his resentment over a family occasion having been invaded and spoiled. Carl Mendip was slightly older than Hewitt and was his immediate senior in the constructional engineering section. He boasted a lot about being able to bank most of his salary, and spent much of his off-duty time sitting in Hewitt's favourite chair extolling the pleasures of bachelorhood. When Hewitt entered the room Mendip already had the dog out of its case and was handing it to Billy.

'Morning, Sammy boy,' Mendip said. 'These things aren't worth the money, you know.'

'It was worth it to me.'

Mendip shrugged. 'I wouldn't have paid it.'

'Did anybody ask you to?'

'In a bad mood, are we?' Mendip examined Hewitt with calm amusement.

Hewitt stared back at him, trying to be impassive, wishing he had controlled his tongue. One man in their engineering section was likely to be transferred to Nimrod, a world which had been broached only recently. As the senior and most experienced man, Mendip had the best chance, but Company policy had dictated that he should also nominate a member of his section for consideration, and – with an unsubtle display of magnanimity – he had put Hewitt's name forward. Ever since then the dominating factor in their relationship was that Mendip's recommendation could be withdrawn by him at any moment. It was a yoke which Hewitt wore with increasing irritation even though he knew the situation was fairly temporary.

'Sorry, Carl,' he said, and turned his attention to Billy, who was sitting cross-legged on the floor with the rigid-limbed dog in his lap. 'What are you going to call it, son?'

'I think I'll call him Bramble,' Billy replied.

'What a name!' Mendip gave a hoot of derision. 'You can't call it that.'

Billy looked puzzled. 'Can't I, Dad?'

'Bramble suits him very well and that's what we'll call him.' Hewitt moved in between the other man and his son and knelt down. He guided Billy's finger on to the activating button and explained what he had to do. Liz came into the room at that moment and watched as Billy held the dog with its face towards him and depressed the button. There was no sound, but the rodog yawned as though wakening from a sleep, its eyes brightened into life, the short legs stirred slightly as they adjusted to distribute the weight, and the ribcage began to pulsate in a simulation of breathing.

'Bramble!' Billy spoke in a rapt voice. 'Bramble!'

Bramble began to wag his tail.

In spite of himself, adult though he was, Hewitt felt a thrill of awe at the achievement of the robotics engineers. 'Set him down and go into the kitchen and see if he'll come to you,' he said.

Billy put the dog on the floor, backed away from it until he was out of sight in the kitchen and called its name. Bramble wagged his tail, then bounded across the room and skidded into the kitchen with the exuberant clumsiness of a real pup. Billy reappeared with the dog clutched to his chest and a beatific expression on his face.

'Can I take him outside, Dad?'

'All right, but don't go far – he still has to learn his way around.' Hewitt was unable to repress a fond grin as the boy ran out into the sunlight at the back of the house. He would have liked to complete the indulgent parent act by standing with an arm around Liz and watching Billy at play, but Mendip's presence ruled that out.

'I hope you get your money's worth out of it,' Mendip said, lowering himself into an armchair. His pale oval face turned this way and that as he surveyed the room.

'Perhaps I already have,' Hewitt answered.

Mendip nodded. 'I guess I'd feel guilty about bringing a kid out here.'

'I don't feel guilty,' Hewitt said quickly.

'Well, maybe I used the wrong word, but you know what I mean – when a kid can't even have a real dog . . .'

'Bramble is programmed to be as good as a real dog. Better.'

'It ought to be better if you're laying out a month's

salary for it. Hell's fire!' Mendip shifted to make himself more comfortable. 'I suppose you and Liz will have to tighten the old belts for a while.'

Hewitt shook his head. 'We don't go out much anyway.'

'That's right – you don't. A place like Mesonia is okay for somebody like me who can get around and enjoy the social life. You'd be surprised at what goes on at some of the parties over on the East Hill, Sammy boy.' Mendip gave a ruminative laugh. 'You know Marie Duchamp, the systems analyst in Structures One? Well, she and another girl . . .'

'Carl,' Hewitt put in evenly, 'what are your plans for today?'

Mendip blinked. 'Plans? I thought I'd just visit with you and Liz. Keep you company.'

'You've no plans to get around a few wild parties?'

Mendip smiled his thin-lipped smile. 'Sammy! You almost sound as if you didn't want . . .'

'Coffee's ready,' Liz announced, coming into the room with a tray.

'I don't know if I should have one,' Mendip said to her. 'I have a feeling Sammy wants me to clear out.'

'Nonsense! You have to stay for a meal now that you've come out this far.' Liz distributed beakers of synthetic coffee, giving Hewitt a reproachful frown as she did so. Hewitt slumped into another chair, sipped the hot liquid and tried to calculate how much he had contributed to his boss's bank balance in the form of free meals in the past year.

'Sam's always grouchy in the mornings,' Liz said. 'Will you try one of these biscuits, Carl?'

'No, thanks.' Mendip patted his stomach. 'I'm keeping my weight down – just in case.'

Liz smiled understandingly. 'When will you hear about the transfer?'

'Not for another four or five weeks, but I'd rather keep myself light. I don't like crash diets.'

Hewitt was tempted to cut in and reprove Mendip, a senior engineer, for talking about weight when he meant mass, but he decided against being petty in the hope that the day could be rescued from disaster. He knew what Mendip meant, anyway. The Ferrari Transfer System – instantaneous travel from one location to another which had similar spatial properties – was technologically superb, but from the practical viewpoint it had a major drawback in that its cost/weight graph took the form of a steeply ascending straight line. No matter how much mass the engineers transferred, no matter how many times they did it, no matter how many refinements or improvements they tried to introduce to the system – the expense of transmitting each and every gram of matter remained at the same astronomical figure.

The harsh economics of the Ferrari Transfer ruled out any prospect of easing Earth's population problems, but by the twenty-second century the world political situation had stabilized enough to permit international funding of a project to seed other planets with the nuclei of human colonies. In philosophical terms, the project was grandiose and far-seeing; in operation terms, it was a matter of paring every cargo down to the absolute miserly limit. The prime qualification for colonists was that they should be slightly built. Even then, they were subjected to rigorous reduction dieting before the outward journey, and were dispatched naked and with all hair removed from heads and bodies. The second qualification for interstellar settlers was, of course, dedication.

Not in utter nakedness, but trailing clouds of glory do we come, Hewitt had often quoted to himself. But on this Saturday morning – with suburban placidity on one hand, and Company politics personified by Carl Mendip on the other – the clouds of glory were not in evidence. He felt that he might as well be incarcerated in some hopeless prairie town back on Earth, that the sacrifices he and Liz and Billy had made were going to achieve little unless he got the transfer to Nimrod . . .

'What are you dreaming about now, Sammy boy?' Mendip said comfortably.

'Dreaming?' Hewitt queried the word, sensitive to his boss's habit of slipping professional criticism into casual conversation. 'I was wondering why they have to take so long to decide who's going and who's staying.'

'The mills of the Company grind slow, but if it'll ease your mind I can let you know your chances aren't too good, Sammy.'

'Why's that? I thought you put in a good assessment for me.'

'Oh, I did.' Mendip looked benign. 'But there's an economy drive on – and there are three of you.'

'Three *people*,' Hewitt said. 'That's the whole point of the operation, isn't it? The idea is to populate planets – not plant flags on them.'

'I know, but it's cheaper to produce the people after you get there.' Mendip looked appraisingly at Liz. 'I reckon that all women in the colonies should be made available to all men who could impregnate them.'

'That lets you out,' Hewitt said, in an automatic response.

Mendip's ice-blue gaze fastened on him in the instant. 'What do you mean, Sammy boy?'

'Nothing.' Hewitt laughed, wondering if his annoyance had driven him too far.

'Your plan wouldn't work,' Liz said diplomatically, smiling at Carl. 'When the word got back to the girls on Earth that you were waiting for them they'd rush the transfer terminal. The system wouldn't be able to cope.'

'You'd still have first claim,' Mendip said, mollified. 'I'm good to my friends.'

Hewitt stood up, went to the rear window and watched his son playing with the dog on the rectangle of mowed grass. The little robot animal was running, leaping, twisting, barking, scampering around Billy in a manner which made it difficult to believe that it was a machine which had been designed by robotics engineers and built in a factory only a few kilometres away. Billy was totally absorbed in his new companion, rolling on the ground and laughing while it clambered over him in a mock attack.

Late that evening when Mendip had left, after consuming two expensive high-protein meals, Liz spent a few minutes tidying the living room. The dog lay quietly on a rug and watched her moving about, its attention directed to one of its secondary owners now that Billy had gone to bed, its brain establishing pathways of familiarity and memory.

'Why don't you leave the place the way it is, and I'll tidy up in the morning?' Hewitt said. 'I'm too tired to do it now.'

'It's tension that's making you tired,' Liz told him. 'You shouldn't let Carl get under your skin.'

'I can't help it. If he's such a hell-raiser why doesn't he go out and do it instead of spending all his time around here?'

'I should have thought that was obvious. Anywhere else he'd have to meet people on equal terms, and he doesn't feel adequate for that. With us, he knows his seniority in the Company gives him the edge he needs, especially with a transfer coming up. He can say anything he wants in our house.'

'It doesn't seem to bother you,' Hewitt retorted.

Liz gave him a level stare. 'It bothers me, but we're dealing with your career, aren't we? After giving up everything we had on Earth, and travelling forty light years, are we going to risk your getting a bad assessment because I couldn't jolly your boss along? It's up to you, Sam – if you want, I'll pour a pot of coffee into his lap the next time he comes near me.'

'I'm sorry, Liz.'

'It's all right.' Liz, graceful in her natural generosity, came to him and kissed his forehead. She knelt down beside his chair and began stroking the dog. It licked her hand.

'Why are you doing that?' Hewitt said in genuine bafflement.

'Dogs like to be stroked.'

'But he's only a machine.'

Liz looked at him with womanly scorn. 'He doesn't know he's only a machine.'

The following four weeks passed more quickly than Hewitt had anticipated. Mesonia was still in an early stage of its development, and therefore was using a nine-day week in which there was only one rest day. The long stints of concentrated effort usually made Hewitt very tired, but Carl Mendip had taken to remaining in the office as much as possible – waiting for a decision about the transfer to Nimrod – and this freed Hewitt to do a number of field trips to outlying communities. He enjoyed the long silent drives through the Earth-like but unspoiled landscapes.

These pleasures were a bonus posthumously conferred on him by Eugenio Ferrari, whose transfer system enabled men to travel forty light years in exactly the same time that it would take to cover four or four hundred. The near-magic of Ferrari's physics meant that mankind could be highly selective about the location of colonies, only establishing them on green and friendly worlds. The colonists were faced with hard work, but little danger or discomfort.

Liz's job as a dental assistant meant she was unable to accompany him on the field trips, but Billy was able to go on days when he was free from classes. He always insisted on bringing the dog, which sat upright on the seat beside him, its brown eyes shining in a semblance of life. Hewitt found himself wishing he understood more about the molecular-circuit electronics of its brain so that he could appreciate what was going on inside the neat, sharp-eared head. All he knew was that the robotics engineers had done their work well, because Bramble had a canine personality all of his own, an individuality which – to Hewitt's surprise – was not entirely tailored to the convenience of his owners. The little rodog liked chewing shoes, for example, and objected noisily when they were forcibly removed from its jaws. It did not eat, but every day lapped some water which was used to keep its eyes, nose and tongue moist, and it frequently overturned its dish, necessitating mopping-up jobs. When accidentally locked in a room it would whine continuously and scratch at the door until permitted to rejoin its owners.

On one occasion, when the dog had been with them about two weeks, it caused a minor commotion in the Hewitt household by disappearing for several hours. Hewitt thought it was stolen and was angry about the loss of a valuable piece of property, but he was even more concerned about Billy's reaction. The boy wept inconsolably and ran around the house, pulling open cupboard doors and calling the dog's name. Later that evening, when Billy was reduced to an occasional exhausted sob, Bramble had been spotted trotting down the avenue towards the house with his head held high, like an animal character in one of the historic Walt Disney cartoons. It transpired that the dog had wandered beyond the area which was properly imprinted on its memory and had spent a long time carrying out a random search for a landmark it knew. Liz had scolded it and slapped its flanks exactly as she would have done with a real pet, and it had responded by scuttling off into Billy's room with its stubby tail between its legs. Billy had been overjoyed at the reunion with Bramble, and it was then that Hewitt felt the first stirrings of unease at the extent of his son's preoccupation with what was, after all, only an assemblage of electronic and mechanical components.

In general, however, Hewitt did not pay much attention to the dog. It was providing companionship for his son in a satisfactory manner, and to that extent it had been a worthwhile investment.

And he forgot about it entirely when the news came through that he – and not Carl Mendip – had been selected for transfer to Nimrod.

Mendip came to Hewitt's desk and watched him for a while with pale, reproachful eyes. 'I expect you're feeling proud of yourself, Sammy boy,' he said eventually.

Hewitt looked up from a site plan he had been pretending to study. 'Not especially. It was all in the luck of the draw – and your recommendation must have helped.'

'Don't you forget it.' Mendip brooded for a moment, unsatisfied. 'You've put on some weight, you know. You're going to have a hard time getting rid of it.'

'Only a couple of standard kilos – I can shed that in a week, easily.'

'Liz has put it on, too.'

'Liz is good at dieting.' Hewitt grew wary, sensing that his boss wanted to mar the occasion for him by whipping up antagonism. 'She can trim down in time for the medical.'

'That's going to spoil things a bit for you – women always lose it in the wrong place.' Mendip cupped his hands in front of his own chest, holding imaginary breasts.

'Secondary sexual characteristics aren't too important to me,' Hewitt said easily, his defences intact. He could swap banter of the most bawdy kind with other men in the office and think nothing of it, but Mendip had a way of particularizing every sexual reference to make it offensive.

'The Company ought to relax the weight rules a little for women,' Mendip continued. 'After all, if they're placing so much emphasis on their role as breeding animals that they're handing out transfers on the strength of it, they should let them keep their tits. What do you say, Sammy?'

'It's a point of view.' Hewitt toyed with a heavy scale rule. One part of his mind admired the craftsmanship with which – in one sentence – Mendip had degraded Liz and denigrated Hewitt's professional standing. Another part of his mind weighed the consequences of flicking the scale rule sideways and shattering Mendip's front teeth. Such an action would result in his transfer orders being cancelled, which was too great a price to pay, but the temptation was considerable.

'Two points of view,' Mendip said.

'If you don't mind, Carl, I'd better get on with this.' Hewitt tapped the site plan. 'I want to leave a clear desk.'

He lowered his head and stared determinedly at the plastic sheet until the other man had moved away and the moment of danger had passed. The tachygram from Earth had come in only ten minutes earlier, and there had been no time to contact Liz with the news. Hewitt decided against calling her from the office because, with Carl Mendip near, it would have been impossible for him to speak in a natural manner. He worked until the middle of the afternoon before acknowledging that his lack of concentration was rendering the exercise meaningless, then he left the office and walked home, pacing himself to arrive at the house soon after the time when Liz would bring Billy home from school. It was a warm day, and he found Billy sitting on the back lawn with a glass of yeastmilk in one hand and a book in the other, while contriving to have one arm around the rodog. Bramble came running to meet Hewitt, wagging his tail in the hope of being stroked. Hewitt, as always, was unable to bring himself to show affection for a machine – regardless of how lifelike it might be – and Bramble, looking mildly dejected, returned to his prime owner.

'Hi, Dad,' Billy called contentedly.

'Hello, son,' Hewitt replied. He went into the house and found Liz examining that week's menu display on their meal dispenser. Her short black hair was combed to the smoothness of an enamelled helmet and she was still wearing the traditional white of the dentist's surgery.

'Oh, you're home early,' she said, with a note of disappointment. 'Why are you home early?'

'What a greeting!' Hewitt slung his jacket over a chair. 'Do you want me to go back to the office?'

'Of course not. It's just that the menu isn't too interesting this week and I thought I might prepare the meal myself.' Liz gave him a lingering kiss.

'There's no need to go to all that trouble – I'll find something I like in the machine.'

'But I'll soon have forgotten how to cook,' Liz protested.

'That's what you think,' Hewitt said triumphantly. 'It'll be quite a while before they have meal dispensers on Nimrod.'

Liz stepped back from him at once. 'Do you mean . . .?'

Hewitt nodded. 'I've got the Nimrod posting.'

'I'm glad for you,' Liz said slowly. She walked to the window and stood with her back to him, looking out to where Billy was sitting on the grass. 'I know it's what you wanted.'

'What *I* wanted? It's a big thing for all of us, isn't it?' Hewitt was disturbed by his wife's reaction. 'It's equivalent to my getting about six promotions all at once.'

'That's why I'm glad for you. I really am glad about it, Sam.' Liz walked to the meal dispenser. 'I guess we'd better forget about a special meal for tonight – we'll have to start cutting down right away.'

'What is this, Liz?' Hewitt caught her arm and turned her to face him. 'Are you afraid of the Ferrari chamber?'

'I'm not afraid. I'll go anywhere with you.'

'But you don't seem . . . Don't you want to see a brand-new world?'

'This one is still pretty fresh after only eight years.' Liz gave him a wise, patient smile. 'Let's be honest about that side of it, Sam – the only reason Nimrod has been chosen is that it's exactly like this world, and exactly like all the others we're colonizing. There'll be no difference.'

'Except that I'll be going in with the rank of Project Leader,' Hewitt said heatedly. 'Or doesn't that count for anything?'

'It counts for a great deal. That's why I'm glad for you.'

Hewitt began to feel desperate. 'Don't keep saying that. Liz, if you didn't want to leave here, why didn't you let me know earlier?'

'Who said I didn't want to leave?'

'You don't need to say it. It's obvious, for God's sake.'

She looked up at him and spoke with the honesty he had always treasured. 'I didn't say anything because everybody was so certain you wouldn't be picked. And the reason I don't want to go is that I believe it would be better for Billy to grow up in one place. The last move upset him, and I think it's too soon for another.'

Hewitt shook his head. 'The Company psychologists advise on that sort of thing.'

'I know. The *Company* psychologists.'

'They wouldn't . . .'

'I'm his mother, Sam, and I know what I'm talking about – but I'm not going to fight you on this thing, because I know Billy will come through it, and I know you'll do everything you can to help him come through it.'

'Of course I will,' Hewitt said, relieved. 'The three of us . . .'

'There's just one condition.'

'Anything you say, Liz. What is it?'

'You have to tell him about Bramble.'

'What is there to tell?' Hewitt gave an uncertain laugh. 'Do you mean you want me to tell him the dog can't go?'

'Yes.'

'Well, I don't mind doing that. Billy's old enough to understand the position.'

Liz went to the door and opened it. 'Go out and tell him now.'

'What's the hurry?' Hewitt said reasonably.

'Sam, go out and tell him now.' Liz spoke in a faint, cold voice.

'All right! All right!' Hewitt went out to the back of the house, approached his son and knelt in the short grass beside him. 'I've got a big new job, Billy – so we're all moving to Nimrod.'

Billy looked all around – taking in the now-familiar view of white-painted dwellings among trees, grasslands sloping down to the river, the valley's palisade of slate-blue mountains – then lowered his head without speaking. The dog stared up at Hewitt from its nest in Billy's lap.

'Did you hear me, Billy? I said we're all going to Nimrod.'

Billy met Hewitt's gaze directly and his round face was momentarily overprinted with an image of the adult he would one day become. 'Dad, I'll do without pocket money for the rest of my life if you don't kill Bramble.'

Hewitt's jaw almost sagged. 'What's all this about killing him? You can't kill a machine, Billy.'

'Don't take him back to the store when we go.'

'But we couldn't leave him running around here. It would be . . .' Hewitt stopped abruptly, having almost defeated his own case by speaking of cruelty. If one could not kill a machine, it was equally impossible to be cruel to it.

'Why shouldn't I take him . . . *it* back to the store?'

'Because they would do something to his head and he wouldn't know us any more. He'd be in a box.'

'It's all for the . . .'

'Dad, let me leave Bramble with somebody, somebody from school, and then someday I could come back and get him. He's got a good memory. He's got the best memory you ever saw! He wouldn't forget . . .'

'Billy!' Hewitt was surprised by the force of his anger. 'There's a four hundred monit trade-in on that machine, and we're not going to walk off and leave it. Now try to grow up!'

He jumped to his feet and was striding back to the house when Bramble came scampering and growling around his ankles. Hewitt gave an irritated flick of his right foot which caught Bramble squarely on the ribcage. The little rodog yelped as it rolled over, then dashed back to Billy. Hewitt slammed the kitchen door behind him and stood there, breathing unevenly, staring at his wife.

'Don't forget,' she said, turning away from him, 'you've still to decide what we're having for dinner.'

Prior to their departure, Hewitt and his wife were awarded three full days of leave from work. The break was officially supposed to give them the chance to make final arrangements, but in fact it was a time of mental preparation for a little death. People who underwent the Ferrari

Transfer simply walked away from all their material possessions, leaving one life as naked as they had entered it, being born into another in exactly the same condition. The only assets they took with them were their personal attributes and skills, plus – by the grace of the Company – their credit ratings.

Hewitt had originally intended to let Billy keep the rodog until the last day, but the boy had stopped eating and spent most of his time in his room with Bramble in his arms. Sometimes when Hewitt was passing the bedroom door he heard Billy whispering to the pet, at others there was a silence broken by painful sobs, and he decided it would be better not to prolong an unhealthy situation.

Accordingly, immediately after breakfast on his first day's leave, he picked the rodog up while it was lapping at its water dish and – without any announcement – took it out to his car. It was not until he saw Billy's shocked face staring at him through a window that Hewitt admitted to himself that he had been hoping to get away from the house unseen. He dropped the warm sentient bundle on to the car's rear seat and drove away with the maximum acceleration the magnetic engine could produce. At the corner of the main road he glanced back once and saw that Billy had run halfway along the avenue behind the car before giving up. He was standing there, helpless. Bramble had raised himself on his hind legs to look out through the rear window, and he gave one low bark as Billy was lost to view.

Hewitt swore savagely, cursing the dog's designers and manufacturers for sins they were unaware of having committed. He slowed the car down and drove into the central area, past the gleaming pyramid of the transfer building, and stopped outside the commissary. When he picked up the rodog it squirmed in his grasp, but in a playful manner, its main objective apparently being to lick his face. Hewitt tucked it firmly under his arm and pushed his way through a transparent door to the domestic electronics department. Burt Pacer, who had sold him the rodog, was again on duty behind the counter.

'Morning, Sam,' Pacer said cheerfully. 'And congratulations – I heard about your transfer.'

'Thanks.' Hewitt set Bramble on the counter, keeping a tight grip of the studded collar as the dog's feet skidded about on the slick plastic. 'I wish I'd known it was coming. I could have saved myself a lot of money and trouble.'

'Didn't it work out?' Pacer lifted the dog in his thin freckled arms and examined it critically while it strove to lick his face.

'Too well – that was the trouble.'

'I might be able to let you have five hundred on it, seeing as how you only had it a few weeks.'

'That would be good,' Hewitt said. 'What'll you do with it now?'

'We'll blank out the brain . . . wipe it, you know . . . and deactivate the mutt and put him back into inventory.'

'Does it take long?' Hewitt was not sure why he was asking.

'About ten minutes should take care of it,' Pacer replied. 'Malcolm Harris does these things because he knows more about molecular logic circuits than I do, but he's out having his coffee right now. Do you want to talk to him about it?'

'No – I just wondered.' Hewitt walked to the door, then turned to look back at the dog which was scrabbling frantically on the counter in an effort to follow him. 'It's a hell of a thing when they have to build robot bloody dogs.'

Pacer shrugged. 'We're a long way from Earth.'

Hewitt nodded and went back to his car. Before moving off he sat and watched the struggling rodog being carried away into the rear of the store. He drove homewards slowly, taking detours and spinning the journey out to fifteen minutes so that Bramble would have been returned to inventory, and the episode finally closed, before he had to speak to Billy again. The first thing he saw when he reached the house was a blue Company car often used by Carl Mendip parked in the driveway. For once, the sight was quite welcome because the presence of an outsider could be useful in keeping emotional pressures down. Hewitt went in through the back door and found Liz alone in the kitchen. Her eyes had a slightly pinkish look, as if she had been crying, but her face was composed.

'Where's Billy?' he said.

'Where do you think? In his room.' Liz's voice was completely neutral. 'Would you like some coffee?'

'No – I have to watch my fluid intake.' Hewitt went through to the living room to where Mendip was prowling around, sipping coffee and examining various small ornaments with critical interest.

'How's it going?' Mendip said with a rare joviality.

'Okay.' Hewitt sat down in his favourite chair.

'I took an hour off to come out and see how you and Liz were getting on.'

'Thanks, Carl.' Hewitt watched as Mendip continued his course around the room, picking up recently-acquired trinkets and setting them down again. The principal items of furniture belonged to the Company and would be renovated for use by another colonist, but Hewitt and Liz had tried to personalize the place to some extent by buying extra pieces, such as flower vases, since their arrival on Mesonia. None of their purchases had been expensive – because of the ever-looming possibility of being transferred – but they helped make a standard Company house into the Hewitt home, and Hewitt disliked the casual way in which Mendip was handling them.

'It's a weird business, being transferred,' Mendip said. 'It would be better if you had a lot of packing to do.'

'Why's that?'

'Keep you busy, keep your mind off it.'

'I'm not bothered,' Hewitt said.

Mendip sniffed disbelievingly. 'Young Billy was crying when I came in.'

'He's upset about the dog.'

'I told you that was a bum investment, Sammy boy. How much did you drop on the deal?'

'Three hundred.'

Mendip hissed his breath inwards. 'Some people shouldn't be allowed out alone.' He picked up a small ceramic glow-clock and dropped it into his pocket.

'Carl?' Hewitt sat upright. 'What are you doing?'

'It's all right – I checked with Liz.' Mendip gave a frosty smile. 'You can't take it with you, you know.'

Hewitt felt himself nearing a dangerous edge. 'Put the clock back,' he said.

'I told you Liz said it was all right for me to take a few things. There's no point in letting the Company have them.'

Hewitt stood up. 'Put the clock back where it was.'

'But what will you do with it?' Mendip made no move to return the clock.

Hewitt considered for a moment. 'On the morning we leave I'll put it in a pile with our other things and smash them up with a hammer. Just to keep the buzzards off.'

'I don't like that remark.' Some of the scanty colour had left Mendip's face. 'I could put in a report about your attitude.'

'And I could put in a counter-report about you being a looter.'

Mendip slowly took the ceramic piece from his pocket

and weighed it in his hand. 'Is this your idea of gratitude, Sammy boy? Is this the way you treat a friend?'

Hewitt put on a look of surprise. 'No. I wouldn't dream of treating a friend this way.'

'I see.' Mendip turned to Liz, who was just entering the room. 'Did you hear that, Liz?'

'I heard.' Liz looked at Hewitt with an impersonal gaze. 'I paid for that clock – so I'm entitled to give it away.'

'What *is* this?' Hewitt said. 'We don't go in for separate ownership.'

'That's what I used to think. Until this morning.' Liz turned to Mendip and closed his fingers around the clock. 'Put it away in your pocket, Carl.'

'Thanks, Liz.' Mendip smiled serenely at Hewitt.

'If you try to leave here with that clock,' Hewitt said in a shaky voice, aghast at what he was doing and yet unable to draw back, 'I . . . I'll . . .'

'It wouldn't be a good idea to hit me, Sammy.' Mendip put the clock in his pocket. 'That way, you'd lose the transfer.'

The words went through Hewitt like a chill wind, enfolding his mind in an icy stasis, bringing time itself to a standstill. He stared helplessly at his wife, and at Mendip, and it seemed to him that they would all be there for ever because he was being required to make decisions of which he was incapable . . .

'Bramble!' Billy burst into the room with a shout and ran to the front window in a blur of bare arms and legs. 'Bramble's come back!'

Hewitt turned disbelievingly and peered out of the window. He experienced a curious blending of relief, affection and pride as he saw the little rodog, compact and jaunty, trotting along the avenue towards the house. Its head and tail were held high and it looked absurdly pleased with itself, again like an animal character in one of the historic Walt Disney cartoons. Billy jumped down from the window seat, was out through the front door in a second and they saw him running across the front lawn. Bramble abruptly gathered speed, and boy and dog met in mid-air, then rolled in an excited, noisy tangle into a flower bed.

'Well, I'll be . . .' Hewitt whispered reverently. 'He must have got away from the store.'

Liz moved close to the window. 'But how did he find his way back?'

'Damned if I know. Billy said he had a good memory, but I didn't think this was possible,' Hewitt said. An instinct made him follow Liz to the window and slip his arm around her. She leaned back against him.

'Better not let the kid get too worked up over it,' Mendip said in an oddly taut voice. 'I'm going back to the office now – I'll drop the dog off at the commissary on my way. Save you the extra trip.' He hurried out of the room. Hewitt ran after him and caught up just as Mendip was grasping Bramble by the collar and pulling him out of Billy's arms.

'Leave the dog alone,' Hewitt snapped.

'What are you talking about?' Mendip faced him on the sunlit grass. 'This isn't a real dog.'

'He's more real than you are, Carl. Put him down.'

'You're not thinking straight,' Mendip said.

'Perhaps not.' Hewitt was dimly aware of neighbours beginning to take an interest in the confrontation. 'But if you don't put him down, I'll put you down.'

'You wouldn't be that stupid,' Mendip said, brushing past Hewitt towards his car.

Hewitt threw a punch which was meant to land on Mendip's chin, but which – because he had not tried to hit anyone since he was a boy – connected squarely with the other man's forehead. Mendip gave a startled moan and dropped Bramble. Hewitt's right hand was aching from the effects of the blow, he knew he was making a fool of himself in front of the entire neighbourhood, and he also knew he was ruining his chances of fast promotion – but he was filled with a sudden gratitude towards Mendip. It was a deep thankfulness for having made him understand what was important in his own life, and it was a thankfulness which could be expressed only by raining blows on Mendip's head and upflung arms. The wild punches, often meeting with sharp elbows, threatened to break Hewitt's own knuckles, but he succeeded in driving Mendip to his knees while Billy backed away holding the dog. Suddenly Liz was beside him, restraining his arms.

'That's enough, Sam,' she said gently. 'I think you've made your point.'

Mendip scrambled to his feet, dishevelled but virtually unhurt. 'You've done it now, Sammy boy,' he panted. 'This has to go on report. You're never going to see Nimrod.'

'You can send me a viewcard,' Hewitt said, through his own gasps. 'Go away, Carl.'

Mendip turned to Liz. 'Of course, it's you I'm most sorry for.'

She held out her hand and smiled. 'We want our clock back, please.'

Mendip took the clock from his pocket, dropped it into her hand and walked to his car without saying another word. They watched him drive away, then Hewitt went into his house, walking slowly and with as much dignity as possible. As soon as he was screened from the view of his neighbours, he held up his skinned and bleeding knuckles, blowing on them to ease the pain.

'Look what I've done to myself,' he said. 'If I'd hit him once more, he'd have won.'

'I'll soon fix those,' Liz replied. 'Wait till I get the medikit.'

A few minutes later, while Hewitt was having his battle wounds dressed, he heard his son laughing outside. He looked out of the rear window and saw Billy and Bramble running down the garden away from the house. They were still gathering speed as they reached the far end of the mowed plot and plunged, unafraid, into the long grass where the rest of the world began.

Small World

I'll do it today, Robbie thought. *I'll run across the sky today*.

He drew the bedclothes more closely around him, creating a warm cave which was precisely tailored to his small frame, and tried to go back to sleep. It was not yet morning and the house was quiet except for occasional murmurs from the refrigerator in the kitchen. Robbie found, however, that making the decision about the sky run had changed his mood, permitted the big and hazardous outside world to invade his security, and that sleep was no longer possible. He got up, went to the window and drew the curtains aside.

The three mirrors which captured sunlight had not yet been splayed out from the sides of the cylindrical space colony, and therefore it was still completely dark outside the house except for the luminance from the streetlamps. The nearby rooftops were silhouetted against the horizontal strip of blackness, unrelieved by stars, which Robbie knew as the night-time sky, but higher up he could see the glowing geometrical patterns of streets in the next valley. He stared at the jewelled rectangles and pretended he was a bird soaring above them in the night air. The game occupied his mind for only a short time – he had never seen a real bird, and his imagination was not fully able to cope with the old Earthbound concepts of 'above' and 'below'. Robbie closed the drapes, went back to bed and waited impatiently for morning . . .

'Come on, Robbie,' his mother called. 'It's time for breakfast.'

He sat up with a jerk, amazed to discover that he had, after all, been able to doze off and return to the peaceful world of dreams after the pledge he had made to himself. All the while he was washing and dressing he tried to get accustomed to the idea that this was the day on which he was going to grow up, to become a full member of the Red Hammers. His mind was still swirling with the sense of novelty and danger when he went into the bright kitchen and took his place in the breakfast alcove opposite his father and mother.

Like most colonists who had managed to settle happily on Island One, they were neat, medium-sized, unremarkable people of the sort who leave their youth behind very quickly, but are compensated with a seemingly endless span of unchanging adulthood. Mr Tullis was a crystallogenetic engineer in the zero-gravity workshops at the centre of the Island's sunward cap – an occupation which was beyond Robbie's comprehension; and Mrs Tullis was a psychologist specializing in verbal communication modes – an occupation Robbie might have understood had she ever talked to him about it. They both examined him critically as he sat down.

'What are you going to do today?' his mother said, handing him a dish of cereal.

'Nothin'.' Robbie stared down at the yellow feathers of grain, and he thought, *I'm going to run across the sky*.

'Noth*ing*,' she repeated, emphasizing the ending for Robbie's benefit. 'That doesn't sound very constructive.'

'The school holidays are too long.' Max Tullis stood up and reached for his jacket. 'I'm going to be late at the plant.'

Thea Tullis stood up with him and accompanied him to the front door while they discussed arrangements for a dinner party that evening. On her return she busied herself for a few minutes disposing of the breakfast remains and, her interest in Robbie's plans apparently having faded, disappeared without speaking into the room she used as study. Robbie toyed with his cereal, then drank the chill, malty-flavoured milk from the dish. He looked around the kitchen for a moment, suddenly reluctant to go outside and face the rest of the day, but he had discovered that when his mother was working in her study the house was lonelier than when he was the only person in it. Taking some candy from a dish on the window ledge, he opened the door and went out to the back garden.

Robbie often watched television programmes which were beamed out from Earth, and so had a fairly clear mental image of how a natural environment should look, but there was no sense of dislocation in his mind as he glanced around him on a quiet, summer morning. He had been born on Island One and saw nothing out of the ordinary about living on the inner surface of a glass-and-metal cylinder little more than two hundred metres in diameter and a kilometre in length. The colony was highly industrialized – because it manufactured many of the components for larger second-generation space habitats – but it had a residential belt supporting over a thousand families. This community, with a fourteen-year history of living in space, yielded valuable sociological data and therefore was preserved intact, even though its members could have been moved on to newer colonies.

None of Robbie's friends was visible in the row of adjoining gardens, so he emitted a sharp, triple-toned whistle, a secret signal devised by the Red Hammers, and sat down on a rustic seat to await results. Several minutes went by without an answering whistle being heard. Robbie was not particularly surprised. He had noticed that – no matter how strict the injunctions were from their leaders at night – the Hammers tended to sleep late in the morning during school holidays. On this occasion, though, he was disappointed at their tardiness because he anticipated the looks of respect from the other junior members when he announced he was taking his initiation.

He munched candy for a few minutes, then boredom began to set in and he thought about asking his mother to take him to the low-gravity park in the Island's outer cap. She had refused similar requests twice already that week, and he guessed her reply would be the same today. Dismissing the idea from his mind, he lay back in the chair and stared upwards, focusing his gaze on the houses and gardens visible 'above' him in the Blue Valley. The layout of the residential areas was identical in all three valleys, and Robbie was able to pick out the counterpart of his own family's house in the Blue Valley and – by looking back over his shoulder – in the Yellow Valley. At that time there was a temporary truce between the Red Hammers and the Yellow Knives, so Robbie's attention was concentrated on enemy territory, that inhabited by the Blue Flashes. He had memorized the map drawn up by his own gang, and as a result was able to pick out the actual houses where the Blue Flash leaders lived.

As the minutes stretched out his boredom and restlessness increased. He stood up and gave the secret whistle again, making it louder this time. When there was no response he paced around the garden twice, making sure that no adults were watching him from windows of neighbouring houses, then slipped into the cool privacy of the shrubs at the foot of the lawn. A sense of guilty pleasure grew within him as he scooped up some of the crumbly soil with his hands and uncovered a small object wrapped in plastic film. Catapults were illegal on Island One – as were firearms and all explosive devices which might be capable of puncturing the pressure skin – but most boys knew about catapults, and some claimed the historic privilege of making them, regardless of any authority.

Robbie tested the strength of the synthetic rubber strands, enjoying the feeling of power the simple weapon gave him, and took a projectile from his pocket. There were no pebbles in the sieved and sterilized soil of the Island, but he made it a practice to collect suitably small and heavy objects. This one was a glass stopper from an old whisky decanter, almost certainly stolen, which he had bought from a girl in school. He fitted it into the catapult's leatherette cup, drew the rubber back to full stretch, and – after a final check that he was not being observed – fired it upwards in the general direction of the residential area of the Blue Valley.

The glass missile glittered briefly in the sunlight, and vanished from sight.

Robbie watched its disappearance with a feeling of deep satisfaction. His pleasure was derived from the fact that he had defied, and somehow revenged himself upon, his parents and all the other adults who either ignored him or placed meaningless restrictions on his life. He also had a ten-year-old boy's faith that Providence would guide the projectile to land squarely on the roof of the gang hut used by the despicable Blue Flashes. His mind was filled with a gleeful vision of one of their full-scale meetings being thrown into panic and disorder by the thunderous impact just above their heads.

A moment later he heard an elaborate whistle coming from one of the nearby gardens and he lost all interest in the now invisible missile. He wrapped up the catapult, buried it, and ran to meet his friends.

The glass stopper which Robbie had dispatched into the sky weighed some sixty grams and had he lived on Earth it would have travelled only a short distance into the air before falling back. Island One rotated about its longitudinal axis once every twenty-one seconds, thus creating at the inner surface an apparent gravity equal to that of Earth at sea level. The gradient was on an entirely different scale to that of Earth, however – falling from maximum to zero in a distance of only a hundred metres, which was the radius of the cylindrical structure.

In the early stages of its flight the gleaming missile decelerated in much the same manner as it would have done while rising from the surface of a planet, but the forces retarding it quickly waned, allowing its ascent to be prolonged. It actually had some residual velocity when it reached the zero-gravity zone of the axis and, describing a sweeping S-curve, plunged downwards into the Blue Valley.

And, because the space colony had rotated considerably during its time of flight, the stopper landed nowhere near Robbie's notional target.

Alice Ledane was lying in a darkened room at the front of her house, hands clasped to her temples, when she heard the explosive shattering of the window which overlooked the rear patio.

She lay still for a pounding moment, rigid with shock, while her heart lurched and thudded like an engine shuddering to a halt. For what seemed a long time she was positive she was going to die, but her shallow, ultra-rapid fear-breathing gradually steadied into a more normal rhythm. She got to her feet and, leaning against the wall at intervals, went towards the back of the house. The mood of calmness and resolve she had been trying to nurture had gone, and for a moment she was afraid to open the door of the living room. When she finally did so her lips began to quiver as the remnants of her self-control dwindled away.

Shards of glass were scattered around the room like transparent petals, some of them hanging by their points from the drapes, and ornaments had been toppled from the small table which sat at the window. The surface of the table was dented, but she could see nothing of the missile which must have been thrown from the back garden. Alice gazed at the damage, knuckles pressed to her mouth, then she ran to the back door and threw it open. As she had expected, there was no sign of the children who for months had been persecuting her with such unyielding determination.

'Damn you!' she shouted. 'It isn't fair! What have I done to you? Why don't you come out in the open?'

There was a lengthy silence, disturbed only by the humming of bees in the hedgerows, then the tall figure of Mr Chuikov appeared at an upper window of the next house. Alice slammed her door, suddenly afraid of being seen, and stumbled back to the front room where she had been resting. She went to the sideboard, picked up a framed photograph of her husband, and stared at the unperturbed, smiling face.

'And damn you, Victor,' she said. 'You'd no right! No . . . bloody . . . *right*!'

While she was looking at the photograph, her hand made its own way into the pocket of her dressing gown and emerged holding a strip of bubbled tinfoil. Alice put the picture down and ejected a silver-and-blue capsule from the strip. She raised the tiny ovoid to her mouth, but hesitated without swallowing it. For the past week – in accordance with Dr Kinley's suggestion – she had progressively delayed the taking of the first cap by an extra hour every day. The aim, the shining goal, was to get through an entire day without any psychotropic medication at all. If that could be achieved just once there would be prospects of further successes and of finally becoming a whole woman again.

Alice rolled the capsule between her finger and thumb,

and knew this was not to be her day of triumph – the children had seen to that. Harold from three doors along the block, or Jean from the house on the corner, or Carl from the next street. With the casual ruthlessness of the very young they had long ago deduced that her illness made her an easy prey, and they had declared a quiet war. Alice placed the capsule on her tongue, yielding to its promise of a few hours of peace, then an irksome thought occurred to her. While she was asleep the broken window in the living room would admit dust, insects, possibly even human intruders. There had once been a time when she could have slept contentedly in an unlocked house, but the world and all the people in it had been different then.

She took the capsule from her mouth, dropped it into her pocket, and went to fetch a waste bin. It took her fifteen minutes to gather up the larger fragments of glass, an armoury of brittle daggers, and to vacuum the carpet until it was free of gleaming splinters. The next logical step would have been to contact the maintenance department and report the damage, but she had had the telephone disconnected a year previously because its unexpected ringing had jolted her nerves too much. She had even, and quite illegally, cut the wires of the public service loudspeaker in the hall for the same reason. On this occasion it would not have taken long to get dressed and go to a phone in the shopping arcade, but Alice shrank from the idea of leaving the security of the house at such short notice. Her only option was to cover the broken window in some way until she felt strong enough to have it properly mended.

In the spare bedroom, the one Victor had used as a workshop, she found a sheet of alloy wide enough to span the window, and a quick search along the shelves produced a tube of Liqueld adhesive. She carried the materials into the living room, squeezed some adhesive on to the metal window frame and pressed the alloy into position. Within a minute it was so firmly in place that it was beyond her strength to move it. Satisfied that her defences were once again intact, Alice closed up the drapes, returned to the front room and lay down on the divan. The rolls of fat which had gathered around her body in a year of housebound inactivity had hampered her in the work she had just done and she was breathing heavily. The acrid smell of unhealthy perspiration filled the room.

'Damn you, Victor,' she said to the ceiling. 'You'd no right.'

Victor Ledane had been one of a team of five who had gone outside the sunward cap of a Model Two habitat to install a parabolic mirror which was going to be used as an auxiliary power source. The work was being done in a hurry against a completion deadline imposed by engineer-politicians back on Earth. As Alice understood it, one of the team had ignored standard procedure and had begun stripping the non-reflective coating from the dish before it was fully secured. Only a fraction of the bright metal surface had been uncovered, but when the mirror accidentally swung free of its mountings a blade of solar heat had sliced open the space suits of two men. And one of them had been Victor Ledane.

Alice and he had been living on Island One for six years at the time. Those had been good years, so absorbing that she had lost contact with her few friends back on Earth, and when the Island's community director, Les Jerome, had asked her to stay on she had readily agreed. She had known, of course, that the sociologists and psychologists were mainly interested in having a genuine space widow on tap, but with Victor gone nothing seemed very important. Obligingly, she had continued to live in the same house, had waited for the promised return of joy, and had tried not to think about the hard vacuum of space which began centimetres beneath the floor.

The trouble was . . . there had been no resurgence of joy.

Eventually she had settled for an inferior substitute, one which was dispensed in the form of silver-and-blue capsules, and now it was becoming impossible to distinguish between the two. The only way to restore her judgment would be to start living without the capsules, getting through one week at a time, but the point that Dr Kinley and the others seemed to miss was that – to begin with – it would be necessary to get through that first, endless, impossible day . . .

Alice fought to hold back the tears of frustration and despair as she realized that, on a day which had begun so disastrously, she was unlikely to hold on as late as noon before seeking relief. It came to her with a rare clarity that, for some people, the burdens of humanity were, quite simply, too great.

There was a gratifying response to Robbie's announcement.

After initial whoops of disbelief the younger members of the Red Hammers lapsed into silence, and Robbie could tell that – already – they were a little afraid of him. He made himself appear calm as Gordon Webb and the three other boys who made up the Supreme Council took him aside for a talk. Robbie went with them, occasionally glancing back at the juniors, and was thrilled to find that David, Pierre and Drew – even Gordon himself – were treating him almost as an equal. They were holding something in reserve, because he had not yet actually made the run, but Robbie was being given a strong foretaste of what it would be like to be a grown-up, and he found it a satisfying concoction. He wondered if his parents would notice a change in him when he went home for his evening meal, and if they would speculate on what had brought it about . . .

'. . . make up your mind which valley you're going to,' Gordon was saying. 'Yellow or Blue?'

Robbie forced his thoughts back to the present, and to the unfortunate necessity of having to qualify for senior status in the gang. Because of the truce with the Yellow Knives there would be less risk in going in their direction, but there would be more glory in a fleeting invasion of Blue Flash territory, and it was the glory that Robbie wanted. The glory, the respect and the recognition.

'Blue,' he said, and then, remembering a line from a television drama, 'where else?'

'Good man.' Gordon clapped him on the back. 'The Flashers are going to be sick. We'll show 'em.'

'We'd better get Robbie's challenge ready,' Drew said.

Gordon nodded. 'Are there any of the Blues watching us?'

Pierre took a small telescope from his pocket, moved out from the shade of the rhododendrons and trained the instrument on the Blue Valley residential section which was visible, at an altitude of some one hundred and twenty degrees, above a strip of sky in which the Earth and Moon could be seen sweeping by every twenty-one seconds. As the distance from where the boys stood to the heart of Blue Flash territory was less than two hundred metres for the most part, the telescope was scarcely necessary, but it was a prestigious part of the Supreme Council's equipment and was always brought into action on such occasions.

'All clear,' Pierre droned presently, and Robbie felt a thrill at being at the centre of such military efficiency.

Gordon cupped his hands around his mouth and shouted instructions to the watchful group of juniors. 'Spread out and keep away from here. Create a diversion.'

The smaller boys nodded dutifully and moved away through the neat little park in the direction of their homes. Robbie was disappointed that they would not be present to see him make his run, but he understood the wisdom of Gordon's precautions. In addition to the risk of alerting the Blue Flashes, there was the more immediate danger of attracting the attention of adults in their own valley.

He went with the Council members to David's home, which was conveniently empty because both his parents were out at work, and they spent some time preparing his challenge. This was a large sheet of paper which he decorated with crossed hammers drawn in red ink. Across the bottom of the sheet, in elaborate lettering which was meant to look like Gothic script, Robbie printed the message: SIR ROBBIE TULLIS, GENTLEMAN SOLDIER OF THE RED HAMMERS, PRESENTS HIS COMPLIMENTS. When the ink had dried, the paper was folded up and tucked into an empty pickle jar, and – as the ultimate insult to the Blue Flashes – a scrap of red cloth was tied around it.

The task was more time-consuming than Robbie had expected and had barely been completed when the day-care matron for the area arrived to give David his lunch. This was the signal for the other boys to suspend operations and disperse to their own homes. Robbie was not hungry, but he went home as usual to avoid giving the impression that anything out of the ordinary was happening. He decided to preserve an enigmatic silence during the meal and, as his mother's thoughts were occupied with her morning's work, there was virtually no conversation. The house was filled with a cool stillness which seemed as though it might go on for ever.

It was with a sense of relief that Robbie finished eating and returned to the sunlit world of comradeship and conspiracy he shared with the other boys of the neighbourhood. Gordon, David, Pierre and Drew were waiting for him in a corner of the park, and as soon as he came near he knew by the solemnity of their faces that something had happened. Pierre, the tallest of the group, was anxiously scanning the vicinity, every now and then pausing to examine some item of suspicion with his telescope.

'Ole Minty saw us,' Gordon explained to Robbie. 'I think he's following us around.'

'Does that mean I can't . . . '

'No chance!' Gordon's twelve-year-old face showed the determination which had made him leader of the Red Hammers. 'We'll wear the old scarecrow down. Come on.'

Robbie tightened his grip on his challenge, which was hidden in the pocket of his jacket, and hurried after Gordon. He was impressed by the way in which the older boy seemed absolutely unafraid of one of the gang's most powerful enemies. Mr Mintoff was the Red Valley's first and only old age pensioner. Robbie knew he must have been a brilliant man to have been allowed to emigrate to Island One in his late middle age, but now he was a solitary figure with little to do except patrol the neighbourhood and act as unofficial policeman. In spite of the fact that he appeared to be senile, and walked with the aid of an alloy stick, he had the knack of divining what was going on in the Hammers' minds and of making sudden appearances at the most inopportune times.

Under Gordon's control, the group walked to the end of Centre Street and stood in a conspicuous knot, giving every indication they were planning mischief, until they saw Mr Mintoff approaching from the direction of the park. They let him get close, then split up and made their way by separate and secret routes to the opposite end of the street, where they again assembled. A good twenty minutes passed before the stooped form of Mr Mintoff caught up with them. Just before he was within hailing distance they disappeared as before, melting into the ample shrubbery of the Red Valley, and came together at their original venue to await their pursuer. The second round of the fight had got under way.

Robbie had been certain that Ole Minty would be forced to concede defeat within the hour, but he displayed a stubborn tenacity, and it was quite late in the afternoon before they saw him give up and turn into the side avenue where he lived. They waited a while longer to establish that they were in the clear, and Robbie's heart began to pick up speed as he realized that all the preliminaries had ended, that it was time for him to make his run . . .

The sidewall of the valley was constructed of smooth, seamless alloy and had a curved overhang which was supposed to make it unclimbable. Island One was an artificial environment, however, and as such it relied on complex engineering systems to maintain its various functions. The systems were designed to be as unobtrusive as possible, and most colonists were quite unaware of them, but children have an intense, detailed awareness of their surroundings, one which often confounds adult minds. Robbie and his four companions went straight to a point where a cluster of hydraulic pipes and valves made it easy to get halfway up the wall, and where a strain monitor installed by a different team of engineers provided a useful handhold at the top. He knew that if he stopped to think about what he was doing his nerve could fail, so he scaled the wall without hesitation and quickly slid on to the outer girder, where he could not be seen by anybody in his own valley. Making sure that his challenge was secure in his pocket, he turned to climb down to the surface of glass stretching away beneath.

And the universe made ready to swallow him.

Robbie froze, his muscles locked by fear, as he looked into the vertiginous deeps of space. The vast, curved window which separated two of the Island's valleys was like a tank filled with black liquid, a medium through which darted stars, planets, the blue Earth, the Moon, seemingly miniature models of other habitats – all of them impelled by the rotation of his own world. The huge plane mirror a short distance beyond the glass did nothing to lessen the fearful visual impact – it created discontinuities, a sense of depths within depths, as bright objects appeared and disappeared at its edges. Adding to the kaleidoscope of confusion were the sweeping, brilliant visions of Island One's sister cylinder, its own mirrors splayed out, which periodically drenched Robbie with upflung showers of white light.

He shrank back from the abyss, fighting to draw breath, face contorted with shock. Something in his pocket clinked against the metal of the girder. Robbie looked down at it, saw the top of the pickle jar containing his challenge, and moaned aloud as he realized he was not free to turn back. He lowered himself to the bottom flange of the girder, stepped out on to the nearly invisible surface of the glass, and began his run across the sky.

The wall of the Blue Valley was less than a hundred metres away, but as Robbie sprinted over the void it seemed to retreat, maliciously, prolonging his ordeal. Each leap over a titanium astragal brought with it a nightmarish moment of conviction that there would be nothing to land on at the other side, and that he would fall screaming into the endless night. And as he neared the midpoint of his run Robbie encountered a new and even more disconcerting phenomenon – the sun had appeared directly beneath his feet. Its reflected light blazed upwards around Robbie, blinding him and producing a nauseating sense of dislocation. He kept on running, but he had begun to sob painfully with each breath and attacks of dizziness threatened to bring him down.

All at once, the wall of the Blue Valley was looming up in front, criss-crossed by the shadows of a lattice girder. He pulled the glass jar from his pocket, hurled it over the wall and turned to run homewards on legs which had lost all strength.

Robbie made it to the centre of the window, to the centre of the fountain of golden fire, before he collapsed. He lay on his side, eyes tight-closed, knees pulled up to his chin, his immature personality in full flight from the world beyond the womb.

'Hold on a moment, Mr Mintoff.' Les Jerome set the telephone on his desk, picked up his binoculars and went to the window. From his office high up on the outer cap of Island One he could see virtually the entire structure of the colony. The opposite cap was at the centre of his field of view, and radiating from it were the three inhabited valleys interspersed with three kilometre-long transparencies. He aimed the powerful glasses at the strip between the Red and Blue Valleys, stood perfectly still for a moment, then picked up the phone.

'I see him, Mr Mintoff,' he said. 'Right beside Frame Thirty-two. Okay, you contact his mother. And thanks for calling – we'll get the little beggar in from there in a hurry.'

Jerome replaced the telephone and depressed the intercom toggle which would let him speak to the chief of his maintenance force. 'Frank, there's a kid stuck out on the glass. Yeah, on Transparency One just beyond Frame Thirty-two. Send somebody out to get him, and make sure a medic goes as well – the brat's going to need a shot of something to calm him down.'

Returning to the window, Jerome leaned on the ledge

and stared at the strange, confined world he had grown to love in spite of all its faults and peculiarities. He had a decision to make, and it had to be done quickly. Strictly speaking, the plight of the boy out there on the glass did not constitute an emergency situation, and therefore he would not be officially justified in closing up the mirrors before the scheduled hour. All three mirrors had to be retracted at the same time, to preserve the Island's symmetrical dynamics, which meant enforcing a universal black-out – and there were many colonists who objected strenuously to that sort of thing. There would be a barrage of complaints, some of them from influential people, but Jerome was a kindly man with two children of his own, and it troubled him to think of a small boy trapped on the glass, suspended in space.

The sooner he could put a semblance of solidity beneath the boy's feet and screen him off from infinity, the better chance the young adventurer would have of emerging from his ordeal without personality scars. He picked up the rarely-used red telephone which would transmit his voice to every home, office and workshop on Island One.

'This is Community Director Jerome speaking,' he said. 'There is no cause for alarm, but we are going to close up the mirrors for a short period. The black-out will be as brief as we can possibly make it, and I repeat there is no cause for alarm. I apologize for any inconvenience that may be caused. Thank you.'

Jerome then contacted his Engineering Executive and gave the order which would bring a premature sunset to his domain.

In the darkened front room of her house, midway along the Blue Valley, Alice Ledane awoke with a start.

She had been skimming on the wavetops of consciousness for hours, sometimes dipping into restless sleep as her private struggle drained her of nervous energy, then surfacing again to feel more exhausted than ever. As was usual on a day like this, she had no idea of the time. She got to her feet, parted the drapes slightly and made the discovery that it was night outside.

Incredulously, she put her hand in the pocket of her dressing gown and found the day's first capsule still there. It was sticky to the touch. She held the tiny ovoid in the palm of her hand for a few seconds, then let it fall to the floor.

Alice went back to the divan and lay down. It was much too soon, she knew, to start congratulating herself on a victory – but if she had managed to get through one day with no outside help there was nothing to prevent her getting through the others which were to follow. Nothing insurmountable, anyway . . .

The sleep which came to her almost immediately was deep and dreamless and long-lasting, in contrast to her previous shallow dozing. It was the kind of sleep which all of life's warriors need to gird them for the morning and the bright light of the sun.

The Kingdom of O'Ryan

The well-dressed stranger sat down, put his attaché case on the floor, crossed his legs and said, 'Is there any insanity in your family?'

I thought immediately of my cousin Trev, who at that very moment was in the next office, squatting inside a packing case lined with aluminium foil and projecting reverent thoughts in the general direction of the star Betelgeuse. Had he finally stepped over the borderline between tolerable nuttiness and criminal lunacy? Was somebody coming to take him away?

'Insanity?' I gave the stranger an indignant stare. 'What a ridiculous question! Has anybody filed a complaint?'

'Don't get me wrong, Mr Cluny.' He smiled and took a business card from his waistcoat pocket. 'I was merely trying to find out if your views on insanity coincide with mine. You see, I divide the insane into only two categories – the unpredictable and the predictable.'

'Do you?'

'Or, to put it another way – the unprofitable and the potentially profitable.'

'Really?' I glanced at the card he had handed me. It read: *Ralph D. Wynter, Computer Systems Consultant.* The after-effects of the previous night's binge were impairing my ability to think, but I was practically certain that Wynter wasn't making any kind of sense. 'I'm afraid I don't quite see . . .'

'In here,' Wynter said impressively, patting his attaché case, 'I have a list of the names and addresses of 400,000 crazy people, and it's worth a lot of money to you and me.'

'That's good to know.' I tried to sound mildly interested and cheerful as I withdrew my legs from the kneehole of my desk just in case it became necessary to flee. Wynter was about forty, with steel-rimmed glasses and a look of square-jawed integrity which would have made him a champion used car salesman, but it was becoming obvious that he had a screw loose. What a way to start the day! I was closeted in my office with a genuine noodle, and the only person I could have called upon for help was my cousin Trev, selfstyled apostle of the Supreme Nizam of Betelgeuse.

Wynter's eyes twinkled behind curved flakes of glass. 'You must be wondering what this is all about. Let me make it clear to you by asking one question – do you ever bet on the horses?'

'What?' I gazed at Wynter with increased perplexity. This was what he called making it clear?

'Do you ever gamble on horse-racing?'

'Never.'

'Why not?'

'Ah . . .' I strove for a succinct way to express my feelings about the evils of gambling. 'I might lose my money.'

'Good man!' Wynter gave me a delighted grin. 'I thought you would have the right attitude, but I wanted to be sure. You see, the crazy people on my list all suffer from the same delusion – they're convinced it is possible to predict the outcome of a horse race.'

'That *is* crazy,' I replied, beginning to relax a little as I sensed that Wynter was not completely adrift from reality and that he was in fact working round, albeit in a peculiar manner, to making some kind of a proposition. 'If there was any way of knowing the winners in advance the profession of bookmaker would never have arisen.'

'Precisely! I can see we're going to hit it off just fine.'

'I don't think so, Mr Wynter,' I said, flipping his business card back across my desk. 'I don't know what all this has to do with computer systems, but I'm a very busy man and I haven't got time to . . .'

'To make yourself a third of a million dollars in less than a month? Tax free?'

My heart wobbled a couple of times like a machine with a defective mounting, and to gain a bit of leeway I said, 'I always pay my taxes.'

That was a lie, of course. The main reason I allowed cousin Trev to stay on in the business was that he was down in the books as receiving a vice-presidential salary of 25,000 dollars a year, whereas he was able to get by quite comfortably on the sixty a week I actually doled out to him. It was tricks like that which enabled me to keep the place on its feet, but even so things were beginning to look pretty bleak and the notion of making a quick killing had a powerful appeal.

Wynter gave me a knowing glance. 'What I mean is that the money will be untraceable, and it will be up to you whether you declare it or not.'

'What money? What *is* this?'

'Before we go into that, you've got to understand fully the nature of the insanity which afflicts compulsive gamblers.' Wynter straightened out his legs and hooked his thumbs into his waistcoat pockets, becoming expansive as he reached a well-rehearsed part of his spiel. 'They actually suffer from *two* delusions, two fantasies which complement and reinforce each other. The first one we've already covered; the second follows on logically from the first – namely that within the horse-racing fraternity there is a select group whose members are kept informed of *all* the hidden variables which affect horses' performances, and who therefore know the result of every race in advance.

'The members of this group are supposed to be a kind of Ouspenskian élite, and the idea that they exist comforts the gambler and prevents him from crashing into the stone wall of reality when the horse he expected to win comes in fourth and costs him a lot of money. His calculations were based on the form book and were correct as far as they went, you see, but the Big Boys knew better because they had access to inside information. It's like a religion – but in place of a Messiah the gambler dreams of a benign Big Boy who will take a special liking to him and pass on crumbs of his esoteric knowledge.

'There's no denying the power of the dream. I've seen a crowded bar emptied in thirty seconds because somebody came in and gave a tip straight from the quote horse's mouth unquote. It doesn't matter how shabby and unlikely the tipster may be, it doesn't even matter for the moment that the whole principle of exclusiveness is being violated – every punter there gets the feeling that he has at last been let in on something and he scuttles off to bet his rent money. Even when the horse loses, as it always does, his faith in the omniscience of the Big Boys isn't shaken – he realizes he has allowed himself to be deceived by a false prophet and is being punished accordingly.'

'It really is pathetic,' I said, 'but I still don't . . .' I broke off as Wynter leaned forward, eyes flaring whitely, and aimed his index finger at the bridge of my nose.

'You and I are going to make that dream come true for a large group of compulsive gamblers.' Wynter's voice was vibrant with evangelistic fervour. 'And we're going to charge them an appropriate fee for our services.'

I sneered. 'A third of a million!'

'For each of us, after we clear our expenses.'

The mention of expenses set off subliminal alarms in my mind, but by then I was pretty well hooked, the more so because I had guessed the general nature of Wynter's plan. I'd say that most people have at some stage in their mental development been intrigued by the story about the man who invents chess for the amusement of an ancient king. He refuses the bags of gold offered as payment, and instead asks for one grain of wheat for the first square on the board, two for the second, four for the third and so on, doubling up every time, and the punchline is that by the time they reach the sixty-fourth square all the granaries in the land are unable to cope with the amount of wheat involved. It's a short step from there to putting that kind of mathematics into reverse and playing around with a dwindling series of numbers, and almost the first notion people come to is that of the seemingly infallible prediction.

I nodded at Wynter's attaché case and said, 'How many names are on your list?'

'Very good, Mr Cluny,' he replied. 'I knew we'd hit it off together. I've got a total of 400,000 names and addresses.'

'How do you know they're the right sort of prospects?'

'The United States, Canadian and Quebec governments have been collaborating on a coast-to-coast study of the social consequences of chronic gambling. I was involved with the data storage and retrieval system, and I managed to get a print-out of the master list. It cost me a lot of money to grease the right palms, but I got what I needed.' Wynter picked up his case and opened it, revealing a massive block of closely printed sheets.

I nodded. 'What sort of breakdown were you thinking of?'

'Well, I plan to use only four-horse and five-horse races.' He was speaking quickly now, giving the impression of a man who was as much obsessed as any of his prospective victims. 'There was a temptation to include a couple of three-horse races to boost the size of the final tiers, but with three horses it would look too easy. There wouldn't be the same build-up of credibility.'

'I'm with you. Go on.'

'We start with a four-horse race and send letters to everybody on the list, introducing them to an exclusive new tipster service which is so confident of its results that it won't introduce any charges for the service until it has given four consecutive winners. That should convince them of our honesty and integrity. Naturally, we divide the list into four blocks of 100,000 and tip a different horse to each. When the race is over, regardless of the result, we'll have 100,000 punters on whom we have created an initial good impression, and we forget about the others.

'We take a five-horse race next and do the same kind of thing, leaving us with 20,000 hopefuls to whom we've given two winners. Another four-horse job boils it down to 5,000, and another one gives us 1,250 clients who have had four straight winners and by this time are convinced they've got a hot line to the Secret Masters of the Turf – and that's when we start introducing a modest fee. I'd say two hundred bucks each for the next tip, giving us a first rake-off of 250,000 dollars.'

'Two hundred each,' I said, slightly taken aback. 'That's stinging them a bit, isn't it?'

'Nonsense! The way these people bet they'll have picked up a bundle on their four winners. That's the beauty of the scheme – nobody really gets hurt.' Wynter paused to dab flecks of froth from the corners of his mouth. 'A five-horse race will reduce them to 250 clients who have had *five* straight winners, and that's where we advise them that we're being pressured by various powerful organizations who resent our helping ordinary gamblers and want us to suspend our operation.'

'Huh?'

'That is vital to the whole plan. It's psychology, you see.

We build up their hopes and dreams, then make as though we're going to dash the cup from their lips. They'll see the pearly gates swinging shut in their faces and they'll do anything to squeeze through the gap. So we tell them that, in view of the great personal risk to ourselves, it's no longer worth carrying on with the service unless we can interest really dedicated gamblers who are prepared to pay 2,000 dollars a time for guaranteed winners.'

'Two grand!' I began to get a cold feeling in my stomach.

'Think *big*, man. The people on my list are reasonably well heeled and they have compulsions. The higher the threshold figure we name the more determined they'll be to get in on it. That's the way they think. For a brief golden hour in their lives they'll have known what it is like to be on the same side as the all-powerful Big Boys, and that's a feeling they won't want to relinquish. I guarantee they'll come through with the money – and that will give us a second rake-off of 500,000 dollars. If it's a five-horse race they'll be reduced to fifty people who have had six straight winners and who will be putty in our hands. I wouldn't want to take undue advantage, of course, so if we stick to the agreed two grand per tip we'll pick off a third haul of 100,000. By then we'll be down to about ten people and well into a diminishing returns situation, but it means that sending out a mere ten letters will net us a useful 20,000 dollars. Add that lot up.'

'I already did – it comes to 870,000.' I swallowed to ease the dryness in my mouth. 'But these figures are too good, aren't they? It can't work out as perfect as that.'

'Oh, there's bound to be a certain amount of wastage and falling by the wayside,' Wynter said unconcernedly, 'but I've only been outlining the basics of the idea. In the actual event I would expect to revive clients who had four winners followed by one loser. Tell them it was the fault of the opposition and offer to let them have future tips at half price. That should bring in more than enough to compensate for erosion in the various tiers and leave some over to offset against expenses.'

Expenses. There was that word again. I mulled it over for a moment and said, 'I get the feeling you didn't pick me purely at random.'

'Of course not! I had to find somebody who controlled a mailing services outfit. It had to be big enough to cope with the first mailing shot, but small enough to keep a lot of nosy employees from screwing things up. It also had to be a place that wasn't doing too well – so that the owner would be properly receptive to a good idea.'

'Hold it right there,' I snapped, squaring my shoulders. 'What gave you the idea that . . . ?'

He silenced me by holding up one hand, palm outwards, and putting on a world-weary smile. 'Don't waste our time with all that stuff, Desmond. I've done my homework very thoroughly and I know *exactly* what sort of financial shape you're in. Okay?'

'Then you should have costed the operation. Even with throwing in the paper at trade price, and fully automatic printing and folding and franking, the cost of 400,000 copies in the mail – even allowing for the new fax mail rates – is going to be . . . is going to be . . .' My voice faded to an undignified croak as I doodled some figures on my blotter.

'I can let you have eight thou in cash to prove I'm on the level, but that cleans me out. You'll have to rack up enough credit to cover the rest of your investment. You can do that, can't you?'

'Yes, but I don't like it.'

'It's only for a couple of weeks, then you can cream it back off the top – before you pick up your third of a million or more. What more do you want?'

'A drink,' I said firmly, producing a bottle of Tucker's Choice from the bottom drawer of my desk. Wynter nodded when I offered him a glass and we sat for another hour sipping bourbon and discussing practical details of the scheme and going over the letters he had already drafted. Sometime during that hour – partly because of the booze, partly because I was desperate for money, but mainly because I was impressed by the thoroughness of Wynter's pre-planning – I became totally committed to the adventure in applied mathematics.

After all, I told myself, *even if it doesn't work out exactly as planned, we're bound to get some money back. It won't be the end of the world.*

Hah!

It was almost eleven when I went into Trev's office and found he was still sitting in his thought projector. He is a very large young man, one of those people who insist on wearing T-shirts and tight jeans on figures which ought to be decently swathed. His face is huge, round and placid, unmarked by earthly cares, covered with the kind of fine golden fuzz that girls shave off their legs. His blue eyes look humorous when there is nothing to laugh at, and gravely concerned when there is nothing to worry about.

'Trev, what are you doing in here at this time?' I said, trying to control my annoyance.

'Having my mid-morning break,' he replied, twinkling.

'How can you have a break before you've even started?' I pointed in the direction of the shop. 'There isn't a single machine running out there.'

His eyes clouded with sorrow, and for a moment I thought I had stirred his conscience. I should have known better.

'Aw, Des, don't tell me you've been at the liquor already.' He heaved himself up out of his foil-lined box, a laborious operation which had to be carried out in stages. 'Have you any idea what that stuff does to your body?'

'As long as it doesn't get like yours . . .'

'Unkind, Des,' he said, but azure gleams showed he was unaffected by the insult. He picked up and swigged from a bottle of his favourite drink, a revolting locally-produced concoction known as Blissfizz, which was pink, opaque and loaded with sugar. It reminded me of calamine lotion, but Trev had been addicted to it since childhood and drank nothing else – a habit which no doubt had a lot to do with his excessive girth.

I decided to try sarcasm. 'What's the good word from Betelgeuse? Have they given you clearance to do some work today, or are you going to be tied up with more important things?'

'I wish you wouldn't talk that way, Des.' He fixed me with a worried stare. 'The emissaries from the Kingdom of Orion are going to land real soon now and put their true believers in charge of the world. I'll probably be in control of the whole continent of North America, but even I won't be able to save you if you go around scoffing like that.'

'I'll take my chances.'

Trev extended three fingers of his right hand and made a priestly gesture. 'May the Supreme Nizam forgive you, Des. I think maybe I ought to intercede with him . . .'

He made as if to climb back into his box, but I grabbed him and pushed his pudgy bulk into a chair. 'Not now,' I said, deciding to steer the conversation on to more constructive lines. 'I've got some important work here. Charity work.'

'You?' Trev took a generous slug of Blissfizz and gave me a look which seemed almost worldly. 'Charity work?'

'I'm a very charitable person, Trev, but lack of money has always prevented me from helping people the way I wanted to.'

'You'd have plenty of money if you didn't blow so much on rotgut whisky and fast cars and painted women,' Trev accused. 'There'll be none of that sort of thing when I'm in control.'

Only the need to be diplomatic prevented me from planting one on his downy chin. During our discussions Ralph Wynter and I had foreseen that some people on the sucker list would make a few discreet enquiries before entrusting us with their cash. For that reason our letters had to be signed by a real person, one with an unblemished record and whose name could be looked up in various directories. Trev was listed as company vice-president, had never been in any kind of trouble and nobody from out of town would have any reason to suspect he was a fully-fledged lollipop farmer – all of which made him ideal for our purpose. Wynter had been dubious before learning that Trev was so naive that he signed all the tax returns I prepared for him without ever reading what they said. He had left it to me to enlist Trev's aid without giving him any real idea of what we were doing.

'I want to atone for all my past sins,' I said, laying on as much sincerity as I could. 'I've thought of a great way of helping thousands of needy people – but I can't do it without your help.'

Trev shook his head. 'I don't know, Des. I'm pretty tied up with my meditation programme and the UFO observations and the meetings of the Orion Society.'

'This won't take up any of your free time, and . . .' I paused as I got a sudden inspiration, 'it would be a way of proving to me that you really do get thought messages from Betelgeuse. I might become a convert.'

'Hey! That would be great, Des.' A faraway look appeared in his eyes. 'If you learned to play the harp I could make you one of the praise leaders in my Grand Temple.'

'We can talk about all that after I've shown myself to be

worthy,' I said quickly, bringing out an advance list of the runners in the second race at Hillston, a meeting due to be held in three days' time, and set it in his lap. 'Have a look at that.'

He studied the sheet briefly then handed it back to me, his moonlike face registering intense disapproval. 'You know what I think about gambling, Des. It's evil.'

'I know that *gambling* is evil, but what I'm proposing has nothing to do with gambling.' I got closer to him by pulling up an empty Blissfizz crate and straddling it. 'Listen, Trev, with the superhuman psychic powers you get from the Supreme Nizam you could easily predict which of these four horses is going to win, couldn't you? There'd be no element of chance involved.'

He pulled back from me, affronted. 'You really do think I'm simple, don't you, Des? You think I'm a moron.'

'What do you mean?'

'Trying to get me to prostitute my divine gifts so that you can make money on the horses.'

'You've got it all wrong,' I said, relieved by the confirmation that he really was simple. 'I swear to you that I wouldn't place a single penny on a horse. I've never suffered from the gambling fever, but others aren't so fortunate. I've got a list of thousands upon thousands of poor wretches whose lives have been ruined because they fell into the clutches of the bookmakers. They're destitute, Trev – but you can help them. You can be their salvation.'

'How?'

'Don't you see? If we tip them the names of a few certain winners they can get their money back from the bloodsuckers. Can't you see the beauty and the rightness of it? We can turn the bookmakers' own weapons against them – make the punishment fit the crime. We might even put some of them out of business.'

'I like it,' Trev mused, a messianic glitter appearing in his blue orbs. 'And you promise you won't take personal advantage of my predictions?'

'Cross my heart!' I gave the list of runners back to him. 'Do your stuff, Trev. Help me fight a holy war against the syndicates.'

'I'll do it. And do you know what, Des? Next time I communicate with Betelgeuse I'm going to give you the full credit for coming up with this idea.'

'Virtue is its own reward,' I said modestly. 'Now, what about this horse?'

He frowned at the list for a full minute, took a thoughtful pull at his bottle of Blissfizz, then shook his head and heaved himself to his feet. My fears that he was going to confess failure were dispelled when he opened a cupboard and took out an instrument I recognized as his UFO detector. This was a small telescope from which he had removed the object lens and in its place had jammed an old-fashioned radio tube. I had looked into it once out of curiosity and had seen nothing but an oily blur of light which split into concentric rings when I moved the telescope's sections – a phenomenon which apparently was enough to convince Trev that he was peering into other planes of existence. He put the UFO detector to his eye, moved the other end of the instrument up and down my list a couple of times and gave a satisfied grunt.

'That's it,' he stated confidently. 'Number four. Realrock Isle.'

'Wonderful! We're in business.' I brought Trev into my office and brandished in front of him the introductory letter from INSIDE INFORMATION INC., which was the name Wynter had dreamed up for our phoney tipster organization. As I had expected, Trev did not even bother to scan the lines of print. His aversion to reading had in the past led to some monumental goof-offs in the mailing service, but now it was proving useful. He was standing there with a look of dreamy fulfilment all over his peach-fuzzed countenance when I handed him a pen.

He stared down at it. 'What's this for?'

'I want you to sign the letter, Trev. It's only right that you should get all the credit. You and the Supreme Nizam.'

'I'm beginning to think I misjudged you,' he said, taking the pen. 'What about putting in the name of the horse?'

'Don't worry – I'll strip that in at the bottom before we go to press.'

Trev nodded, satisfied, poked his tongue out of the corner of his mouth the way he always did when he was writing, and signed his name with a flourish. *Trevor Q. Botley*. I whisked the letter away from under his hand, led him to the door and told him he was free to return to his thought projector if he wanted to bring Betelgeuse up to date on all that had been happening. Unbelievably, he shook his head.

'I'd rather get to work,' he announced. 'This is no time for sitting around. It's a time for action.'

'Action?' A sense of unreality stole over me. 'Are you feeling all right?'

'This is important work, Des – not one of your trivial money-grubbing commercial exercises. In a project like this you'll find me zealous, industrious and untiring. You'll see.'

Coming from anybody else those words would have been disquieting – I would have much preferred to carry out the mailing shot alone and unobserved – but in the case of Trev I was not unduly worried. When it comes to serious work he has an attention span of about three seconds and a lizard-like tendency to remain perfectly motionless for hours at a time. I led the way into the shop and got down to work immediately.

Up until around 1990 the reproducing of 400,000 copies

of even a single-page letter would have been a task of considerable magnitude, but the advent of gamma ray multi-sheet printing changed all that. Simply by placing the master copy on a block of treated paper and giving it a short burst of non-divergent radiation I was able to print 5,000 good copies at a time. It took me fifteen minutes to prepare the first 100,000 copies of the letter, those bearing the name of the horse Trev had selected. I passed them over to him for feeding through the Mailomat IV, the lightning-fast robot which began printing each with a name and address from Wynter's list, folding, sealing, franking and stacking them in well-secured bundles.

True to form, Trev fell into a near-cataleptic trance in the middle of the operation. That gave me ample opportunity to peel the name of his horse off the master, strip in another one and print a further 100,000 copies. At that point Trev, apparently deciding he had had enough of being zealous, industrious and untiring, ambled off to his office to have his customary lunch of a quart of Blissfizz and a bag of nauseating confections known as Coco-blobs. It was a full hour before he returned, and by then I had printed two more 100,000 lots with the names of the remaining horses and was running them through the Mailomat.

He blinked with surprise as he glanced around the shop and saw the stage the job had reached. 'Say, you've really been going some.'

'A strange force seemed to be driving me onwards.'

'I'm proud of you, Des,' he said. 'And I want you to know you'll get your due reward for all this work.'

I gave him a suitably enigmatic smile.

There now had to be a three-day break in the proceedings, time in which to let the letters reach their destinations and be studied in 400,000 homes.

As there was nothing I could do until the chosen race at Hillston had been run, I worked hard for the rest of the day on routine contracts and that night – partly as a celebration, partly to relieve nervous stress – blitzed a couple of my favourite clubs with all the vigour of Genghis Khan and Attila the Hun rolled into one. Next morning I woke up beside a sweet young thing called Kristine, who demonstrated her essential good nature by giving me a couple of Superseltzers and remaining silent while I dressed and tottered off to work.

I got to the office shortly after eight and was brewing coffee when, to my astonishment, Trev opened the door and rolled in with a news sheet tucked under his arm. He was wearing a dark blue T-shirt on which he had painted the major stars of Orion. As usual the constellation was somewhat lacking in grandeur because the central part of it was lost in the fold beneath his squabby breasts, but his round face was more animated than I had ever seen it.

'Boy, you sure look a mess,' he said, inspecting me with a show of concern.

'Never mind how I look. What brought you in so early?'

Trev unfolded his paper. 'I've been making my selection for today,' he said importantly, 'and it's Lightburn in the . . .'

'Hold it!' I snatched the paper from his grasp and dropped it into a waste bin. 'There isn't going to be any selection today.'

'But I thought we were going to rob the bookies to help the poor.'

'We are, Trev, we are – but not every *day*! We've got to allow time for the poor to collect on the first bet so that they'll have money for the next one.' Looking at Trev's perplexed expression I thought of a way to explain the dwindling scale of our charity work. 'Besides, what we did yesterday cost me a lot of hard cash – I'll have to concentrate on some ordinary work for a while, then see how many more needy people we can help. The list probably won't be as big next time.'

'Sorry, Des,' he said, looking contrite. 'I didn't realize the way it was.'

'It's all right.' I patted him on the shoulder and eased him out of the office. 'Just you leave the boring old practical details to me. All you've got to do is come up with the winners when we need them. Okay?'

'You can count on me.' He lumbered away amid a creaking of floorboards, leaving me staring thoughtfully into the coffee percolator. One thing I had not anticipated was my cousin actually taking an interest in what was going on in the shop – even when running off leaflets for his own Orion Society he was wrapped up in daydreams so much that he would let any kind of mistake go by. On one lovely occasion he had issued a news sheet, typed up by a semi-literate temp, which had referred all the way through to the Kingdom of O'Ryan. To me it had looked better that way, more appropriate somehow, but apparently a few of the faithful were pretty annoyed about the blunder and had threatened to depose Trev.

Later in the day, when Ralph Wynter called in with a draft of the second message from INSIDE INFORMATION INC., I told him I was thinking of cutting Trev out of the operation and simply stripping in his signature on future letters. Surprisingly, he was against the idea.

'What we're doing isn't actually against the law,' he said, staring meaningfully through his steel rims, 'but there are large sums of money involved. Some people might get angry and there might be some embarrassing investigations and publicity. It might be advisable for us to take a long vacation.'

'And leave Trev to face the music? I don't know if I could do that.'

'Nobody's going to touch *him*. From what you told me, he's got the best defence in the world – his innocence. How could anybody even think of leaning on a simpleton who genuinely believed he was a holy crusader?'

I nodded, impressed by the slippery quality of Wynter's mind, and we went on to talk about more important things. Trev's behaviour continued to worry me though. Something about the project, as he understood it, seemed to have caught his imagination and his interest was still as high as ever when Monday – the day of the selected race – came round.

On several occasions when I went into his office I found him sitting in his thought box running his UFO detector up and down racing sheets, pausing only to munch a Coco-blob. Right up to the start of the race I was fretting about what I was going to say to him if, as was likely to happen, the 'wrong' horse came in first, and so it was with some trepidation that I called up the afternoon's sports pages on the Cathodata set in my office. I needn't have worried, however – Realrock Isle had walked it by ten lengths. A combination of relief and unexpected excitement sent me sprinting in to give Trev the news.

'Naturally Realrock Isle won,' he said in a mild voice, arching his eyebrows at me. 'What did you expect?'

Only then did I remember the rules of our game. 'Of course, I knew it *had* to win if that's what the thought voices told you,' I mumbled apologetically, doing my best to cover the slip. 'It's just that when you're not used to this sort of thing it seems sort of . . . miraculous.'

'You've so much to learn,' he sighed, passing me a handful of racing sheets upon which one horse in every event had been underlined in red crayon. 'Take your pick from that lot.'

'Thanks, Trev.' I flicked through the sheets and was pleased to see that he had covered the race Wynter and I had selected for our next mailing – a five-horse affair the following Thursday at Argent Heights. This time the Supreme Nizam of Betelgeuse, speaking through the medium of a defunct thermionic valve shoved in the end of a Woolworth telescope, had decreed that a nag called Wheatgerm would be first past the post. I got Trev to sign the second letter and, leaving him to his meditations, went out to the shop and started to work.

This time I only had to deal with the 100,000 people from the original list who had been given the winner, and it was a comparatively easy job to split them into five lots of 20,000 and tip a separate horse to each lot. Just to be on the safe side in case Trev came out to do a little work, I put spare letters tipping Wheatgerm on top of each pile – making it look as though the entire mailing said the same thing – and only removed them as the piles were going into the Mailomat. The precaution proved unnecessary, because it was almost quitting time before Trev roused himself and by then all 100,000 letters had been loaded into the pneumotube and were well on their various ways.

I began to feel easier in my mind about how the operation was shaping up, and celebrated by going out on the town that night with an exotic young lovely who was a snake dancer at Lord Jake's Revue Bar. She ate enough to choke one of her pet pythons, but I had no qualms about the expense – I could feel it in my bones that all my troubles, financial and otherwise, would soon be a thing of the past.

The first faint intimation that my skeleton is a lousy fortune teller came on Thursday afternoon when Wheatgerm romped home so far ahead of the rest of the field that he was nearly placed in the previous race.

Judging by the odds he came in at the bookmakers were as surprised as I was, so I did a slightly peculiar and uncharacteristic thing. I *knew* that Trev had no cosmic forces working for him, and that it isn't really remarkable for somebody to pick two winners in a row, and yet I was unable to resist digging out the handful of racing sheets he had marked and comparing them with the Cathodata results. The way it worked out, he had chosen some thirty horses and out of that number precisely three, including Wheatgerm, had been winners.

To me that figure seemed about average for somebody making blind stabs with a pin, or even with an old radio tube, so I damped down the sparks of the crazy idea that had begun to glimmer at the back of my mind and began to think about the next phase of the project. We were down to 20,000 people who had been given two winners and now the mechanical side of the operation was becoming child's play. Trev made things easier by spending more and more time in his thought projector while he pored over racing sheets, and once again I didn't even have to ask him to pick a horse in our next four-horse race. He had chosen an animal called Prismatic and as it was the odds-on favourite I wasn't too surprised when it won fairly comfortably. Trev received the news with a calm shrug and handed me another bunch of marked-up sheets, including one on which he had underlined a horse called Foreign Exchange in our next four-horse race.

Pleased with the way we had settled into an undemanding routine, I split the remaining list of 5,000 clients into four equal lots, tipped each lot a different horse and had the whole mailing completed in less than half an hour. Past experience had taught me to be extra careful when everything in the garden seems lovely, but I was so bemused by the nearness of the first pay-off that I let myself be lulled into that famous false sense of security, and was totally unprepared for trouble when it came.

I had spent an entire evening at my apartment with

Ralph Wynter, splitting a bottle of Tucker's Choice and perfecting the text of the letter we were going to send to our reduced roll of 1,250 lucky people who – when the fourth race was run – would have received advice of four straight winners. Even though I say so myself it was a masterpiece of psychological manipulation, one which played on their quasi-religious hopes so accurately that they were bound to fall over themselves in their rush to mail us their money. With the serious business completed, Ralph had called up a couple of well-endowed working girls he was friendly with, and we had spent a few hours sampling what a more poetic person might have called the garden of earthly delights.

I think I was still wearing a self-satisfied smile when I got into the office next morning and began to tidy up some routine business matters. Hard work is a good way to pass the time. The race we were interested in was at noon, and within seconds of its completion the result was flashed up on my Cathodata screen. A horse called Lamplighter had won by two lengths. Trev's selection, Foreign Exchange, had come in last, but all that did was prove that his previous record of success had been what I always knew it to be – pure dumb luck. Whistling cheerfully, I isolated the list of 1,250 people who had been tipped Lamplighter and went into the shop to send them the offers they wouldn't be able to refuse. Visions of a promised land of dollar green pastures were shimmering before my eyes.

So intent was I on the good work that I almost keeled over with shock when, a few minutes later, a crash of breaking glass followed by a tremulous and unearthly moan drowned out the faint whir of the machinery.

I spun round, dry-mouthed, and saw Trev standing in the doorway of my office. To be more precise, his great bulbous form was slumped against the jamb and one hand was pressed to the narrow margin between his eyebrows and hairline that he regards as a forehead. His face was pale as he lurched away from the door and crunched towards me through the fragments of the Blissfizz bottle he had dropped. I backed off from him, fearful that his mind had finally snapped.

'It's all over, Des,' he said in a hollow voice. 'I'm undone. The Supreme Nizam has abandoned me.'

'He'd never do a thing like that,' I soothed, wondering what in hell had happened. 'Not to you.'

He rolled his eyes, horribly. 'I must have transgressed, Des. That's the only explanation.'

I was still trying to figure out what explained what when my gaze was drawn to a point behind Trev, to the electronic glow emanating from my office which told me I had forgotten to switch off the Cathodata set. That explained everything. It was obvious that Trev had wandered in there and somehow had concentrated on the screen long enough to discover his prediction for that day's race had been wrong – and, to say the least of it, he was reacting badly. He was swaying around like a balloon man anchored only by his shoes and there was a real danger of some of my best equipment being toppled and damaged. Cursing my carelessness, I fought to steady him up, but it was like trying to wrestle a zeppelin full of water.

'I'm unworthy, Des,' he groaned. 'I'm going to be cast into the outer darkness. Woe is me.'

Staggering around under each surge of his weight, I strove desperately for some way out of the jam and almost sobbed with relief when inspiration came. 'Why are you saying these things, Trev? Would the Supreme Nizam keep giving you winners if he thought you were unworthy?'

He steadied up slightly. 'But I got it *wrong*. I saw it on the screen.'

'Saw what?' I queried. 'Lamplighter came in first – just like you predicted.'

'Huh?' A flicker of hope appeared in his eyes. 'I . . . I was nearly sure I marked a different horse. Foreign something or other.'

'Perhaps that's what *you* meant to do, Trev, but you're forgetting that Another was guiding your hand.' I groped around in the inside pocket of my jacket, carefully counting sample letters from the last mailing, and whipped out one I knew to bear Lamplighter's name. 'I mean, it's down here in black and white. You can't argue with that, can you?'

'You're right,' he whispered, a look of joy appearing in his eyes. He let go of me and hurried away, but not before I saw that he was on the verge of tears.

I felt a twinge of guilt over having conned him and made up my mind to give him a bonus, maybe fifty or a hundred bucks, when the big money came in. The first thing I did, however, was to search out and destroy all the racing sheets he had marked, then I unplugged the Cathodata and removed its fuse to forestall any further trouble. After that I completed the mailing and, having made sure that Trev wasn't within earshot, telephoned Wynter to let him know that the gravy train was about to arrive.

Actually, I saw very little of Trev during the next few days – he seemed to have taken up permanent residence in his thought projector – and that was just as well because the flood of mail which began to arrive was, of course, addressed to him. And it's no exaggeration to describe it as a flood!

I have to confess that right up to the moment it happened I didn't really believe the scheme would pay off according to plan. Deep down inside me there had lingered a fragment of scepticism which sneered that it was all too good to be true – but I was wrong. The loot came winging from all over the continent. Well over 200,000 dollars arrived in the space of three days, all of it in the form of cash or open postal drafts as we had specified in the letter. Among the bills there was a surprising number of sincere little thank-you notes from people who were moved by Trev's apparent philanthropy, but when we had separated those out and burned them Wynter and I were left with great heaps of beautiful, glorious, untraceable money. We felt like lying down and rolling in it.

After a hectic bout of celebrations we sent the usual spread of tips on a five-horse race to almost 1,250 paid-up clients, and I took a little time off to buy a new car and restock my wardrobe with the classiest gear I could find. When the race had been run we then had close on 250 people who were convinced that their benefactor – Trevor Q. Botley – was the greatest thing since silent cornflakes, and to them was sent the letter which revealed that the syndicate bosses were turning nasty and that in view of the huge risks involved the only way INSIDE INFORMATION INC. could stay in business was by upping the ante to two grand a throw. To the thousand disappointed clients who had been tipped the losing horses we sent an entirely different letter which apologized for the mistake, hinting that powerful enemies had been the cause, and offering the next guaranteed winner for a mere hundred dollars.

Once again I began to experience sneaking doubts – after all, two thousand dollars is a lot of money – but I needn't have worried. Nearly half-a-million promptly arrived in registered envelopes, most of which also contained embarrassingly fervent letters of gratitude. Even Ralph Wynter was surprised by the response we got to the auxiliary missive. It seemed that many of our clients were quite prepared to forgive Trev for one little slip, and to prove it they coughed up to the tune of an extra 70,000 bucks. For days as we went through the lucrative final phase of the operation I wandered around in a dreamy euphoria, giggling aloud every now and then, and trying to understand why I had ever bothered to work when making real money was so ridiculously easy.

During that period Trev went on signing letters without reading them, and making predictions about horse races without even bothering to check the results. Apparently his traumatic moment of doubt and subsequent renewal of belief had attuned him more closely than ever to his ethereal friends in the residential section of Betelgeuse. It made him less aware of what was going on in real life. I was glad about that because his success rate continued to be abysmal and it would have been awkward for us had he found out what a rotten prophet he actually was.

The daily ritual of sorting the mail and dividing the spoil meant that Wynter was now spending quite a bit of time in the office, and inevitably there came the point at which I had to introduce him to Trev. My cousin put on a performance which under other circumstances would have embarrassed me to death.

'Forsake your worldly ways,' he said to Wynter, ignoring his outstretched hand. 'The emissaries from the Kingdom of Orion are coming. They'll be here soon.'

'Is that a fact?' Wynter winked at me. 'How soon?'

'Real soon.' Trev spoke with priestly assurance. 'The Supreme Nizam of Betelgeuse has decreed it.'

'Yes, but *how* soon?'

Trev stared upwards for a moment, apparently seeking guidance from a light fixture in the ceiling. 'Ten o'clock Thursday morning.'

'That's nice,' Wynter chuckled. 'He'll be just in time for coffee.'

Trev gave him a look of mingled disdain and pity, turned on his heel and strode out of the office. He slammed the door so hard the pressure wave almost made my ears pop.

'You were right about that guy,' Wynter said, sticking his tongue out of the corner of his mouth and making an idiot face. Perhaps I had some remnant of family feeling for Trev, but Wynter's remark and the way he delivered it annoyed me. Also there had been a strange glint in Trev's baby blue eyes, a hint of intensity I had never seen before which made me wonder what was going on inside his head.

'You shouldn't have pinned him down to an exact time like that,' I said. 'I don't like the idea of popping his bubble.'

Wynter shrugged carelessly. 'Relax, Desmond. Nobody can pop that kind of bubble.'

For some reason I couldn't quite put my finger on the comment gave me a chilly feeling, as though somebody had opened a door nearby and admitted a coiling snake of cold air.

By the time we got near the final greatly reduced stakes, Wynter and I had settled into a routine. Every morning about nine we picked up the mail, took it into my office, locked the door and began the pleasurable task of opening the envelopes and sorting and dividing the money. Had we used the simplified scheme there would have been very little mail to deal with at that stage, but Wynter's idea for 'reviving' clients who had been given only one loser was still yielding fair returns, and Thursday morning produced sizable stacks of money, postal drafts and letters of worshipful gratitude.

'This is okay, but I'm packing it in tomorrow,' Wynter announced, polishing his steel rims with a tissue. 'It's vacation time and I can feel Rio calling. You should pull out as well.'

'Expecting trouble?'

He tapped a pile of letters. 'Some of the people who went down are a bit churned up about it, but I don't think they're a real threat. The ones I'm worried about are the characters who want to come round here and kiss your cousin's feet. They could descend on us at any time – and that's something I hadn't planned for.'

'I see what you mean,' I said. 'Perhaps I ought to . . .'

I never got round to finishing the sentence because at that moment I became aware of something very odd that was taking place right before my eyes. My desk faces the door of the office, only a few paces from it, and from where I sat I could see with perfect crystal clarity that the aluminium shootbolt was sliding back – all by itself! I had fitted that bolt personally and knew there was no way of moving it from the far side of the door, so the sight of it quietly slipping back through its guides did peculiar things to my stomach. Wynter noticed the startled expression on my face, but before I could say anything to him the door was flung open and Trev came striding into the room. He was wearing his best Orion T-shirt, the one on which he had sewed the gold epaulettes, and was brandishing his UFO detector.

'The appointed hour is nigh,' he boomed. 'It's almost ten o'clock, and time for you to repent and . . . and . . .' His voice faltered as his gaze was drawn towards the desk and took in the heaps of envelopes, letters and money.

'Why didn't you lock the door?' Wynter said accusingly.

'I *did*,' I whispered, but there was no time to explain about the self-propelled bolt for Trev was advancing on me with anger and reproach in his eyes. He looked bigger than ever, oddly majestic.

'Des, Des,' he said, eyes burning me like blue lasers, 'why have you committed this terrible sin? You gave me your word.'

'This isn't what it looks like,' I replied hurriedly, trying to calm him down. 'Ralph and I have started this little mail order business. It's nothing to do with the horses. We sell . . . we sell . . .'

'Bibles,' Wynter put in.

I nodded emphatically. 'Bibles.'

A story like that would have satisfied the old familiar Trev, but this new and rather disquieting one snatched up a handful of letters and subjected them to intense scrutiny. 'You're lying to me, Des,' he said. 'You've been lying to me all along. These people believe in me, and you've been lying to me all along. These people believe in me, and you've been taking money from them. I'm disappointed in you.'

'I've had enough of this crap.' Wynter stood up and motioned for me to do the same. 'Let's throw the clown out of here.'

'Good idea,' I said, suddenly realizing how dumb I had been to let somebody like Trev knock me off balance. Wynter and I were closing in on him when the second very strange thing occurred.

'*Do not move*,' Trev commanded, raising his UFO detector as though it were some kind of talisman, and on the instant of his speaking I was gripped by a sudden and complete paralysis. Unable to believe what was taking place, I frantically willed myself to move forward and nothing happened – I was frozen into the immobility of a statue. Wynter was similarly petrified, locked in mid-stride, and judging by the expression on his face he was very unhappy about it.

For a moment Trev seemed almost as surprised as we were. His gaze shuttled between our faces and the UFO detector a few times, and I saw a look of wondering surmise appear in his eyes. He raised the detector again and, with his lips working silently, pointed it at one of my filing cabinets. The cabinet immediately turned into a stack of Blissfizz crates.

'It has happened,' Trev breathed. 'It's all coming to pass. The Supreme Nizam is rewarding the faithful.' A faint halo sprang into being around his head as he waved the modified telescope again and turned the money on my desk into a small heap of withered leaves. Wynter gave a strangled moan.

At that point the evidence in favour of Trev's weird theories about the Kingdom of Orion was becoming pretty convincing, but in spite of everything I still couldn't accept them. Fantastic things, miraculous things, were happening all round me – but there had to be a better explanation than that the Supreme Nizam of Betelgeuse was dropping in to visit my simple-minded cousin. I sometimes get flashes of intuition, and at that moment my mind suddenly seized on the last word Trev had uttered – faithful. Faith, somebody once said, can move mountains. Trev had always had faith, lots of it, but not enough to make any difference to anything in the material world, so the inference was that he had obtained reinforcements. And I – God help me – had been instrumental in bringing up those reinforcements.

Thanks to my trickery and manipulation of him, Trev was genuinely convinced he could predict the future, and furthermore there were many people throughout the country who also believed in him because they had had incontrovertible 'proof' of his powers. Wynter had stressed the religious element in the make-up of the compulsive gambler, and indeed we had relied on it to make the scheme work. I have never been mystically inclined, but in the moment of stress I could see clearly that the faith and fervour of our remaining clients was forming a reservoir of psychic power which Trev could tap at will. He had become a miracle-worker. In a way it was almost surprising that his transformation had not occurred at an earlier stage in the game, but perhaps the mental force of 5,000 people who are fairly well convinced of something is less than that of fifty who are total believers.

The insight I had received was a terrifying one, but it provided some sort of explanation for what was going on – and it also showed me a possible way out of the situation. The key factor was Trev's own faith in his powers, and if I had built that faith up I should also be able to tear it down and restore him to his former state of ineffectual goofiness.

'I have a confession to make,' I said to Trev, relieved to find he had left me the power of speech. 'Ralph and I *have* been making money out of this thing with the horses. We've been duping people all along. It was what we set out to do, right from the beginning.'

Trev eyed me with sorrow. 'You're a broken reed, Des.'

I nodded. 'The point is, Trev, that we even duped you. Nearly all the predictions you made about the races were wrong. I fooled you into thinking you were getting them right.'

'That doesn't make sense,' he said, giving me a calm and pitying smile. 'You showed me the letters yourself. And why are the people I helped still sending you their money?'

'But those are only a fraction of the number we started out with.'

'That's right,' Wynter chimed in, apparently sensing what I was trying to do. 'You see, my whole plan was based on starting off with a huge . . .'

'Silence!' There was a look of Mosaic anger on Trev's round face as he turned on Wynter. '*You* are the one who corrupted my cousin, *you* are the serpent – and you shall be punished accordingly.'

He raised his UFO detector, waved it once – and Wynter disappeared. For a second I thought he had simply been dematerialized, then I saw there was a tiny speckled snake wriggling on the floor right where he had been standing. I stared down at it in dismay. Trev, revealing a ruthless streak I didn't even know he possessed, completed Wynter's punishment by raising one of his boots and stamping hard on the snake, converting it into a revolting mess.

'My God,' I quavered. 'This is terrible.'

'You have nothing to fear from me,' Trev said. 'You are a weak man, Des, prey to all the desires of the flesh, but you have a hidden core of goodness. I have forgiven you for your sins and will give you a place by my side as soon as . . . Well, as soon as . . .' His words tailed away uncertainly.

I had been staring at him for several nervous seconds before it dawned on me that he had no idea what to do next, that he was all dressed up with supernatural powers and epaulettes on his T-shirt, and had nowhere to go. My gaze followed his to the clock on the office wall. The time was ten after ten, which meant that the Supreme Nizam was late for his appointment. Trev gnawed his lower lip and I could see he was having difficulty in reconciling himself with the notion that a Lord of Orion could have human faults such as tardiness.

'How about that?' I said, seizing the chance. 'It's way after ten and there hasn't been any cosmic visitation. Can't you see what this means, Trev? It proves . . .'

'Clam up,' Trev said irritably and, having seen what he could do to people who displeased him, I clammed up. He brooded for a moment, his face looking more and more like that of the Trev I knew, and I began to hope against hope that the bubble of his beliefs had been punctured. I studied his halo, trying to decide if it had shrunk or grown dimmer. It may have been my imagination at work, but it seemed to me that his aura really was on the wane.

I was beginning to feel quite optimistic about my chances of escaping from him when he got one of his inspirations. He raised the UFO detector to his eye and aimed it at the ceiling. There was a moment of silence and then, to my consternation, a look of inhuman elation spread over his chubby features. He snapped the telescope shut, almost dislodging the radio tube from the end of it, and turned to me.

'I've been a fool,' he said, beaming. 'I don't know what came over me, Des. All that stuff about the Supreme Nizam coming here – it was pure nonsense.'

'Don't worry about it,' I soothed, hardly able to credit my luck. 'Anybody can make a little mistake.'

Trev shook his head. 'It wasn't a little mistake, Des – I got the message completely wrong. You see, the Supreme Nizam wants me to go to *him*!'

'Hold on a minute,' I said, my voice rising into a bleat of alarm as new vistas of peril opened up in my mind.

'I don't have a minute.' Trev raised his arms and now he really was huge and awesome. 'My work on Earth has ended. The time has come for me to lead the faithful to the Kingdom of Orion.'

I made an attempt to pull his arms down again, but I was too late.

The floor gave a sickening lurch, the office walls dissolved and blew away like mist, and all at once I was standing with Trev at the centre of a circular landscape about the size of a football field. It was a surrealistic landscape, dotted with ornate fountains and artificial-looking trees covered with small tufts of white. Beyond the perimeter was a hard blackness, and when I turned to my left I could see the blue-white disk of the Earth floating on a background of stars. I moaned aloud as it came to me that I was out in space and travelling through the interplanetary void in a kind of environmental bubble conjured up by Trev. I fell on my knees before him and tugged at the hem of his T-shirt.

'Have mercy on me,' I pleaded. 'I don't want to go to Betelgeuse – please send me back to Earth.'

'Can't do that,' he said in a voice full of compassion. 'Earth is no more.'

He made a casual gesture with his UFO detector as he spoke, and the Earth winked out of existence.

I cringed away from him. 'Wha . . . what have you *done*, Trev? All those people . . .'

'Not all of them.' He gave me one of his terrifying indulgent smiles. 'The harvest of the faithful is safely gathered.'

At that moment I became aware that there were about fifty people wandering around the circumscribed Dali landscape, their faces blanked out with shock. I recognized several as members of Trev's Orion Society, and could only surmise that the rest were 'all-winner' clients of INSIDE INFORMATION INC. The whole affair must have been even more traumatic for them than it had been for me, but I didn't get time to sympathize with their plight.

Trev waved his telescope and suddenly all of us were dressed in unisex garments which took the form of ankle-length robes. I looked down at the unfamiliar object which had materialized in my hands and saw that it was a small harp.

'Come, my children,' Trev called in a voice of thunder. 'Come and sing the praises of the Supreme Nizam of Betelgeuse, who has called us to our rightful places in the Kingdom of Orion. The journey will take many years, but do not worry – there is an abundance of food and drink. Now, *sing*!'

Raising our voices in unison – because there is no way

to disobey Trev's commands – and with me plinking dispiritedly on the harp, we began to sing.

That was three years ago and we've been travelling through space ever since. I've become as fat as a hippo through lack of exercise and having to get all my nourishment from the Coco-blob trees and the Blissfizz fountains. With Trev in complete control of things here inside his space bubble life is, as you might imagine, hellishly boring – no booze, no decent food, no sex, and we spend sixteen hours a day singing the bloody awful hymns he composes.

I don't mind telling you, the only thing that keeps me from going mad is trying to figure out what is going to happen when we finally get to Betelgeuse.

Dream Fighter

Rowan and his wife had to carry their own cases up three flights of stairs and along a sad brown corridor. Some of the lighting fixtures were broken, and the others served only to create dirty orange smudges on the walls. Jane stopped outside the room the desk clerk had assigned them and looked about her with a mixture of disdain and weariness.

'Some hotel,' she said. 'Why do you allow Sammy to book us in to places like this?'

'It's only for one night,' Rowan told her.

'It's always only for one night. I can't go on like this much longer, Victor.'

'We'll be taking a break soon.'

'I don't see how. The money you get for one fight these days barely sees us through to the next.'

'It's better than no money, which is what we'd have if I . . .' The weight of the cases in Rowan's hands suddenly became unbearable. 'Do you mind if we continue the conversation inside? If we're paying for the room we might as well make use of it.'

Jane nodded, turned the key in the lock and pushed the door open. Just beyond it, in the shabby dimness of the room, stood a grinning, scaly horror – part man, part dragon – which raised a clawed hand in menace. Jane drew breath sharply, but stood her ground.

'Victor,' she said. '*Victor!*'

'I'm sorry,' Rowan mumbled. He closed his mind, painfully, and the creature vanished into nothingness.

'You're losing control.' Jane strode forward, through

the spot where the apparition had been, and slung her case on to a bed. 'Isn't that a sign it's time to quit?'

'How in hell can I quit?' Rowan kicked the door shut behind him, dropped the cases, and lay down on the other bed. The soft, walnut-sized bump on top of his head was throbbing, aching, flooding him with disquiet. He cupped his hand over it, feeling the unnatural warmth through his cropped hair, and tried to relax.

'Victor, you're in no condition to fight.' Jane spoke softly as she knelt beside him. Grateful for the warmth in her voice, Rowan turned to his wife. The years had honed the original prettiness of her face into taut, economical planes which Rowan saw as beauty.

'I'll be all right,' he said. 'If I beat Grumman tonight the purse will be enough to let us . . .' He stopped speaking as Jane began to shake her head.

'Victor, you've lost twelve fights in a row. Against third-raters. And Grumman's supposed to be *good*.'

'Perhaps he's not all that good.'

'He's too good for you.' There was no malice or reproach in Jane's words. 'Five years ago it would have been different, but now . . . I mean, I can't understand how Sammy even got you the fixture.'

'You know who to put your money on, then.' Rowan was referring to his wife's small ritual bet, which lately had become a monetary sacrifice.

'Never,' she said. 'Now, you'd better get some rest.'

Rowan closed his eyes and courted sleep, but his nerves were charged with awareness of the contest which was only a few hours away. There was an agitation, a restless traffic along all his neural pathways, and his exo-brain – that seat of supranormal power – seemed to crouch on top of his skull like a tiny animal with a disparate life of its own, scheming and dreaming . . .

* * *

The taxi in which Sammy Kling rode down town had been old even before they had ripped out its gasoline engine and put in a battery-powered unit. He perched on the narrow rear seat, staring out at the shabby streets with eyes which had lost some of their usual glitter. *How come*, he asked himself, *that so many good cities got clobbered in the Dust-Up, while dumps like this survived*?

He was a flinty little man, normally immune to his surroundings, but he was in a mood of vulnerability brought on by the telephone call he had received some minutes earlier. It had lasted about twenty seconds, consisting of nothing more than a terse instruction from Tucks Raphael, Grumman's manager, to meet him at his hotel. Raphael had hung up without waiting for Kling's assent.

The fact that he could be treated in such a manner, Kling realized, was an indication of how far he had sunk in the world. There was a time when he had owned pieces of four good fighters, but one had died and two had burned up. The one who remained, Vic Rowan, was fading fast and should have been put out to pasture years earlier. Kling had, of course, brought on other men, but his judgment was not what it used to be – or the game was changing – and none of them had amounted to anything. Now he was paying the penalty for being a loser – living in cheap hotels, eating synthetic pap, having to go running when men like Tucks Raphael crooked their fingers.

When the taxi dropped him at the Sheraton he paid, without any argument, the exorbitant sum demanded by the driver and went inside. Raphael's suite was only on the fourth floor, but Kling – too dispirited to walk – paid the elevator surcharge and rode up. Two hard-looking men showed him into the well-lit silvery room where Raphael was lounging in a deep chair and making a telephone call. Raphael had grown fatter and shinier in the years since Kling had last seen him, but Kling's attention was absorbed by the younger man who was standing at a window. Built more like an old-style boxer than a dream fighter, Ferdy Grumman had pale grey eyes fringed with white lashes. In contrast to the powerful musculature of his body, his mouth was small and womanly, pursed in permanent distaste. His scalp was shaved to reveal the irregular blister of exo-brain centred on top of his skull.

Kling stared at him for a moment, then – as their eyes met – he felt an icy sensation of dread, a fierce projection of hatred, and he knew at once that Grumman was a borderline psycho, a man whose main reason for fighting was that monsters were devouring his soul. He quickly averted his gaze and saw Grumman's pink lips twitch in satisfaction.

Poor Rowan, Kling thought. *Poor, gentle, faded-out Rowan hasn't a chance. Tonight could finish him.*

The thought inspired in Kling a rare flash of guilt about his profession. Several different kinds of mutant had appeared in the human race in the years following the Dust-Up, all of them characterized by the extrusion of extra-cortical tissue through the fontanelle. There were the straightforward telepaths – many of whom had been killed before the UN had extended special protection – and there were the seers, and those with limited powers of telekinesis. Their abilities had proved useful to society in one way or another, and they had found profitable roles, but there had also been a sprinkling of Unclassifiables, including those individuals whose 'gift' it was to make others see things which did not exist.

They functioned partly by instinctive control of radiation fields around them – the images they created could be photographed – but there was also an element of telepathy, because the visions were much more realistic and more detailed to the naked eye than to the camera. In a tired and shabby world the opportunity for a new kind of spectator sport had been seized at once, and the trade of dream fighter had come into existence. There were countries where the sport was illegal because of the psychological wear and tear on the combatants, and – in the dreadful presence of Grumman – Kling understood the reasoning . . .

'Hello, Sammy,' Raphael said, setting the telephone down. 'How've you been?'

'Okay, Tucks. I'm getting along okay.'

Raphael smiled disbelievingly. 'Have you met my boy Ferdy?'

'No. Hello.' Kling nodded towards Grumman and looked away again, unwilling to face the eyes. Grumman did not acknowledge the greeting in any way.

Raphael's smile broadened. 'Right, Sammy, we get down to business. My Ferdy is going to be the next area champion and I'm making him contender before the end of the year.'

'That's fast,' Kling commented, knowing it was expected of him.

'You bet it's fast. That's why he's got to get in ten straight wins in the next five weeks. That's my programme for him, and I'm not taking no chances with it. No chances at all.'

Kling nodded. 'Why did you want to see me?'

'It's like this. Ferdy will destroy Vic Rowan tonight, but because this is a big operation with a lot of heavy money involved, I'm handing you two K. For insurance, if you know what I mean.'

Kling fought to control the pounding in his chest. 'You want Vic to throw the fight?'

'He won't be throwing it,' Raphael explained with mock patience. 'I'm generous. I'm giving you and Rowan a thousand each just to accept defeat gracefully.'

'It's a waste of money,' Grumman said in a sullen monotone. 'I'm going to turn Rowan's brain into mush and let it run out of his eyes.'

Raphael waved him to silence. 'What do you say, Sammy?'

Kling's brain was analysing the situation with cryogenic efficiency. Rowan was going to lose, anyway. The last shreds of his reputation were going, and it was becoming difficult to match him. He was so certain to lose that there was no need even to tell him about the fix. And with two thousand monits in his pocket he, Sammy Kling, could quit the fight game and go into something which offered better returns and more security. The decision was easy to make.

'You've got yourself a deal, Tucks,' he said. 'The figure was two K?'

'It's all there.' Raphael took a long envelope from an inner pocket of his jacket and handed it to Kling.

'Thanks, Tucks.' Kling turned to leave and was almost at the door when Raphael called him.

'Sammy! Vic Rowan used to be good, didn't he?'

'People say that.'

'Just remember,' Raphael said. 'You and Rowan have taken my money. I've bought you. And if there's any funny business tonight I'll put you both through the meat grinder. Got it?'

Kling nodded silently and hurried out of the room.

Rowan brushed his hair, trying not to touch the now-burning lump, and turned to his wife. 'Are you coming to the fight?'

'To help carry you out afterwards?' Jane exhaled a cloud of cigarette smoke. 'No, thanks.'

'I've only been carried out once.'

'It doesn't matter. Besides, I've heard how Grumman

fights and I don't want to see it.' She continued flicking the pages of a magazine with studied disinterest. Jane was always tense and withdrawn just before a fight, but this time something in her manner alarmed Rowan.

'You'll be here when I get back, won't you?'

'I've nowhere else to go, Victor.'

'I . . .' Rowan gave up the struggle to find the right words. He closed the door and went down the three flights of stairs to where Sammy Kling was waiting with a taxi. The little man looked perfectly normal but a vague signal from his exo-brain suggested to Rowan that Kling had things on his mind.

'All right, Sammy?' he said as he got into the waiting vehicle.

'*I'm* all right,' Kling replied gloomily. 'A bit worried about you, though.'

'Why?'

'I don't like some of the things I hear about Grumman. Listen, Vic, when you feel him getting the edge on you – don't wreck yourself trying to stop him. Just bow out, huh?'

Rowan felt a stab of annoyance. 'Why is everybody so worked up about Ferdy Grumman?'

'I don't think you should risk getting your brains scrambled, that's all,' Kling muttered. 'It's up to you, of course.'

'I know it is.' Rowan sat without speaking for the rest of the short journey to the stadium. He knew he was going to lose again, that he no longer had the vital drive to win, but some remnant of his former self resented being written off so casually. The perverse notion crossed his mind that it would be worth beating Grumman for nothing more than the pleasure of seeing Jane's face when she heard the news.

At the amber-lit stadium he got the checking-in formalities over as quickly as possible, and was glad to reach the solitude of a preparation room. It was an important part of the system that dream fighters did not meet prior to a bout, especially in the final minutes when antagonism was high and control of their powers most likely to slip. He lay on the simple bed and half-heard, half-felt the occasional eruptions of cheering from the crowd in the arena above. Grumman and he were fourth on the bill, a good position, and the audience would be receptive when they went on. Lying perfectly still, scarcely breathing, Rowan made himself ready for the struggle ahead.

When the signal came – a double chime from the loudspeaker on the wall – he rose without haste and went along the corridor to the ramp which ascended to the arena. A strongly-built man he recognized as Grumman emerged from another corridor and reached the foot of the ramp at the same time. Rowan was instantly aware of his opponent's chilling psychic aura, but he went through it, like a swimmer breasting an icy tide, and held out his hand.

'I've heard a lot about you,' he said.

Grumman looked down at the outstretched hand and conjured a piece of brown, smoking filth into it. The image was too close to Rowan's sphere of influence to last for more than a fraction of a second before he blanked it out of existence, but the accompanying mental shockwave had the force of a physical blow. Face unchanged, pale eyes staring, Grumman walked on up the ramp. Rowan followed him, barely aware of the reverberating announcements which boomed across the amphitheatre, cursing himself for having given Grumman the opportunity to take the psychological advantage.

At the head of the ramp, one on each side, were two low circular bases. Grumman went to the one on the left. Rowan turned right and was still a couple of paces from his base when there was an abrupt silence, followed by the sound of a woman screaming. He spun and found himself facing a thirty-foot-high demon.

A red light began flashing in the judges' kiosk, to indicate that Grumman had made a foul play by leading off before the signal. Rowan's senses were swamped by the reality of the beast towering over him. He had seen many monsters during his career, beings designed to inspire fear and thus weakness, but this one was in a class of its own. Its face was a compound of things human and things animal, and of things the earth had never seen. Its body was grotesquely deformed, yet true to alien symmetries – black, powerful, matted with hair in some places, glistening naked in others. And above all, the demon was obscene, massively sexual, with an overpowering realization of detail which had the intended effect of cowing the beholder's mind. Rowan was closest to the apparition, and he took the full projected force of it.

He moved backwards, instinctively, and felt his way on to his base, filled with an intense reluctance to go on with the fight. It would mean entering a strange intimacy with the demon's creator, and that was something which should not be asked of him. He considered quitting in that first moment, by stepping down from the base, then came the understanding that he was reacting exactly as his opponent intended, which was something a dream fighter should never do. That was what such contests were basically all about – the forces of nightmare, the conquering of minds by the use of no weapon but fear itself.

Habits developed over many years caused him to probe at the towering demon with intangible sensors, and he found the image *hard*. That meant Grumman was playing a one-shot, concentrating all his powers into a single protagonist with which he intended to win the contest. The discovery surprised Rowan, because it hinted at a lack of flexibility which was dangerous for any fighter trying to make the big time. He gathered his strength, opened the shutters of his mind, and put up a scaly, slope-shouldered dinosaur, equal in height to the demon but many times greater in apparent mass. There was a gasp of appreciation from the encircling terraces.

Rowan caused the dinosaur to lunge forward, but the black demon – moving with incredible speed – swung a razored hand at its throat. And connected. The movement was carried out so naturally, with such a co-ordinated and perfect simulation of reality, that Rowan was momentarily convinced, and – in being convinced – yielded control of his own image. There was a huge fountaining of dark blood and the dinosaur fell sideways, its head almost torn off. Rowan automatically dissolved the writhing creature into nothingness, while he fought to regain control of his own terror. Caught unawares, he had still been involved with the dinosaur when it was killed, and now a part of his subconscious knew what it was like to be ripped asunder by organic knives. Unbidden, in spite of all his efforts to prevent it, a lethal fear began to seep through him.

The demon shook knotted arms above its head in silent triumph, and a seemingly-tiny Grumman performed the same gestures, like a puppet gyrating at the feet of its master.

Rowan forced himself to rally. His exo-brain was on fire, pulsing with agony, but he took command of it, and – perhaps reacting against the demon's associations with evil – put up a giant knight in full medieval armour. The warrior was equipped with a two-handed sword which he swung against the demon in a glittering sweep, but the blow never landed. The demon was too fast, too ferocious. Again Rowan was convinced, and again he yielded control. The bright armour was slashed open like foil, the blood spurted, and another part of Rowan died.

After that he tried a two-headed python which was torn apart even as it materialized around the demon's neck. And a bat-winged creature which Grumman's demon dismembered with contemptuous ease.

Each time, Rowan was unable to disengage quickly enough, and the resulting neural punishment brought him to his knees. His exo-brain was a blob of white-hot metal searing through his skull. He clasped the top of his head with both hands and rocked backwards and forwards, peering through slitted eyes. The crowd, sensing that the crisis point had been reached, ceased to make any sound.

It's time to step down, Rowan told himself. *You don't have to die again. Just step down off the base, and it will all be over, and you can have a rest.* His involuntary swaying movements grew more violent as his body, unconcerned with matters of pride or prestige, fought against the dictates of his intellect.

'Go ahead, old man – fall over.' Grumman's gloating whisper reached him across stellar distances. 'This is the time to do it. Just fall over.'

Rowan stared at him uncomprehendingly. Everybody expected him to do the same thing. Jane. Sammy. Grumman. They all wanted him to fall over. In a way it seemed a good idea not to fight any longer, and yet . . .

Rowan brought his eyes to a focus on the opposite base, and made an astonishing discovery. Grumman was concentrating his attention on Rowan, indulging a personal enmity, instead of monitoring the image which loomed above him. Rowan glanced upwards and saw that the edges of the huge demon had softened slightly, that some of the oppressive detail had been allowed to blur. He waited for a full second while, from the depths of his memory, he summoned up an old friend – one who had settled many issues for him in the past.

Valerius was a professional soldier, a scarred and

weather-beaten veteran who had served with three different legions in Syria, Gaul and Britain. He had withstood rain, snow and desert heat with equal stoicism, and he had slain the varied enemies of Rome with impartial efficiency, regardless of whether they wore silks or skins, regardless of which gods those enemies believed to be giving them protection. He was a stolid, unimaginative man – as plain, functional and uncompromising as the short sword he carried – and in all his years of service he had never encountered a creature which could survive having an iron blade driven through its guts. And, as Valerius saw things, this meant that no such creature existed.

Rowan – knowing by heart every detail, every rivet and thong of the legionary's equipment and armour – snapped him into existence in micro-seconds. He was much smaller than the demon, a sign that Rowan's strength was nearly spent, but his sword was sharp, and he struck with economical swiftness. The blade went deep into the demon's protruding belly, and pus-like fluids gouted. Rowan heard Grumman grunt with pain and surprise, and he guessed at once that the younger man had never experienced neuro-shock before.

This is what it's like, he thought savagely, directing on to the demon a flurry of hacking blows which transmitted their fury to its creator, convulsing him with sympathetic shock. Grumman turned his eyes upward, guiding the black demon as it made a snapping rush, but Valerius – his body protected by the long Roman shield – struck at the face with almost clinical exactitude.

Grumman whimpered and fell backward from his base. His demon vanished as he struck the floor.

The fight had ended.

In spite of his exhaustion, Rowan kept Valerius in existence long enough for him to acknowledge the cheers of the crowd with upraised sword, and then gradually dissolved him out. *They shouldn't have written us off*, he told the fading warrior. *They should never write a man off.*

It was late, and the stadium had emptied, before Rowan broke free of the local sports reporters. He had spent some time trying to find Sammy Kling, and finally had had to go to the promoter's office alone and collect the winner's purse, a cheque for five hundred monits. Puzzled by Sammy's absence, Rowan waited on the front steps of the building for a few minutes, nodding as the box-office staff bade him goodnight and the stadium was sectionally plunged into blackness. He debated calling a taxi, then decided that walking back to the hotel would ease the dull pounding in his head. The after-taste of victory was less pleasant than it had seemed in memory.

He lit a cigarette and walked north on a shadowed street.

The car drew in beside him with feline swiftness, its sleek haunches speckled with rain, and four men got out of it. They closed on Rowan without speaking. Sensing their purpose, he ducked his head and tried to run, but two of them hit him at the same time, with what felt like mailed fists, and he went down. Within seconds he had been dragged into an alley, and there followed a nightmarish period during which he was systematically kicked from neck to groin. Eventually the blood-red explosions of pain seemed to diminish and he realized, with gratitude, that he was escaping into unconsciousness.

'That's enough,' a voice said from somewhere above him. 'He's got to know what's happening.'

The assault on his body ceased, and the dim figures re-deployed. In the faint light from the street one of them appeared to be holding an ordinary garden spade. Rowan became aware of an even greater threat than that of simply being bludgeoned, and he tried to fight against it.

'Hold his head steady.' The dark figure moved over him, foreshortening like Grumman's demon, and his head was clamped in place on the wet concrete.

'No,' Rowan pleaded. 'No!'

'Yes, Rowan,' the voice told him. 'And don't say you weren't warned.'

The spade drove downwards across his skull, shearing through skin and extraneous brain tissue alike. And, in that ultimate pang of agony, Rowan was born into the world of normal men.

Perhaps two hours elapsed before he found the strength to get to his feet and resume walking back to the hotel. The streets seemed unusually quiet, but he was unable to decide if the impression was a genuine one or something subjective, stemming from the newly-found silence within his head. Occasional cars ghosted by without stopping, their occupants undisturbed by the sight of a drunk staggering homewards with a bloodied handkerchief pressed to his scalp.

The hotel lobby was deserted, enabling him to climb the three flights of stairs without being seen. When he fumbled open the room door there was darkness beyond, but the tiny beacon of a cigarette near the window signalled that Jane was awake and waiting for him.

'Where have you been, Victor?' she said quietly. 'What happened to you?'

The concern in his wife's voice reminded Rowan that she had her own kind of dreams, better dreams than those which had just ceased to dominate his own life.

'What do you want first,' he said, forcing his body to remain upright for the necessary moment, 'the bad news, or the good news?'

The Cottage of Eternity

When a young man devotes a lot of time to a scheme – a scheme which culminates in his slipping a vital question to a young woman – he usually feels pleased when she says yes. With Barney Seacombe, however, things were different. On hearing the affirmative answer he had at first refused to believe his ears, then had come the numb conviction that his life was in ruins.

The question was one he had rehearsed many times, and he uttered it with a brash and breezy confidence. 'Have you,' he said, 'a vacancy for a nuclear physicist?'

The young lady, a clerk in the employment exchange in the rural community of Daisyford (population: 8,324), glanced through the card index on her desk and said, 'Yes.'

'That's a good one.' Barney chuckled to show his appreciation of the witticism, then returned to the serious business of the day. 'Now, where do I sign on and how soon can I have some money?'

The young lady gave him a look of cool reproach. 'There's no question of your drawing benefit while there is suitable employment on offer.'

'Wait a minute,' Barney protested. 'I've got my old mother to look after – I can't go away off to Aldermaston or Windscale or somewhere like that.' The part about his mother was a lie – she was being quite well looked after by her current boy friend – but he had thrown it in to win sympathy.

'The vacancy is in Gibley End,' the young lady said, keeping her sympathy to herself.

Barney shook his head in disbelief. 'But that's only three miles from here.'

'I know.'

'There aren't any nuclear establishments there.'

The young lady's eyes flickered like those of a bad poker player. 'Are you refusing to consider this offer of employment?'

'Give me the address,' Barney said, acknowledging defeat. He left the employment exchange and stood for a moment in the sunshine of a glittering spring morning.

The main street of Daisyford was a scene from a tourist poster, painted in exuberant acrylics, but Barney was not in an appreciative mood. When entering university he had chosen to concentrate on nuclear physics for no other reason than that it was a field which offered zero employment opportunities in his home area. The plan was that, having prolonged his education for as long as was humanly possible, he would return to Daisyford and settle down to a state-financed life of fishing the numerous local streams and sipping real ale in the equally numerous local hostelries.

It had seemed a good plan, virtually foolproof, and the last thing Barney had expected was for it to go awry on the first day, especially on account of someone who styled himself:

Arthur Haggle, Squientist,
Gibley Castle,
Gibley End,
Herts.

He thought hard about the name and address which had been supplied to him and, as he rode his motorcycle through the lanes which tenuously connected Daisyford to Gibley End, his natural optimism began to return. Gibley Castle was too old and dilapidated to have been taken over by a research organization looking for low-cost accommodation, so the whole business was either a mistake or a hoax which had been perpetrated on the humourless clerks of the employment bureau.

Squientist, indeed, he thought scornfully as his engine pulsed its note into vistas of quiet fields. *What a give-away! If the idiots in the dole office had any brains they would have realized immediately that there's no such word.*

By the time the compact grey mass of the castle came into view, hulking up incongruously from pastures and ploughed fields, Barney was rehearsing a jocular account of the expedition for his friends in the Daisyford Arms. He was slightly taken aback, therefore, to find on drawing near the old building that a gleaming letterbox had been fitted into the gnarled timbers of the main entrance, and that above the letterbox was a brass plate engraved with the words: A. HAGGLE, SQUIENTIST.

Frowning a little, Barney took stock of the building's exterior and noted the renovated stonework and freshly painted window frames. Gibley Castle was a comparatively modest affair, more like a manor house with delusions of grandeur than a proper castle, but it appeared that someone with money had taken up residence in it. Perhaps, Barney speculated, he had been too quick to assume that no research company would have bought the place. Perhaps there really was a prospective employer lurking inside. Perhaps – Barney's spirits quailed at the thought – he was on the verge of obtaining work and would have to spend the forthcoming summer at a desk instead of lingering on the banks of murmurous streams. Numb with apprehension, he thumbed the new electric bellpush and waited to see what fate held in store for him.

After a minute's delay the door was opened by a thin, middle-aged man whose rusty black suit, walrus moustache and white-gleaming cranium made him look like a character from a Mack Sennett comedy. His gaze hunted suspiciously over Barney's face, and Barney – with a swift, sure instinct – knew that here was a man with whom he could never form a working relationship of any kind. He made an immediate decision, assuming he was looking at Haggle, to flunk the job interview in as spectacular a manner as possible.

'You must be Seacombe, the one they phoned me about,' the man said in a fussy voice. 'I must say you don't look like a nuclear physicist.'

'Cyclotrons weigh thousands of tons,' Barney explained. 'That makes it difficult for me to wheel one up to people's front doors and ask them if they have any atoms they want smashed.'

Disappointingly, Haggle appeared not to notice the sarcasm. 'You'd better come down to my laboratory – we can talk better down there. Quickly, man!'

He closed the heavy wooden door and took Barney through an antechamber, a hall, and into a small elevator. The elevator was smooth in operation, but seemed to go an inordinate distance into the earth. When it stopped Haggle led the way into a tunnel-like corridor. The passageway was warm and dry, and was illuminated by modern electric light fittings, but Barney began to feel cool fingers of unease caressing his spine. It was quite obvious that he had descended into the castle dungeons in the company of a complete stranger whose motives and intentions were shrouded in mystery. Barney tried to draw comfort from the fact that Haggle resembled a silent movie comedian, then recalled that as a child he had been terrified of silent movie comedians because, one and all, they looked like frightening maniacs.

'Mr Haggle,' he said brightly, 'what exactly *is* a squientist?'

Haggle replied without looking back. 'I presume you've heard of a squarson?'

'Can't say I have.'

'What's the education system coming to? If you look squarson up in the dictionary you'll find it means a squire who also happens to be a parson. I'm a squire who happens to be a scientist.'

'I see.' Barney was still turning the explanation over in his mind when they reached the end of the passage and were faced with a massive steel door set flush with the surrounding stonework. Haggle straightened his tie, smoothed a fringe of hair down over his neck, rubbed the toe of each shoe against the back of his other leg, then took a remote control box from his pocket and pressed a button on it to operate the door. Barney's apprehension increased as the door swung open a short way with a muted electrical hum, giving him his first glimpse of a large, dimly-lit room of cavernous aspect. He followed Haggle through the narrow opening, glancing about him with some disquiet as the door quickly whispered shut at his heels, imprisoning him in an ambience of vaulted ceilings, floor slabs which were big enough to cover graves, and thick pillars behind which armies of shadows lay in ambush.

Remembering the way in which Haggle had preened himself before entering, Barney looked around him – half-expecting to see an occupant, possibly a woman – but the chamber was empty except for a scattering of benches, equipment cabinets and a large divan bed. For no reason he could explain, the sight of the bed in such an unlikely setting brought Barney's skin up in goose-pimples, strengthening his resolve to get out of Gibley Castle in a hurry and never come back.

'This is my laboratory,' Haggle announced, 'and it's where you'll be doing most of your work.'

You want to bet? Barney thought. He said, 'What kind of work are you engaged in?'

'Research into the fundamental nature of particles. I have only recently hypothesized an entirely new class of particle.'

'Really?' Barney felt a faint stirring of professional interest. 'What properties do your particles have?'

'Size.'

'Size?' Barney considered the word, trying to place it in context with other scientific whimsicalities such as strangeness, colour and charm. 'For a minute I thought you meant *big* particles.'

'I do.' Haggle's eyes glittered briefly. 'My particles can be a metre and more in diameter, with corresponding volume.'

'I see,' Barney replied, meaning exactly what he said. It had finally become clear to him that Haggle not only looked crazy – the little man was a genuine lunatic. And, with the cunning of the true madman, he had successfully inveigled Barney into his underground lair . . .

'I can handle all the practical work, looking after the particle detectors and so on, but I need an assistant to deal with the theoretical side,' Haggle said, giving Barney a penetrating stare. 'How are you on theory?'

'Very sound,' Barney said, realizing the time had come to start disqualifying himself in no uncertain manner. 'Of course, I've thrown out all that garbage about wave mechanics and distribution probabilities and so forth.'

'You have?' Haggle looked suitably perturbed.

'It's totally unnecessary. Needless complication.' Noting that Haggle was reacting in a satisfactory manner, Barney warmed to his subject. 'What these modern eggheads don't seem to realize is that Neils Bohr's model of the atom was absolutely correct. Particles really are like little snooker balls – all different colours, all bumping into each other – and I can explain any interaction on that basis. It's quite simple, really.'

Haggle took a step backwards, the stricken look on his face making it obvious that he felt he was the one who was incarcerated with a lunatic. 'Are you feeling all right, Mr Seacombe?'

'I feel fine.' Barney put on a broad smile. 'I hardly ever get the headaches now.'

'I'm glad to hear it,' Haggle said, moving towards the door. 'Thanks for coming to see me, Mr Seacombe. You realize, of course, there are other applicants . . .' He broke off as a telephone began to ring somewhere in the shadowy reaches of the room. 'Will you excuse me?'

Barney, now feeling he was in control of the situation, made a generous gesture of acquiescence. He watched Haggle disappear into a cell-like room adjacent to the main chamber and a few seconds later there came faint and fragmentary sounds of a telephone conversation. Humming a popular tune, his mind full of green visions of the afternoon's fishing, Barney sauntered around the nearby benches examining the various items of equipment without much curiosity. He was pleased at having managed to think his way out of a tricky situation and he resolved that he would never again allow anybody or anything to spring surprises on him.

At that moment – as though to demonstrate the vanity of such thoughts – Fate confronted Barney Seacombe with the two biggest surprises of his life.

Within the space of five seconds he saw a ghost and fell deeply, irrevocably in love.

The ghost was in the form of a slender young woman with an oval face, large eyes, long hair and a style of dress which – to Barney's startled and inexperienced eye –

might have dated from the Restoration. She was partially transparent, glowed with a delicate violet radiance, and was beckoning for Barney to join her in the shadowy area behind one of the largest pillars.

His first and natural impulse was to take flight, perhaps emitting a scream or two for good measure, but that was counter-balanced by an emotion of an entirely different nature. Barney, although a presentable young man, had never had much success with the girls of his own generation, most of whom regarded him as being too dreamy. Undeterred, he had continued to cherish the belief that one day he would meet a genuine soul-mate, a girl predestined to be his and his alone, and when that happened both he and she, without a word being spoken, would experience a pang of recognition, ecstasy and fulfilment. Now, gazing silently at the girl, he knew that his faith had been vindicated.

In his daydreams the event had been scheduled to take place in a crowded room – the onlookers largely made up of insensitive females who had previously rejected him – but the meeting itself was all that mattered, and Barney was not going to be put off by a few peripheral drawbacks. Here, in the converted dungeons of Gibley Castle, he had found the light of his life, and it mattered little to him that some kind of slip-up in the celestial book-keeping had resulted in his being born a few centuries too late for true love to run its normal course.

Smiling a tremulous smile of hope and joy, he went towards the beckoning figure. He was rewarded with an answering smile, but it faded almost at once and was replaced by a look of haunting anxiety.

'Please do not leave,' she said. 'Please stay here. Please do not leave me here with . . . *him*.'

Barney was not sure if he had really heard her voice or if the words had merely echoed in his mind, but the plea for help was unmistakable. 'Do you mean Mr Haggle?' he whispered.

'Yes, yes. I implore you to save me from him.'

'But you're a ghost, aren't you?' Barney glanced down at the girl's figure to confirm his diagnosis and made the discovery that her semi-transparent state of being made it possible for him to see a variety of distracting curves beneath the insubstantial dress. 'What can . . . ? What can . . . ?' He made a valiant effort to gather his thoughts. 'What harm can he do you?'

'He is keeping me a prisoner in this terrible place,' she said, her ethereal features registering distress.

'But . . . I thought a ghost could just flit through walls.'

'If I could do that,' the girl said, and it almost seemed to Barney that a note of impatience was creeping into her voice, 'I would hardly be standing here now, would I?'

'You should nip out through the door next time he opens it. You could pass through him, couldn't you?'

'And mingle my body with his! How can you suggest such a thing?'

'Sorry. I guess I wasn't thinking. You see, this is the first time I have ever . . .'

'There is no time to talk,' the girl cut in. 'Will you please help me?'

'Gladly. What do you want me to . . .?' Barney stopped speaking as a faint *ting* from the telephone signalled that Haggle had just hung up, and in the same instant the girl disappeared. He turned away from the empty space she had occupied and, more than a little overwhelmed by what had happened, prepared himself to face the mysterious Mr Haggle, squientist and abuser of pretty ghosts.

'Sorry about the interruption,' Haggle said, walking towards the door.

'It's all right.' Barney gave a hearty laugh to conceal his nervousness. 'I really had you going a minute ago, didn't

I? All that nutty stuff about particles looking like snooker balls! Sometimes I let my sense of humour run away with me.'

Haggle's heavy moustache twitched several times. 'You mean, that was a joke?'

'Of course!' Barney spoke quickly, anxious to gain the initiative. 'Look, Mr Haggle, I've been weighing up your new concept of large-volume particles and I think it's absolutely brilliant. In fact, I'm so impressed by it that I'm prepared to come and work for you without payment – the privilege of helping in your great work would be all the recompense I would need. What do you say?'

Haggle looked furtively gratified. 'You wouldn't expect any salary at all?'

'Not a penny.'

'And you'll bring your own lunch?'

Stingy swine, Barney thought. 'I'll bring some for you, as well. My mother is a great cook.'

'Well, in that case,' Haggle said, in the manner of one who was yielding to a generous impulse, 'I'm prepared to take you on for a trial period. You can start work immediately.'

'Wonderful!' Barney found it quite easy to sound enthusiastic despite his aversion to work, especially of the unpaid variety. His intention was to remain on the premises only until he had rescued the translucent damsel, and with any luck that task might be completed in a matter of minutes. And as a first step he would have to speak to the girl again and find out exactly why she was unable to pass through the stones of the castle walls like any other spirit. He looked around the shadowed recesses of the room, hoping to catch another glimpse of her, but all the corners and niches remained impenetrably dark.

'. . . particles, which I have named maryons, can easily penetrate solid screens up to a tenth of a metre in thickness,' Haggle was saying, 'but the evidence seems to show that they can be trapped in a container whose walls are more than half-a-metre in thickness.'

'Really?' Barney tried to bring his thoughts to bear on the other man's preposterous notions about particle physics.

'Yes. And according to my understanding of wave mechanics, that establishes them as objects whose associated wave functions decrease to 1/2.7 of their full amplitude at about 0.1 metres from their boundary. Do you agree?'

'Absolutely,' Barney said, still covertly scanning his surroundings.

'Their wavelength must be of that order of magnitude – so what sort of rest mass would they have?'

'Huh?' Barney floundered for a moment and then, realizing he would have to play along with Haggle until there was an opportunity to be alone, took a calculator from his pocket and fingered its buttons. 'It looks like the rest mass would be less than an electron's by a factor of around 10^{16}. That's pretty small.'

'So it wouldn't take much energy to accelerate a maryon to Earth escape velocity?'

Barney did more calculations, all the while wondering at what point Haggle would begin to appreciate the absurdity of his own theories. 'Only 10^{-38} joules.'

A gleam appeared in Haggle's slightly protuberant eyes. 'Would the pressure of the solar wind be enough?'

'More than enough.'

'*Hah!*' Haggle began to pace the stone floor, his hands fluttering like white moths. 'This confirms all my ideas.'

'Does it?' Barney's wariness of the little man returned as a strange thought began to take shape at the back of his own consciousness. Haggle's large-volume particles were the product of an eccentric mind, but it was possible to suspend disbelief for a moment and predict that if they did exist they would be very rare on Earth because the solar wind would sweep them away into space. The only places where they might be found would be inside buildings with very thick walls – for example, in the dungeon of an old castle. It looked as though Haggle had come to the same conclusion and had designed his underground laboratory as a sort of bottle for capturing maryons.

Was it possible, Barney wondered with a growing sense of excitement, that Haggle's arrangement for trapping non-existent particles was also responsible for imprisoning the ghost? If so, all he had to do to set her free was to get Haggle out of the way and open the door. It was all quite simple and straightforward, and yet alarm bells had begun to clamour in Barney's subconscious, warning him that he had not taken his idea to its logical conclusion, that there were implications he had overlooked. The girl – whose name he had yet to discover – had given him the impression that Haggle was *deliberately* preventing her escape. And it was odd, very odd indeed, that the postulated physical characteristics of Haggle's strange particle should be exactly the same as . . .

'What's the matter with you, man?' Haggle moved closer to Barney, one of his eyes narrowing critically while the other grew correspondingly larger. 'You look like you've seen a . . .'

'I haven't,' Barney cut in. 'I haven't seen anything.'

'You weren't listening to a word I was saying.'

'It's just that I'm rather tired,' Barney said. 'Haven't slept much lately. Worrying about not getting a job.'

Haggle scowled his dissatisfaction. 'I have to go upstairs for a while. Can I trust you to familiarize yourself with the equipment and not fall asleep as soon as I leave?'

'Of course,' Barney said eagerly, pleased at the prospect of being alone with his ghost-girl. He hurried to one of the benches and stared fixedly and conscientiously at the instruments on it until Haggle left. As soon as the door had swung shut behind the little man Barney turned and walked towards the dark area where he had last seen the ghost. She appeared to him almost immediately and he felt an upsurge of tenderness and concern as he saw that she was more distraught than ever.

'You mustn't worry,' he soothed. 'I'll get you out of here in no time. You'll see.'

She shook her head. 'I can scarcely believe it. After being bricked up in a cell for almost three hundred years I have begun to feel that I shall never escape.'

'Bricked up in a cell!' Barney was horrified. 'Who did that to you?'

'My uncle – Lord Cyril.'

'But what made him do such a terrible thing?'

The girl lowered her gaze. 'I fancied myself in love with a stableboy. My uncle said that if I could not find it within myself to behave like a lady it was incumbent on him to remove me from all worldly temptation by locking me in the castle dungeon.'

Barney felt a twinge of jealousy towards the long-dead stablehand and was at once consumed by intense curiosity about how far the affair had progressed. Unable to think of a diplomatic way of obtaining the information, he asked the girl's name and was told that it was Mary Grey. Further questioning revealed that Mary had died of pneumonia soon after her incarceration and that her uncle, who probably had not intended things to go that far, had hidden his misdeed by having her cell bricked up. Mary's ghost had been imprisoned there for almost three centuries – until Haggle had knocked the wall down in the course of constructing his laboratory.

'In a surfeit of joy I made myself visible to him, wishing to express my gratitude,' Mary said. 'You can imagine how quickly my gratitude turned to fear and loathing when I discovered the kind of creature Mr Haggle is. Not only has he continued to keep me prisoner here, but he has made me the object of his base and carnal lusts.'

'I'll kill him,' Barney gritted, quivering with rage. 'I'll go up there now and tear him from limb to . . .' He paused in mid-vow as certain practical difficulties in what he had just heard presented themselves to his mind. 'Um . . . if it's not too delicate a question . . . what exactly did he do to you?'

The violet radiance of Mary's face deepened to magenta. 'He asked me to disrobe for his vile pleasure.'

Barney gave a relieved sigh. 'At least he isn't able to . . .'

'Not yet,' Mary said in a tragic voice.

'Not yet?' Barney frowned at her in bafflement. 'I'm sorry, but I don't see . . .'

'He is not a well man. His heart is not strong, and that is why he spends most of his time in this room. Some day, perhaps quite soon, he will die, then he and I will be locked in here for ever – and I will not be able to escape him.'

Barney gave a low whistle, words failing him as one part of his mind took in the full extent of Haggle's nastiness, while another was swamped with speculations about the sexual proclivities of disembodied spirits. Mary had certainly retained all the externals of a nubile female, but Barney found it difficult to envisage, for example, the production of spectral hormones. A possibly vital clue lay in the fact that Mary, who had been a ghost for rather a long time, still thought like a woman and apparently was confident that Haggle's ghost would act like a predatory male. It was a subject to which Barney had never devoted any thought and he found it intriguing.

'Mr Seacombe!' Mary silently stamped her foot. 'Are

you going to help me, or are you content to stand there dreaming?'

'I'll help you, of course,' Barney said fervently. 'I'll get you out of here in no time – all I have to do is open the door.'

'How will you do that?'

'Nothing to it! I'll just grab the handle and . . .' Barney's voice faltered as he noticed that the inner face of the door was a smooth sheet of metal, devoid of any manual controls.

Mary toyed with one of her tresses. 'Mr Haggle always opens it with a magic box.'

'There's nothing magic about it,' Barney explained. 'It's a remote control device operating on radio or ultrasonic frequencies. Very common. Very simple.'

'Have you got one?'

'Ah . . . no.'

'Can you make one?'

'No, not in here.'

'In that case,' Mary said, 'it cannot be as common or as simple as you appear to think.'

'You don't understand,' Barney replied, suddenly aware that seventeenth century girls could be as irritatingly illogical as their space age counterparts. He took out his nail-file, went to the door and – trying to look as though he knew what he was doing – inserted the sliver of metal into the hairline crack at the door's edge and wiggled it up and down. The door swung open immediately.

Barney's delight at this unexpected development was tempered, however, by the discovery that Haggle was framed in the narrow aperture, holding his remote controller in one hand and a mug of coffee in the other. He advanced quickly into the laboratory and the door swung shut behind him.

'I've brought you a drink,' Haggle said, looking almost affable. 'Something to pick you up a bit.'

Barney checked discreetly to confirm that Mary had vanished, then accepted the mug. 'This is most kind.'

'Think nothing of it. Living alone has made my manners a bit rusty, but I do want you to be comfortable.'

'Thanks a lot.' Barney sipped the coffee and deduced from its flavour that it had been made from some rather inferior brand of powder, but at the same time he was intrigued by Haggle's desire to be hospitable. It appeared that the little man, in spite of some serious character defects, had a better side to his nature. *It just goes to show*, Barney mused, *nobody is all black*.

'How is your coffee?' Haggle said, watching Barney with a look of intense solicitude.

'It's very nice.' Barney made an appreciative slurping sound. 'Delicious.'

Haggle looked pleased. 'I'm glad to hear it – most poisons spoil the taste of a drink.'

'I'm an anti-caffeine man myself,' Barney riposted, 'but I wouldn't go so far as to call it . . .' He stopped speaking as a curious tingling sensation spread through his limbs, making it difficult for him to move, and causing him to fix Haggle with a look of abject pleading. 'You *are* talking about caffeine, aren't you?'

'Hardly.' Haggle took the mug from Barney's numb fingers and put it aside. 'Caffeine takes decades to kill a person, but the substance I put in your drink will do the trick in about fifteen minutes. You can consider yourself well and truly dead.'

Barney had read somewhere that the imminence of death was a powerful aid to concentration, but he found himself unable to string two thoughts together as Haggle caught his toppling body and dragged him to the door of the laboratory. It obviously took most of the little man's strength to get both of them through the narrow opening during the brief period in which the door was ajar, and when it closed again Haggle leaned against a wall, panting and clutching his chest. As soon as his breathing steadied he bundled Barney into the elevator and thumbed the top button on the control panel.

'You're not going to get away with this,' Barney said, aware that the near-final utterance sounded disappointingly like a line from an old B-movie.

Haggle appeared not to mind the lack of originality. 'I'll get away with it, all right. After all – what motive could the police establish?'

'Motive? I'll tell you what motive.' Barney paused for a moment, his brow wrinkling. 'Why *did* you do it?'

'Bringing you here was part of an experiment,' Haggle explained, smirking. 'I did need some theoretical help, but I was also interested in finding out if Mary would be visible to other people. I guessed from the expression on your face that you had seen her when I was on the phone. That was why I went out and left you alone with her.'

'I take it that the lab is wired for sound,' Barney said, getting his first inkling of what had been going on.

Haggle nodded. 'You take it correctly. I suspected Mary might try to be unfaithful to me – there's a touch of the wanton in that girl – and when I heard you begin plotting with her so readily I realized you would have to be put out of the way.' Haggle's brows drew together. 'It's a fine thing when you invite someone into your home and the first thing he does is try to steal your wife.'

'Mary isn't your wife,' Barney protested.

'She soon will be.' A look of lascivious anticipation appeared on Haggle's face. 'I don't think I'll have long to wait until I'm free of this mortal shell.'

Barney felt a strong desire to take part in the little

man's discorporation, but as his paralysis was now almost complete he concentrated instead on assuaging his curiosity. 'Do you reckon that male and female ghosts are able to . . . you know . . . ?'

Before Haggle could reply, the elevator came to a halt and the door slid aside to admit strong sunlight from a conservatory which appeared to have been constructed on the roof of the castle. Haggle manhandled Barney out of the elevator and unceremoniously dropped his body on the rush matting of the floor. The rough treatment caused Barney no pain, a reminder that he was close to death. He gazed up through the glass roof, into the clear blue vault of the sky, and made the astonishing discovery that he was unafraid. Previously, death had always been equated in his mind with total extinction, but he had learned a lot in the past hour. He had met Mary, had fallen in love with her, and passing from this world into the next merely meant that . . .

'There's something you seem to have forgotten,' he said, experiencing a pang of mingled triumph and joy as the new thought was born in his mind. 'You're doing this to keep Mary and me apart, but when it's all over I'll be a ghost – just as she is – and then we'll be together. What do you think of that?'

'I think you must be as moronic as you look,' Haggle said contemptuously. 'Have you learned nothing in the past hour? Why do you think I went to all the trouble of bringing you up to the roof? Answer me that.'

'I . . . ' Barney struggled unsuccessfully against a wave of mental confusion. 'Can you give me a clue?'

'What name did I give my new particle?'

'Ah . . . the maryon.'

'And what is the name of the young lady down in my laboratory?'

'Mary, of course, but I don't see . . .' Barney lapsed

into silence, teetering on the edge of a philosophical chasm which abruptly yawned before him.

'I named the whole class of particle after her, you oaf.' Haggle's eyes bulged with excitement as he glared down at his victim. 'Human ghosts and my large-volume particles are one and the same thing! It may be that all the matter in the universe is made up of greatly condensed maryons – that concept could reconcile the religious and scientific views of creation, but it's outside the scope of my researches. It was enough for me to prove that a ghost is a particle with the properties we discussed earlier, because it explains so much about psychic phenomena.

'Maryons can pass through thin partitions, but not thick walls – that's why ghosts are most often found in very old buildings, although if the human body has chains or ropes around it at the time of death they can hold the ghost in place, too. A maryon has very little rest mass, but if it gets speeded up or agitated for some reason, perhaps because of anguish, its mass increases and it is *less* able to penetrate walls. That explains why ghosts are usually unhappy, and the increase in mass also accounts for most poltergeist phenomena. A massive high-speed ghost could easily knock over a vase.'

Haggle squatted down beside Barney, his face twitching in scientific fervour. 'Now do you see why I brought you up to the roof to die? You yourself worked out that the pressure of the solar wind would be enough to sweep a ghost, or maryon, away into interstellar space. That's why the world isn't crowded with ghosts; that's why vampires are so careful to avoid sunlight. And that's why, young Seacombe, you won't be able to try coming between Mary and me again.

'As soon as you die you'll be on a one-way excursion out of the solar system. Have a nice trip!'

Haggle rounded off his discourse by giving vent to a

maniacal giggle. Barney, all other recourse denied to him, tried to spit in the little man's gloating face and discovered that the paralysis had now spread to his lips and tongue. He was unable even to swear. He had time for one searing stab of regret over having failed Mary, for having doomed her to an eternity closeted in an underground prison with a monster like Haggle . . .

Then he died.

On his way up through the stratosphere and the various radiation belts surrounding the Earth, Barney noticed quite a large number of other ghosts of many shapes and sizes, all being carried in the same direction by the inexorable pressure of the solar wind. The sun, mother of all life, was heartlessly driving away its young. Events had been proceeding at a bewildering pace, but his training in the science disciplines had not quite deserted Barney and he was quick to notice that he was travelling much slower than the rest of the ghostly multitude. They were whipping past him at accelerations he guessed would soon take them close to the speed of light, while he was progressing at a fairly moderate pace which gave him plenty of time to look around.

I'm a massive ghost, he deduced. *And if Haggle is right, it's because of the heartache I feel over . . .*

At that moment the cratered sphere of the moon swung into his field of vision and, aided by his spectral senses, Barney saw the satellite's conical shadow extending and tapering out into space behind it. He was approaching the moon's orbit with increasing speed, and until that moment had no idea he was capable of some independent motion, but a kind of instinct took over, he darted sideways on a vectoring course, and before he knew it had come to rest in the calm and pressure-free volume of space which was the shadow of the moon.

With the brilliant disk of the sun screened from his view, Barney found he could see with great clarity, and the first thing he noticed was that his immediate vicinity was quite thickly populated with other ghosts. He rotated himself into the attitude they had all adopted – feet towards the moon – and examined his neighbours with some interest. There were myriads of spirits in a variety of costumes which spanned ages and cultures. Many of them were congregated in large groups, but some were flitting about in restless isolation. Very much aware that he had been extremely lucky to escape being blown away into the reaches of interstellar space, Barney paused for a moment to collect his thoughts and then approached a chubby, benign-looking man – clad in Victorian tails, a stand-up collar and top hat – who was regarding him from the fringes of a nearby group.

'Allow me to welcome you to the afterlife and to congratulate you on your quick thinking,' the portly gentleman said. 'My name is Joshua Simms.'

'Quick thinking?' Barney began to feel he had lost the power of thought altogether. 'I'm sorry, but I . . .'

Simms smiled approvingly. 'Oh, yes – you were very quick. Most fledgling souls get swept away into infinity before they know what is happening to them, but you were perspicacious enough to realize that the shadow of the moon is a sanctuary, and you got into it just in time. Physicist, are you?'

'Yes. How did you guess?'

'We get two main classes of people in here, apart from those who are lucky enough to be carried in by accident,' Simms said, waving expansively at the surrounding ghost population. 'Astronomers and physicists – people whose professional training enables them to appreciate the advantages of this select volume of space. We think of ourselves as a kind of élite, although in recent years there has been an unfortunate influx of spirits whose only qualification is that when they were corporate they read that fantastic rubbish scribbled by Bertie Wells and his followers.' Simms lowered his voice to a confidential level. 'Naturally, nobody bothers with them.'

'Naturally.' Barney struggled to assimilate the flow of new data. 'So it's all true – a ghost is akin to a large-volume particle.'

'Of course! Though we're not elementary particles, needless to say. We have highly complex structures.'

'But if space is full of ghosts why haven't astronomers detected them?'

'They have, but they don't realize it,' Simms said scornfully. 'The very low mass of a ghost leads to a very large shift in any radiation which strikes its surface and is scattered by it. All short wave radiation, such as light and infrared, is scattered at radio frequencies – so ghosts are a major source of cosmic radio noise.'

'This is all too much for me,' Barney said feebly as radical new ideas about the nature of reality swarmed in his mind.

Simms nodded sympathetically. 'It's obvious that you have been ill-used by Fate, my friend. You are very massive for a ghost, which means you are burdened with regrets. Did you, by any chance, commit suicide?'

'No, I was murdered – and the rat who did it has got my girl.'

'How distressing for you!' Simms patted Barney on the shoulder. 'But take my advice, my young friend – put all thought of your mortal existence out of your head, and, above all, don't contemplate going back to Earth to haunt your murderer. If you join one of our debating societies or discussion groups you will have the inestimable privilege of conversing with Galileo, exchanging scientific ideas with the two great Isaacs, Newton and . . .'

'What did you say?' Barney cut in. 'What was that about going back to Earth?'

'Some misguided souls do it,' Simms said, shaking his head in disapproval. 'They never achieve anything, of course. All that happens is that they eventually get swept away into infinity. It doesn't bear thinking about.'

'How could anybody possibly return to Earth?' Barney said casually, disguising his intense interest in what he had heard.

'It can only be done safely during a lunar eclipse, when the Earth's shadow forms a corridor linking it to the moon. Some poor tormented souls cannot wait that long, however . . .' Simms indicated the distraught-looking individual ghosts who were restlessly keeping themselves apart from the groups, '. . . and they try to get back during an ordinary full moon, when the tip of the Earth's shadow comes near us. It means crossing a stretch of open space, which is a hazardous enterprise, but I daresay some of them must manage, otherwise the full moon would not be so prominent in the history of superstition.'

'That's right,' Barney said, a desperate resolve forming itself in his mind. He still felt a powerful yearning to be with Mary, a fact which was slightly puzzling considering that neither he nor she had any physical presence to speak of; he would never rest until he got her out of Haggle's clutches; and, in the name of both justice and revenge, he craved the chance to punish the little man for all his evil ways. And if the achievement of those goals necessitated crossing the brink of hell itself – so be it.

It occurred to Barney, as he quietly slipped away from Simms, that he had grown up a lot since setting out on his bicycle from the Daisyford employment exchange only two hours earlier.

* * *

After waiting three days for the time of the full moon, Barney traversed some thousands of kilometres of open space and reached the shadow of Earth with comparative ease. He did not deceive himself that the crossing had been without risk, however – he had seen other ghosts, presumably less massive than himself, being swept away by the unrelenting pressure of the solar wind. Their cries of despair faded quickly as they were accelerated off into some unknown and remote part of the galaxy.

Barney tried not to think about their ultimate fate as he arrowed down the cone of dark stillness, identified the continent of Europe with his spectral vision, and homed in on southern England which was settling into a night of peaceful slumber. Picking out familiar landmarks, he flitted over Daisyford, and briefly considered dropping in to see his mother before deciding that the ensuing complications would be too much for him to cope with on top of his other problems. In any case, she was likely to be busy with her boyfriend.

He descended on the roof of Gibley Castle, passing through the glass of the conservatory with ease, and came to rest with a jolt on the ancient fabric of the building proper. Haggle had been right, he realized – a particle with the wave functions peculiar to a ghost was unable to pass through thick stonework. Barney glanced around and was relieved to see that his mortal remains had been tidied away. He went to the small shed-like structure of recent origins which capped the elevator shaft, and found he was able to penetrate the thin sheeting of its door with very little difficulty. He sped down the shaft, coming out at successive floors to explore the castle, and eventually was drawn by the bright lighting of a small apartment on the ground floor.

On entering the room Barney saw that it was furnished as a kitchen. The black-suited figure of Haggle was sitting at a table, poring over a book and sipping a cup of chocolate. During his three days of waiting behind the moon Barney had nurtured a plan to lurk around near the laboratory door until Haggle opened it, and then to slip inside without being seen, but at the sight of his enemy his self-control snapped. Haggle was seated under a shelf which was laden with heavy porcelain jars, and before he had considered the consequences Barney – driven by ungovernable fury – was whirling around the room at an ever-increasing rate, like a particle in a cyclotron, trying to dislodge the jars. As his speed built up his mass increased accordingly, as dictated by the laws of physics, and the ceramic containers began to vibrate and stir under the multiple impacts of his ghostly form.

Haggle looked up from his book, his eyes widening in alarm. He turned his gaze towards the overhead shelf, saw one of the jars toppling down on him, and threw himself clear an instant before it shattered on his chair.

Barney came to an abrupt halt, his disappointment giving way to relief as he belatedly realized the position he would have been in had Haggle met a well-deserved end. With the little man dead there would have been no physical agency for opening the laboratory door and Mary would have continued languishing in captivity. Barney, knowing he was invisible because of the brightness in the kitchen, paused beside Haggle and was concerned to see that he was clutching his chest with one hand and holding on to the table for support with the other. Perspiration beaded out on the white dome of his head. He emitted a strangulated gasp, staggered out of the kitchen and lurched along a passageway to the elevator.

Barney stayed close behind him the whole way down to the dungeon level, hovering solicitously as Haggle clawed the remote control box out of his pocket and opened the laboratory door. Steeling himself to endure the unpleasant intimacy of partially occupying the same space as Haggle's body, he went through the narrow aperture with the little man. The heavily shielded door swung shut behind him and, his whole body suffused with tender longing, he cast about him in the hope of espying Mary and once again hearing her voice. She was not to be seen.

'There's no point in your hiding, my proud beauty,' Haggle croaked, hobbling towards his bed. 'I have a feeling I'm soon to be released from this physical shell, and when that happens . . . you and I . . . you and I . . .' The excitement of visualizing what he would do when he finally came to grips with Mary apparently placed too great a strain on Haggle's system. He gave a quavering moan and collapsed unconscious on the bed. Barney gazed at him anxiously, half-expecting to see an astral body arise from the mortal clay, but rapid shallow movements of the chest told him that Haggle was still in the land of the living.

'Mary! Where are you, Mary?' Barney kept his voice low. 'It's me – Barney. I've come back to rescue you.'

'Oh, Barney!' There was a flicker of soft radiance in one of the darkest niches of the room, and Mary came into view and glided towards him.

At the sight of her Barney felt a pang of desire which almost frightened him with its intensity. He was impelled towards her, but stopped short of actual contact, partly because he was afraid of offending her innate modesty, partly because of the startled expression on her face.

'Mr Haggle *did* poison you,' she gasped. 'I had hoped that part was untrue, that he was only taunting me.'

'It was true, all right,' Barney said. 'The little swine gave me a lethal dose of something. I don't care about that, though – it didn't stop me coming back for you.'

'But you are a ghost – just as I am.'

'I know.' Barney got an impression that Mary was not

as pleased to see him as she ought to have been. 'What difference does that make?'

'What difference? You were not able to open that door when you were alive,' Mary said, a note of asperity creeping into her voice. 'How do you propose to do it now that you are dead?'

'I . . . Well . . .' Barney gave the door a look of baffled resentment.

'If Mr Haggle dies now the three of us are going to be cooped up in here for ever. Have you thought of that?'

'No, I haven't,' Barney said hotly. 'All I've been able to think about was seeing you again. I've crossed the depths of space to be with you, because I loved you, hoping that you loved me in return – but I realize now that I was wrong. I'm sorry if all I succeeded in doing was to anger you, and in future I'll try to stay out of sight to spare you further annoyance.'

Barney made to turn away, but during his impassioned speech a misty expression had appeared in Mary's eyes and she reached out to take his hand. The contact gave Barney a pleasurable thrill.

'Do you really love me?' she said softly.

'You know I do. You must know.'

'And I have similar feelings for you, though we have scarcely met,' Mary said wonderingly. 'I don't know why that should be, because I'm a spirit now and I haven't been troubled by such desires since I quit my mortal body.'

'I can't understand it, either.' Barney took Mary's other hand in his, completing a circuit which intensified his feeling of delight. 'There's nothing in the rules of particle physics to account for it, unless . . . unless . . .'

'Don't question it,' Mary whispered urgently, moving close to him. 'Hold me, Barney, hold me.'

'Darling!' Barney took her in his arms, and in the

instant their bodies met a pang of orgasmic rapture fountained through him with an intensity he could never have imagined, obliterating his senses, filling him with the joyous realization that his whole life had merely been a prelude to this divine moment. He clung to Mary, and she to him, and time itself seemed to cease.

'My love,' Barney said eventually, surfacing through a golden haze of pleasure, 'do you know what has happened to us?'

Mary laid her head on his shoulder. 'Yes – our souls have united in heavenly bliss.'

'That's one way of putting it,' Barney replied. 'But I think I understand everything now. You were once a woman and I was a man, and a trace of sexual difference is carried over into our present state, a difference represented by the antisymmetric wavefunctions characteristic of particles which obey Fermi-Dirac statistics. You have half integral spin in one direction, and I have it in the opposite direction, and when we paired up together we fully occupied the available energy state. That's what gives us this feeling of bliss and . . .'

'Don't try to analyse it,' Mary said. 'Just tell me we will always be together like this.'

Barney smiled at her. 'Of course we will. Just the two of us.'

'That's what you think!' The voice of Haggle, loaded with gloating malice, interrupted the lovers' communion, and when they turned towards the bed they saw his ghost-figure spring up from congruency with a lifeless body. He came towards them, face contorted, limbs quivering with pent-up emotion.

Mary shrank away, hiding in Barney's embrace. 'Mr Haggle has died! Oh, Barney – what are we going to do?'

'It looks as though you've already done it, you shameless wanton,' Haggle hissed. 'You betrayed me with this young jackass the minute my back was turned, but I'll have my revenge. You'll see! The three of us are going to be in here for a long time, and I'm . . .'

'Correction,' Barney put in, sounding relaxed and unconcerned. '*You* are going to be in here for a long time – but Mary and I are leaving almost immediately.'

Haggle looked alarmed for a moment, then a sneer tilted his walrus moustache. 'And how do you propose to get out?'

'Through the walls, of course.' Barney was aware of Mary looking up at him with an expression of surprise, but he continued to stare Haggle straight in the eye.

Haggle gave a derisive laugh. 'You young fool! You've learned absolutely nothing.'

'I've learned how to do this.' Barney put out his right hand and thrust it into the stone wall beside him. His hand and arm slid into the ancient masonry with no trace of resistance. Mary gave a cry of wonderment.

'But that's imposs . . .' Haggle darted at the wall, bounced off it and stood glaring at Barney with impotent fury.

'There's no point in your trying it,' Barney told him. 'You see, it's hard enough for an ordinary ghost to penetrate a thick wall, and for a ghost like you – bursting with anger and hate – it's quite impossible. You'll be trapped in here until the building crumbles.'

'So will she,' Haggle snarled, pointing at Mary. 'She was in here for three centuries without being able to escape.'

'Ah, but that was before Mary and I were bonded.' Barney gave Mary a reassuring squeeze. 'The probability density distributions of our wavefunctions are now finite beyond the boundaries of this room, which means that we can tunnel through the walls and exist outside. I'm using the word "tunnel" as it is employed in quantum mechanics, of course, to account for the passage of an electron through a potential barrier in a . . .'

'I don't believe all this theoretical twaddle,' Haggle snapped. 'You can't leave me here alone.'

'We can,' Barney said sternly. 'In fact, we have very little choice in the matter. If you consider this room as a quantized space, then the three of us can't continue to exist inside it without violating the Pauli Exclusion Principle.'

'Balls to the Pauli Exclusion Principle.' Haggle's voice thickened with venom. 'There's one thing you've forgotten – the solar wind! If you go outside this castle you'll be blown away into the depths of space.'

'I would have dreaded that at one time,' Barney admitted, 'but not any more. Now that I'm pair-bonded with Mary I can see that it's our natural destiny to journey across the universe together, exploring all the wonders of creation hand-in-hand, meeting and welcoming cosmic travellers from other worlds. I'm not daunted by that prospect, and I don't think Mary is.' Barney glanced down at his partner and gave her a fond smile. 'Are you, sweetheart?'

'Not as long as we're together,' Mary said. 'Eternity seems as friendly and homely to me as a rose-covered cottage in which the love you and I have for each other will flourish and blossom, and will continue to do so long after the stars have grown cold and the galaxies have returned from their lonely flights and new cycles of . . .' Her words faded away as, still exchanging looks of mutual adoration, she and Barney faded into the stonework and were lost to view.

'Pompous bores,' Haggle muttered to himself. 'If that's what pair-bonding does for you, they can keep it. I think I had a lucky escape.' He squatted on the floor, produced an insubstantial pack of playing cards and settled down to the first of many, many games of solitaire.

In the Hereafter Hilton

The apartment was neat, stylish and comfortable – not at all like a machine designed for killing people.

For a few seconds after the entrance door had locked itself behind him, Renfrew stood perfectly still, taking stock of the place, trying to identify the most likely sources of death. The kitchen – always the most complicated room in any habitat – was one area that obviously had to be avoided. Every particle of food and drop of liquid was suspect in case poisons had been administered; the appliances could have been wired in such a way as to electrocute the unwary user; and the bright-lettered canisters could be bombs which would explode on removal of their lids. Even the simple act of opening a cupboard door might release a cloud of instant-acting gas into his face, and one startled intake of breath would be enough to . . .

If you want to stay alive, Renfrew thought, *keep out of the kitchen*.

From his position near the entrance he could see into the bathroom, and that also looked dangerous – too many chromed fittings which could spring bad surprises. He was going to survive the mandatory seven days in the apartment, of that much he was sure, but to do so he would have to be fantastically careful. The best plan, the one he had already decided upon, was to make himself as comfortable as possible in the centre of the living room floor and to remain there until the seven days were up. It would not be easy or pleasant – the matter of bodily functions alone would see to that – but it was a straightforward choice between life and death, and Renfrew much preferred being alive.

He walked into the living room and checked it out against his requirements. It measured roughly ten by ten, had blue wall-to-wall carpeting, and was furnished with a good-quality settee, easy chairs and occasional tables. Several original paintings, restful abstracts featuring the exact blue of the carpet, adorned the cream-coloured walls. The room could have belonged to a youngish, intelligent, not-excessively-trendy person living just about anywhere between New York and Los Angeles – except for two atypical features. One was the complete absence of windows, and the other was the display tube built into the wall above the artificial fireplace.

On the screen, in pulsing amber sans serif lettering, were two words – JURY OUT.

Renfrew examined the room critically and decided at once that the largest table, positioned near the middle of the floor, would have to be moved against one of the walls to give him the clear central space he needed. When the room armed itself against him, as it was practically certain to do, he was not going to risk even the most fleeting contact with any of the artefacts it contained. For all he knew, every piece of furniture in the apartment would begin to ooze contact poison as soon as the jury returned the verdict of guilty, and he wanted to be sure he would not roll over in his sleep and touch something.

The table was surprisingly heavy when he tried to move it and for a moment Renfrew feared it was anchored to the floor. He changed tactics, pushing instead of lifting, and this time the table slid fairly easily, creating deep furrows in the carpet. When it had come to rest against the wall, he stepped back with widespread arms and gauged the size of the area he had cleared. It appeared ample for his needs.

This seems a shade too easy, he thought, his confidence faltering. Nobody knew what percentage of condemned murderers actually lasted out the week – it was the practice, for humane reasons, to whisk survivors off to colony worlds in total anonymity and secrecy – but if the system could be beaten merely by camping out in the centre of a room would they not modify it? Was there a chance that the carpet itself could become toxic? Or that rapiers zipped upwards through the floor during the night?

No, that wouldn't be fair, Renfrew decided, his fears abating somewhat. That way the apartment would be nothing more than an execution chamber, and the whole point of the Capital Punishment Reform Act of 2061 had been that it removed the awful foreknowledge of death – the feature of earlier systems to which humanitarians had most strongly objected. There had to be some prospect of getting through the week alive, and if others had done it then so could he. It was simply a matter of intelligence, determination and self-control.

And of lasting for seven days without a drink of water.

The prison micropedia had been annoyingly imprecise about how long a man could survive on zero liquid intake. Some of the quoted authorities had avoided giving any estimate at all, and others had been content to state that death would occur after seven to ten days. The spread, Renfrew supposed, was due to factors such as the size, weight and general health of the subject and the rate of water loss from the tissues, and in that respect he was doing all he could to tip the balance in his favour. He was naturally pudgy around the middle, and throughout the four days of his trial had loaded all his food with salt and had drunk copiously of tea, coffee, milk and water. His tendency to retain fluids, something he had often bemoaned in the past, had enabled him to increase his body weight by approximately ten pounds – equal to a one-gallon reservoir of life-giving liquid.

That alone would probably be sufficient to ensure his survival, but Renfrew had gone further. Knowing in advance that he would be stripped of all personal possessions before being installed in the apartment, he had taken time after breakfast to spray most of his skin with an antiperspirant which, fortunately, was quite odourless. He suspected that its effectiveness would fade rather quickly, but by closing his pores and preventing evaporation for even part of a day it was giving him that extra edge in the battle for life. Only two more measures remained to be taken.

Renfrew glanced at the screen above the fireplace, checking that the jury were still deliberating. He had been in the apartment less than five minutes, but his defence had gone so seriously awry that he was half-prepared for a verdict to be reached in record time. Fortesque, the young state-appointed attorney, had tried to make capital from the fact that the store security guard shot by Renfrew had himself been indicted, only a year earlier, for the manslaughter of an unarmed kid who had tried to run off with a tray of gold rings. The proposal had been that Renfrew was defending himself against a trigger-happy zealot, but the members of the jury appeared not to have been impressed. It had been obvious to Renfrew that, to a man, they were in favour of trigger-happy zealots and would have been pleased to employ teams of them to safeguard their own property. At that point he had begun thinking very hard indeed about ways of surviving for a week in – to give the apartment one of its more popular labels – the Hereafter Hilton.

The first of the remaining precautions was to reduce evaporation of bodily moisture even further by turning the heat down. Renfrew located the thermostat and adjusted it to its lowest level. He then went into the kitchen, filled a tumbler with water and began sipping it with the intention of increasing his fluid reserves. The notion of filling all available vessels and laying in a week's supply of water was tempting, but he put it aside as being too dangerous. Any microscopic bubble in a glass could be a poison container to be opened by remote control as soon as the jury had pressed thirteen buttons and fed their votes into the computerized system. He had almost finished the glass of water when a low but insistent chiming sound filled the apartment. He set the tumbler down, went back into the living room and saw that the wording on the screen had changed.

It now said: JURY VOTING.

'Vote early and vote often,' Renfrew said aloud in jocular tones, trying to neutralize the spasms of alarm he had felt on realizing that the time for theorizing was over, that his very existence was now being laid on the line. He took a cushion from a chair and set it in the middle of the floor, then hesitated, frowning. A cushion was just as much an artefact as a microwave oven, just as capable of being booby-trapped. He skimmed it back on to the chair and squatted on the carpet, his face turned towards the screen as he waited for the final announcement. In addition to his fear he could feel powerful undercurrents of excitement, and it came to him that the provisions of the 2061 Act had been successfully implemented in the present system. He was about to be sentenced to death – yet he had absolutely no sense of imminent doom.

The inevitable reaction to the steady increase in violent crime had begun in the last quarter of the twentieth century with one state after another reintroducing the death penalty. By the middle of the twenty-first century capital punishment had become almost universal, coast to coast, and the moral dilemma facing the legislators had grown in proportion. How could one condemn killing on the one hand while going on taking human lives with the other? Variations in the actual method of execution had been tried, but the principal objections to legalized killing had remained the same – it was totally inhuman to tell a man exactly when and how he was going to die, then leave him to sweat out his time, counting off the weeks, days, hours, minutes, seconds. And if the State was inhuman, could its subjects be expected to be otherwise?

It was basically a question of how to be cruel in a kindly way – and a workable answer had come along in 2061. The lengthy, soul-destroying delays of earlier systems had been eliminated by direct implementation of the majority vote of a thirteen-man jury, and the dreadful certainty of death had been replaced by the challenge of a week in the Apartment. Not only were the exact time and method of execution decently shrouded in mystery – there was a ray of hope that the grim event could be avoided altogether. And that made all the difference.

Analysing his own feelings, Renfrew found that he was tense, alert, stimulated and – above all – confident that he was going to beat the system. There remained only a trace of furtive, niggling doubt. His idea seemed foolproof, but it had been rather too easy to conceive. It had, in fact, been the first scheme to blossom in his mind, and he knew perfectly well that he was anything but a genius – if he could come up with a successful plan anybody could do it. Did that mean that nobody but the occasional moron ever paid the supreme penalty? Or was there some factor he had overlooked?

There was another chiming sound and the message on the screen was replaced by a new set of words scribed in raw crimson: VOTING COMPLETED – AWAIT VERDICT.

On the lower part of the display a sweep hand began

remorselessly erasing a sixty-second clock. Renfrew shifted to a more comfortable posture, making sure he was in the exact centre of the cleared area of carpet. *I'm going to be all right*, he thought. *All I've got to do is stay put for seven days*.

He was glancing around the room, assuring himself that nothing could go wrong, when his gaze picked out two vertical cracks in the skirting board of the wall opposite him. It looked as though a small flap-type door had been built into the base of the wall. He stared at the door, feeling oddly threatened as he tried to guess its purpose. It was nothing to do with ventilation, too awkwardly positioned to be an electrical system access hatch, too small to be a cupboard . . . Renfrew's eyes widened as he noticed the slightest trace of wheel marks fanning out across the carpet from the flap and understanding blossomed in his mind.

Robotic cleaners!

The apartment was as immaculate as only an automated cleaning system could make it, which meant that at night when the occupants were asleep in bed silent little machines came out of the walls and scavenged every speck of dirt. But he wasn't going to be in bed! He was going to be laid out on the floor while the busy robots came nosing and nuzzling around him, and any one of them could be capable of killing him in a dozen different ways. How fast did they travel? How many were there? Could he avoid them?

Renfrew looked at the clock. It had devoured most of itself. Only twenty seconds were left until the apartment declared war on him.

He half-rose, his face turning towards the kitchen. Was there time to run in there, snatch up the lightweight table and get back with it? Would he be safe squatting on top of the table? What if . . . ?

His hands fluttered to his mouth as he heard the final chime which signalled the jury's verdict. He glanced involuntarily in the direction of the screen, then froze, his chin sagging with incredulity as he read the three words electronically emblazoned across the face of the tube.

VERDICT: NOT GUILTY.

The breath left his body in a noisy, quavering sob. He pushed a hank of hair away from his forehead as though giving himself a better view of the glowing words might change their import. The message remained the same. Against all the odds, his defence counsel had succeeded in carrying the jury. He was a free man!

Renfrew got to his feet, shaking his head in wonderment, suddenly conscious of how much he had been dreading the seven-day ordeal that had lain ahead. He took a last look at the apartment, gave a low chuckle which expressed relief and an almost insupportable feeling of happiness, then strode to the entrance door with a buoyant tread, keyed up for his first taste of liberty in many months.

The doorknob did not turn when he grasped it.

Instead, it fired a cloud of poison through the skin of Renfrew's palm, a poison which was so swift-acting that he had no time to realize he had been tricked by executioners who, in their determination to be humane, were not above telling a little white lie.

Amphitheatre

The retro-thrusters were unpleasantly fierce in operation, setting up vibrations which Bernard Harben could feel in his chest cavity.

He had little knowledge of engineering, but he could sense the stress patterns racing through the structure of the shuttle craft, deflecting components and taking them close to their design limits. In his experience, all machines – especially his cameras – gave of their best when treated with the utmost gentleness, and he wondered briefly how the shuttle pilot could bear to subject his craft to such punishment. *Every man to his trade*, he thought, for the moment incapable of originality, and as if to reward him for his faith the precisely-timed burst of power came to an abrupt end. The shuttle was falling freely, in sweet silence.

Harben looked upwards through the crystal canopy and saw the triple cylinder of the mother ship, the *Somerset*, dwindling to a bright speck as it slid ahead on its own orbit. The shuttle was brilliantly illuminated from above by the sun, and from below by the endless pearl-white expanses of the alien planet, which meant that every detail of it stood out with a kind of phosphorescent clarity against the background of space. Up at the front end the pilot was almost hidden by the massive back of his G-seat. He sat without moving, yet controlling their flight. Harben felt an ungrudging admiration for his skill, and for the audacity which enabled him to drive a splinter of metal and plastics down through the all-enveloping cloud layers to a predestined point on an unknown world.

At that moment Harben felt a rare pride in his humanity. He turned to Sandy Kiro, who was in the seat next to him, and placed his hand over hers. She continued to stare straight ahead, but the fullness of her lips altered a little and he knew she shared his mood.

'Let's claim this planet tonight,' he said, referring to a secret game in which love-making established their title to any place in which it occurred.

Her pale lips parted slightly, giving him the answer he wanted, and he relaxed back into his own seat. In a few minutes the silence of their descent was replaced by a thin, insistent whistle as they penetrated the uppermost layers of the stratosphere, and the ship began to stir in response. Presently its movements became more assertive, more violent, and when he looked up front Harben saw the pilot had abandoned his God-like immobility and was toiling like any other mortal. Quite abruptly, they were surrounded by greyness and the space shuttle had become an aircraft contending with wind, cloud and ice. Their pilot, his stature reduced in proportion, might have been a twentieth-century aviator trying for a touchdown in an unpredicted storm.

Sandy, unaccustomed to blind planetfalls, turned anxiously to Harben.

He smiled and pointed at his chronometer. 'It's almost time for lunch. We'll eat as soon as we set up camp.'

His apparent preoccupation with domestic routine seemed to reassure her, and she settled back with a tentative preening of her shoulders. Again his trust in the pilot was justified. The ship broke through the cloud cover and steadied in its course as a grey-green landscape materialized below – ranges of hills, terraces and ramparts formed by broken strata, dark vegetation, and a pewter filigree of small rivers. Harben assessed the view with professional speed, took a panoramic camera from his breast pocket and recorded the rest of their descent. In a surprisingly short time the pilot had grounded the shuttle amid a turmoil of vertical jets, and the three of them were outside and testing their Northampton-made boots against wafers of alien shale.

'That's the Bureau's radio beacon,' the pilot said, pointing at a squat yellow pyramid which clung like a limpet to the rocky surface a hundred metres away. He was a competent-looking boy with fine gold hair and a bored manner which, in view of his extreme youth, Harben thought to have been cultivated.

'You dropped square on to it, didn't you?' Harben said, testing his theory. 'Nice flying.'

The pilot looked gratified for an instant, then got back into his vocational stride. 'It's ten minutes off local noon. The shuttle will be back here at noon six days from now – that's giving you ten minutes more than the charter called for.'

'Generous.'

'We're like that, Mr Harben.' The boy went on to explain the cost penalties involved if they failed to rendezvous promptly, and to check that their chronometers were properly set to cope with Hassan IV's day of almost thirty hours.

'The shuttle will be here on time,' he concluded. 'You can be assured of that – though I don't know if I'll be the pilot.'

'Oh, I hope it is you,' Sandy said, joining in Harben's game. 'I was really impressed. David, isn't it?'

'That's right.' The pilot was unable to hold back a wide smile. 'I have to go now. Good hunting!'

'Thank you, David.' They picked up their field packs, retired to a safe distance and watched the shuttle rise vertically for a few metres before vectoring its thrust and swooping upwards into the clouds. It was lost to view long before the irregular, surging echoes from its jets had subsided, but it was not until the final whisper had faded – dissolving their perceptual link with the rest of mankind – that Harben became fully aware of the planet on which he was standing.

Visibility was surprisingly good, considering the amount of moisture in the air, and he could see complex perspectives of grey hills, interlocking wedges of vegetation, and bodies of water which were leaden, black or soft-glowing silver depending on the direction of the light. The temperature was in the region of ten degrees and a breeze was blowing steadily from the east, laden with ozone and the smell of mosses and wet rock. There were no birds, nor any immediately visible signs of animal life – though Harben knew the area was the haunt of one very special creature, the one whose killing technique he had been commissioned to film.

'What a nice boy,' Sandy said lightly.

'He's gone,' Harben reminded her, gently making the point that it would be best to put the ways of Earth behind them and concentrate on successfully interacting with the new environment. Their marriage covenant had only two months to run and, although he had repeatedly sworn to her that he intended to renew, he suspected she did not fully believe him and had come along on the current expedition with some idea of cementing a bond. He would have been pleased had it not been for the fact that a previous team had disappeared without a trace while filming *ET Cephalopodus subterr. petraform*. His attempts to persuade her not to come had been resisted on grounds he believed were emotional rather than logical, and in the end he had assented on condition that she bore a full working load, both mental and physical.

'Let's go,' Harben said. 'With any luck we'll find a good site in less than an hour, then we can eat.'

Sandy shouldered her pack willingly and they set off in a direction which was virtually due north by their compasses. Harben could actually see the point he was aiming for – a notch in an east-west rampart about eight kilometres away – but he made a careful note of the bearing so that they could return in the foggy conditions which were common throughout the region. In keeping with the agreement that Sandy was not to be sheltered in any way, he insisted that they carry their energy guns at the ready – hers set for a slightly divergent beam which would compensate for any lack of expertise, his own adjusted for maximum-intensity convergence at five hundred metres. There was no evidence to suggest that the Visex team of two years earlier had encountered a fate more sinister than, say, falling into one of the numerous underground rivers, but Harben had agreed with his employers that they should take as few chances as possible.

Sandy and he continued north, zigzagging on tilted platforms of sedimentary rock, and gradually reached a softer terrain where the tricky shale gave way to a blackish sand in which thrived shrubs and ground-hugging creepers. In some places the surface was infested with saltatorial insects which leaped from underfoot with audible pops, causing Sandy to flinch away from them. Harben assured her their metallized field suits were proof against much larger creatures, and after a short time she began to take his word for it. She was a travel journalist whose previous experience had been on resort worlds, and he was relieved to see how quickly she adapted to Hassan IV.

Presently they drew near the natural gateway to the north and, as he had hoped to do, Harben found signs of *ET Alcelaphini*, the gnu-like animals which were the principal prey of *petraform*. The tracks fanned outwards from the notch in the encircling cliffs and dispersed into the rocky tableland from which Harben and Sandy had just emerged.

'This is good,' Harben said. 'I think we're on a main migration route to the south.'

Sandy glanced around her. 'Shouldn't we have seen some of them?'

'No – that's the whole point. The females slow down a lot when they're getting ready to drop their young, and they and their mates become super-cautious. That could be why our friend *petraform* evolved the way he did.'

An expression of distaste appeared briefly on Sandy's classically feminine features. 'Don't refer to those things as our friends, please.'

'But they're going to bring us a lot of money,' Harben protested, smiling. 'And that's the second friendliest thing anybody can do for you.'

'They're horrible.'

'Nothing in nature is horrible.' Harben raised his compact binoculars and felt a pang of excitement as he scanned the flat ground immediately south of the pass. The angles were too acute for good observation, and his view was obscured by boulders and vegetation, but he thought he could see no less than three horseshoe formations of grey rocks. They were like miniature and incomplete versions of terrestrial Druid circles, each about five metres in diameter. Harben's pleasure mounted as he counted the stones and confirmed that there were seven in each circle. Most significant of all was the fact that in each case the gap, where the eighth stone should have been, faced due north – in the direction from which the quasi-gnu came every spring in search of the lush pastures needed by their young.

'In fact, everything in God's garden is lovely,' Harben said.

'What do you mean?'

'I think we've hit the jackpot first time. Let's go – I'm hungry.'

As they approached the circles Harben discovered that the site was even better for his purpose than he had at first supposed. He had four automatic cameras in his pack and right away could see vantage points in the shape of trees and boulders where they could all be hidden and serviced. There was even a small, wind-hewn monolith just to the north of the group of circles which would enable him to get high-angle shots to improve the visual texture of the completed film. He became so absorbed in plotting camera locations that his attention wandered from Sandy and it was only when he noticed she was unconcernedly walking straight ahead that he became alive to the danger.

'Sandy!' He touched her arm. 'Where do you think you're going?'

She froze, sensing the warning in his voice. 'What's wrong?'

'Nothing – but stay here with me.' He waited until she had positioned herself slightly behind him, then pointed out the three circles. 'Those are what we've come to film.'

She stared at the flat ground, uncomprehending, for almost a minute before – guided by his gyrating index finger – she picked out the loose patterns among the natural scatter of rocks. Her pallor grew more pronounced, but he was glad to see that she held her ground without flinching.

'I thought they'd look more like spiders,' she said. 'Or octopuses.'

He shook his head. 'If they looked like anything but ordinary rock formations they'd starve to death. Their whole survival plan depends on suitable prey walking straight into their arms.'

'Then . . . those rocks aren't real.'

'No. They're arms in which most of the power of movement has been traded off against the ability to simulate stone. I suspect you could even tap them with a hammer and not know any difference – as long as you were standing outside the circle.'

'What would happen if you were inside it?'

'The eighth arm would probably get you.' Harben continued the impromptu lesson in extra-terrestrial zoology by pointing out the shallow depression at the 'entrance' to each circle. It was there, under a camouflage of pebbles and grass, that the whip-like eighth arm was coiled in readiness to snap itself around any creature unwary enough to enter the circle.

Sandy was quiet for a moment. 'What happens then?'

'That's what we're here to check out and put on film,' Harben said. '*Petraform* seems to have the same body plan as an ordinary cephalopod, which means the mouth is in the centre of the circle, but we don't know how long the processes of killing and ingestion actually take. For all we know, when it gets hold of an animal it simply waits until the beast has died of fright or starvation, and then absorbs it.' Harben paused for breath, his eyes still assessing the photographic potentialities and limitations of the scene.

'You know, Sandy, this is the big one I've been looking for – the one that'll set me up for life. I can see it going out on every TV network there is.'

'I'd like a hot drink now,' Sandy said. 'Can we put up the shelter?'

'Sure.' Harben led the way to a suitable spot, spread out the shelter's base sheet and triggered a built-in gas cartridge to erect the pliant hemispherical roof. He was an exceptionally tall man, with a long back and slightly stiff limbs which did not readily fold into cramped spaces, but he was undisturbed by the prospect of six nights in the tiny inflatable. The rewards promised to be so great that his next field trip, assuming he chose to go out again, would be made in ostentatious luxury. He took twelve flat autotherm trays – guarantee of two hot meals a day – and handed them to Sandy, who stacked them in the shelter with her own supplies. While she was heating cans of coffee he moved off to an appropriate distance and manually dug a latrine, an ancient procedure still in favour because of its superb cost-effectiveness.

He was folding up the lightweight spade when a wisp of sound reached him. With a tingling sense of shock he realized that Sandy, who was a good fifty metres away from him, was speaking to someone in normal conversational tones. Harben ran a short way towards her, then stopped as he saw that – as had to be the case – she was completely alone. She was kneeling with her back to him, apparently opening the coffee cans.

'Sandy,' he shouted, not sure of why he was alarmed, 'are you all right?'

She turned and he saw the look of surprise on her face. 'Bernard? What are you doing over there? I thought you were . . .' Sandy stood up, looked all around her and began to laugh.

He crossed the intervening space and accepted a coffee. 'Most people take years of this sort of life before they go crazy.'

'I thought you were right behind me.' She sipped her drink, somehow managing to look feminine, even fashionable, in the silver-grey quilting of a field suit, and her eyes steadied on the flat space dominated by the stone circles. 'Bernard, why are there no animal bones over there?'

'They get eaten. If they were left sitting about they might scare off other prey, but it's most likely that they get absorbed for the mineral content. Hassan IV has some funny gaps in its geochemistry, especially where metals are concerned.'

'What a place!'

'All part of nature's rich tapestry, lover.' Harben finished his coffee, appreciating its warmth, and put the can down. 'I'm going to set up the auto-cameras in case there's some action soon.'

'I'll stay here and put some notes together for an article.' Sandy gave him a wry smile. 'I might as well make some money, too.'

Harben nodded. 'I'd want you to stay here anyway. It's best to leave as little spoor and scent as possible around the place.'

He took the four automatic cameras from his pack, slung the rifle on to his shoulder and walked towards the circles. The cloud ceiling had come down low enough to hide the tops of the tallest trees, but close to the ground the air had the clarity of glass. He kept his gaze fixed on the innocuous-looking rock formations, wondering if the bizarre creatures waiting below ground could feel the vibrations of his footsteps and were preparing themselves in anticipation of his walking into a trap. *Tough luck, rocktopus,* he thought. *I'm not going to feed you – you're going to feed me.*

There were two trees conveniently positioned on each side of the subject area, and he clamped cameras to their trunks, checking the coverage they provided as he did so. The small monolith to the north was easy to climb by the outer face and he installed a third camera on top of it. Two largish boulders were available on the south side as camera mounts. He chose one which was beside a deep-looking pool, hoping that some of the quasi-gnu would be attracted towards the water, thus providing extra film sequences he could use. An advantage of the holofilm system he employed was that it had unlimited depth of focus and a very wide recording angle, which meant that long shots, close-ups, panoramas and framed sequences could be prepared afterwards, at will, through selective processing of one roll of film. Harben was leaning on the boulder and smoothing out the plastic dough of a mounting pad when he became aware of Sandy standing behind him.

'What do you want, Sandy?' he said, not hiding his annoyance. There was no reply. He turned to remind her that she should have kept away from the area, but there was nobody near him. A sudden heightening of his senses made the moisture-laden breeze cooler and the murmur of streams louder. He allowed the strap of his rifle to slip from his shoulder, transferring the weight of the weapon to his hand, and at the same time he scanned the vicinity, satisfying himself there were no places of concealment. A full minute dragged by while he held the defensive pose, but there was no movement except for the slow drift of downward-reaching fingers of mist.

Finally, with the clamour in his nerves gradually abating, he turned back to the camera and completed the task of setting it up. When he had finished he checked the operation of the hand-held remote controller and walked thoughtfully back to the shelter. One explanation for what had happened was that Sandy and he were more jumpy than they realized – walking the face of an alien world was a supremely unnatural experience; another was the possible presence of hallucinogens in the atmosphere. Official survey samplings had indicated a standard mixture of gases, but that did not exclude local or temporary variations. He decided to monitor the performance of his own sensory apparatus for a few hours before saying anything to Sandy.

As soon as he had rejoined her she triggered one of the autotherm trays and they ate their first meal on Hassan IV. Harben periodically checked the approach from the north with his binoculars, and between times tried to decide if he was perceiving his surroundings in a completely normal manner. There was no repetition of the delusion, but as he moved around the camp there were moments, always as he was relaxing his vigilance, when he got an unaccountable feeling he was in a party of three. The impressions were so vague and fleeting that they could have been a consequence of his edginess, and he learned to dismiss them. Sandy, dictating notes into a recorder, appeared to be untroubled.

Late in the afternoon Harben detected a movement in the folds of grey rock to the north, and he made ready with his main camera, snorting with excitement as he checked its settings. A few minutes later two animals which bore a superficial resemblance to antelope came through the pass, delicately picking their way over the broken ground. One was a doe, and even at a distance it was obvious she was soon to give birth.

Being careful to remain in cover, Harben filmed their progress. As the animals began to draw level with him he saw that what he had taken to be the doe's tail was actually two spindly legs of her nascent fawn projecting from the vagina. His heart began a steady pounding as the animals reached the flat area where the *petraforms* lay in waiting. He pressed a button on his remote controller, setting the four automatic cameras in operation, and watched through his viewfinder as the quasi-gnu reached the deadly circles.

As though guided by a powerful instinct, they threaded a path through the danger zone – passing within a metre or so of the ill-defined perimeters – and continued southwards into the safety of the higher ground. Harben shut down his cameras, wondering if the disappointment he felt was being shared by the three immobile predators lurking below the surface. He turned to Sandy, who had been watching the animals through her own binoculars.

'Too bad,' he said. 'Still, we couldn't really expect to connect first time.'

She looked at him with sombre eyes. 'Bernard, was the female giving birth?'

'She wasn't far off it.'

'But that's awful! Why don't they stop and rest?'

Harben smiled at her concern, suddenly reminded of how little she knew about wildlife. 'Animals like that, which stay alive through being able to run fast, usually keep on the move. Especially if they feel threatened. When she drops the fawn it'll have maybe five minutes to learn to walk – then they'll be on their way again.'

Sandy glanced about her and shivered. 'I don't like this place.'

'It's the same on any Earth-type planet,' he told her. 'You can see the same sort of thing back in Africa.'

'Well, I'm glad that one got away. It would have been too horrible if those monsters had caught the mother.'

It was not a good time for an argument, but Harben decided he should straighten out Sandy's thinking before she actually witnessed a kill. 'In nature there aren't any monsters,' he said. 'There aren't any good guys or bad guys. Every creature is entitled to take its food, and it doesn't matter whether that creature is a robin or a rocktopus.'

Sandy shook her head, lips compressed. 'There's no comparison between a robin and one of those . . . things.'

'They both have to eat.'

'But a robin is only a . . .'

'Not from a worm's point of view.'

'I'm cold,' Sandy said, looking away from him. All at once she seemed absurdly small and defenceless, and he felt a pang of remorse over having allowed her to accompany him to a world which was so foreign in every way to her own milieu.

There were no more sightings that day, and as soon as it began to get dark Harben laid out the alarm cord in a large circle around the shelter. Sandy crawled into their artificial cave almost immediately, but Harben sat on the ground outside it for another hour, staring into the total blackness and listening to the complex, conflicting whispers of nearby streams. Once he developed a conviction that he was being watched, but none of the green-glowing needles on the alarm panel even trembled, and he concluded there was still some tension lingering in his nervous system.

When he moved in beside Sandy she moulded her body into his so that they fitted together as neatly as two spoons. The love-making they had planned earlier in the day would have relaxed Harben and made it easier for him to sleep, but – sensitive to her mood – he made no advances. He lay awake for a long time, enduring the stretched-out hours and waiting impatiently for the morning.

The return of daylight, the aromas of hot food and coffee, the purposeful domesticity of the morning chores – all combined to elevate Sandy's spirits, and Harben felt a corresponding lift within himself. He moved around a lot, driving the stiffness from his limbs, and talked rather more than was necessary about their plans for the next few years. Sandy may have realized he was scheming to influence her attitude towards his work as a whole, and to the Hassan IV expedition, but there was no adverse reaction on her part. She even started a running joke based on the notion of treating the planet as a luxury resort in an article for a travel magazine.

Harben's principal concern while this was going on was that during the night the cloud ceiling had descended almost to ground level. He kept a watchful eye on it as he ate and was relieved to find that the sandwich of clear air was – in response to the action of the invisible sun – gradually growing wider, revealing more and more of the high branches of trees. It gave him the sense of being at the bottom of a glass of aerated water which was steadily clarifying from the base upwards. As soon as the northern hill slopes beyond the pass had come into view he raised his binoculars and at once saw a small herd of quasi-gnu patiently filtering down through rocky obstacles.

'I think we're in business,' he said, sliding his hand through the wrist-strap of his main camera. 'Perhaps you should stay here.'

He doubled over and ran to a hummock from the lee of which he had a good view of the flat area and the sentient circles. A glance at the remote controller told him the automatic cameras on their vantage points were ready to function and, as a precaution against being forgetful in the forthcoming excitement, he switched them on early. He sensed Sandy taking up a position close behind him, but was too busy getting long shots of the approaching herd to speak to her. The quasi-gnu were emerging from the pass and their leaders were heading straight for the waiting circles.

Harben watched the entire scene in enlargement through his viewfinder as the herd of about twenty came level with him and began crossing what, for them, was the danger zone. Again, as though protected by an extra sense, the animals threaded tangential courses between circles. He was beginning to think none of them would make the fatal mistake when a large buck, which was being followed by a pregnant female, walked into the nearest circle. Harben's mouth went dry as the creature, unaware of its peril, stepped over the depression marking the *petraform*'s eighth arm. It crossed the ring of stones which were not stones and, moving with a stately nonchalance, passed safely out the other side.

Harben's disappointment was as sharp as a blow. *Could the petraform be dead? Would he have to look for another site?*

He tensed again as the doe followed her mate's footsteps into the circle. There was an explosive flurry of movement in the entrance depression. A slim black tongue snapped upwards and, with an easily audible whipcrack, coiled around the legs of the partially-born fawn which protruded from the doe's haunches. The doe screamed in terror and immediately came to a standstill.

I'm going to be rich, Harben exulted, as he jumped to his feet to improve his camera angle.

At the doe's cry of pain and fear the rest of the herd, with the exception of her mate, bolted off to the south. Their hooves drummed briefly, then there was silence broken only by the plaintive bleating and snuffling of the captured animal. The buck watched her, helplessly, from a safe distance as she shifted her feet, inching backwards as the leathery black arm of the *petraform* increased its tension, threatening to drag the fawn from her womb. Harben guessed she could have ejected it easily and made her escape, but that the maternal instinct in the species was too strong to permit the sacrifice of her young. And as he watched, keeping his camera trained on the struggle, the doe's dilemma became more urgent – the *petraform*'s other seven legs had begun to stir like giant snails. The living stones churned the wet soil as they closed in on the trapped animal.

'Bernard!' Sandy's voice came from some distance behind Harben, and was followed by the sound of her footsteps as she ran towards him. On one level of his consciousness he was slightly surprised – he had been certain Sandy was close by him – but his attention was concentrated on the natural drama being enacted before him.

'Bernard!' Sandy arrived at his side, breathing heavily. 'You've got to *do* something!'

'I'm doing it,' he said. 'I'm not missing a thing.'

As the doe became aware of the arms closing in on her, elongating as they came, she gave a convulsive movement and the full length of her fawn's forelegs came into view, followed by its head. Sandy gave a low sob and stepped past him, and from the corner of his eye he saw the metallic lustre of the rifle in her hands. He risked looking away from the viewfinder long enough to grasp the weapon, and used his superior strength to twist it out of her grasp.

'You've got to help her, Bernard.' Sandy beat ineffectually on his shoulder with her fists. 'I'll never forgive you if you don't help her.'

'There's no point.' He fended Sandy off, knowing that subsequent processing would eliminate the effects of camera movement. 'This is the way nature intended the rocktopus to provide for itself. What you're seeing now has happened billions of times before we got here, and it'll happen billions of times after we've gone.'

'I don't care,' Sandy pleaded. 'Just this once . . .'

'Look at that, for God's sake!' Harben shouted.

Through the viewfinder he saw the ground suddenly begin to open beneath the doe's feet. The rocktopus was ready to feed. As the surface supporting her began to shift and dissolve, the doe's courage failed her and she lurched towards safety. The fawn fell behind her and, on the instant of being born, disappeared into the waiting mouth. Freed of her constraint, the doe leaped effortlessly over the advancing arms of the *petraform* and galloped to the waiting buck. Both animals fled into the surrounding greyness and were lost to sight.

'I've got to have this.' Harben was only dimly aware of Sandy's whimpering as he ran forward, past a tree, into the flat area to get a downward view into the predator's maw. She kept beside him, pulling desperately at the rifle in his left hand.

He pushed her away, intending to continue running to the centre of the flat area, but his wrist was gripped with a force which brought him to a standstill with an arm-wrenching jolt. Sandy screamed his name with a new urgency. Harben swung round angrily and found he had been snared, anchored to the ground, by a thin black cord. He tugged at it disbelievingly and an identical cord sprang from another point and encircled his ankles. Within a second a dozen others, pulsing with eager life, had coiled themselves around his limbs, rendering him helpless. He looked about him in desperation and saw that Sandy was going to her knees amid a similar web of tendrils.

'*The gun!*' Her voice shrilled into the topmost registers. 'Burn them off!'

As though her words had been understood by a mind other than his own, new cords wrenched the rifle out of his grip. Harben was barely aware of this – because all of the flat space surrounding the three stone circles had begun to writhe with black feelers which waved in the air like wind-blown grass. And then, as the ultimate horror, the trees and boulders forming the outer circle began to change shape, to move inwards. Even the surface of the dark pool humped upwards into a pseudopod of black jelly.

The shifting and loosening of the ground beneath his feet brought a total, though belated, understanding to Harben – the entire area was part of one huge, complex and hungry beast of prey.

He fell to his knees as the glistening cords increased their multiple tensions, and he felt the surface gently parting to receive him, yearning, beginning to exert suction. Sandy was almost hidden from view by skeins of black threads. A strange, sad humming filled the air.

Harben raised his gaze skywards as he gave vent to one last bellow of fear and despair, but the protest died in his throat as he saw something – something incredible – moving in the cloud ceiling above him.

There was a humanoid figure, unnaturally tall, difficult to focus on because it slanted in and out of visibility in a way which had nothing to do with obscuration by mist. It was sheathed in prismatic colours and carried glimmering artefacts. A tongue of blue-white incandescence stabbed downwards from it, a scream which Harben felt rather than heard vibrated through the vastness of the plasm beneath him, and suddenly he was free to move. The thickets of black tendrils had vanished into hidden pores.

He staggered to his feet, caught Sandy's hand, and they half-ran, half-waded towards the safety of the firm ground beyond the circle of boulders and trees. As they passed a weirdly misshapen, but now immobile, tree Harben glanced back and glimpsed the rippling, polychromatic figure suspended among a swirl of vapours. He could not distinguish the eyes, but he knew the being was looking directly at him, into him, through him.

Know that you were wrong, my friend. The door to an intellectual furnace was opening, and its fire washed through Harben's mind. *I, too, am a recorder, but my experience far surpasses yours. Entropy demands that all living things shall die – but Life is counter-entropic, and that must apply in particular as well as in general. If you surrender the ability to sympathize with the individual, you will become isolated from Life itself . . .*

There was a shifting of super-geometries, and the figure vanished.

* * *

By the time Harben had broken camp the arena in which they had almost died looked exactly as it had done before. The trees looked like ordinary trees, the boulders and pool were indistinguishable from natural features of the landscape, and in the centre the three stone circles were quiescent. A thin, steady drizzle was gradually erasing all signs of disturbance from the surface layer of soil.

The sedatives she had taken had quelled the trembling of Sandy's limbs, but her face was pale and distracted as she looked at the deceptively peaceful scene. 'Do you think,' she said, 'that it's all part of the same organism?'

'I doubt it,' Harben replied as he opened a valve to deflate the shelter. 'I'd say the three in the middle have some kind of symbiotic relationship with the big brute.'

'I don't see why it let the herd pass on through, then went for us.'

'Neither do I – yet. It might be because it's mineral-hungry and we carry so much metal. Look at the way the material of our suits perished in a matter of seconds.' Harben got to his feet as the shelter subsided. 'Can you roll this up?'

Sandy nodded, and her troubled gaze steadied on his face. 'Where are you going?'

'To pick up the automatic cameras.'

'But . . .'

'It's all right, Sandy. I'll be safe as long as I stay outside the circle.'

She approached him and took his hand in hers. 'Are you going to take the film back with you?'

'You're still in shock, little girl.' Harben laughed incredulously, withdrawing his hand. 'That stuff is worth a fortune, especially if our visitor registered on it. Of course I'm taking it back.'

'But . . . don't you remember what he said?'

'I'm not sure that he said anything, and what there was of it didn't make too much sense to me.'

'He meant we all have to die – but not for the benefit of an audience.'

'I told you it didn't make sense.'

'It's very simple, Bernard.' Sandy's eyes were dulled with drugs, and yet were oddly intent. 'When you point your camera at any creature you make it special. You enlist the sympathy of millions of viewers, and if our sympathy isn't worth anything . . . what are we worth?'

'I've never had myself valued.'

'He was filming us, but he didn't let us die.'

'Sandy, this is just . . .' Harben began to walk away, then he saw that she was crying. 'Listen to me,' he said. 'The fawn is dead and gone, and there's nothing anybody can do about it. And you'll notice that *he* didn't kill that brute off. It's all right again, and it's going to go on feeding itself in the only way it knows how. For all we know, that's what happened to the Visex team a couple of years ago.'

'It's a pity you weren't here to film that.'

'You'll feel better when I get you away from here,' Harben said curtly. He turned from her and collected his cameras at the points where they had fallen, being careful not to set foot within the circle of menace. Sandy's last remark had stung him, but his thoughts were becoming preoccupied with new plans for the future. Quite apart from having yielded the fleeting but newsworthy contact with the super-naturalist, Hassan IV was an even richer treasure house than he had dreamed, one which could be exploited only through years of dedicated work. Already it was obvious that Sandy would not want anything to do with it, and that fact posed serious problems with regard to their marriage covenant.

Later, as they were crossing the uplands on the

approach to the radio beacon, he realized he had come to a decision. He felt unexpectedly guilty at the prospect of broaching the subject while she was still so badly shaken, but he was entering a vital phase of his career and would have to learn to move quickly in everything he did.

'Sandy,' he said quietly, taking her elbow, 'I've been thinking things over, and . . .'

She pulled her arm away from him without turning her head. 'It's all right, Bernard – I don't want to stay married to you, either.'

Harben stood still for a moment, staring at her retreating back, experiencing an emotion compounded of puzzlement and relief; then he adjusted his camera pack to a more comfortable position and continued picking his way across the wet, grey shale.

Frost Animals

The period of weightlessness had been very brief, but its psychological aftermath was profound. Hobart could see and hear the difference in his fellow officers as they moved about the upper deck's rest room; and within himself he could feel a mixture of emotions – relief, expectation, nostalgia – which were going to make the remaining days of the voyage tedious. There was an irony in that fact, he realized. After weeks of steady deceleration the ship had cut its speed to a level at which the time dilation effect was negligible – but now his impatience to reach home had intervened to slow down subjective time. He was pondering the matter when the tall, angular figure of Harry Stiebel, the day exec, came into the room with a pile of fax sheets curved over his arm.

'Earth is still there, folks,' Stiebel called in a professionally jovial voice. 'Still abiding away for all it's worth. That's good to know, isn't it? Hands up everybody who thought the Earth wouldn't still be there.'

'Why shouldn't it still be there?' said Os Milburn, the chief systems engineer, who was seated near the door. 'Eighteen years without your smart-assing around has probably rejuvenated the place.'

'Have a reorientation kit, lover.' Stiebel threw a fluttering bundle of paper on to Milburn's lap and began working his way around the room, distributing the sheets with unnecessary vigour and a surprising amount of noise. Hobart watched his progress with affection and respect. Stiebel was completing his fifth trip to the Sirian system, which meant he was more than a hundred years old in

Earth chronology, yet he showed no symptoms of dislocation. Thin, square-shouldered, invariably cheerful, he seemed determined to diffuse his normal life span over as many centuries as company regulations and Albert Einstein would allow. It was an ambition of which Hobart stood in awe.

'One for you, Denny,' Stiebel said as he reached Hobart. 'See what you've been missing.'

'Thanks.' Hobart took the proffered sheaf and began to flick through pages that clung together electrostatically. Switching off the main impulsion torch for two minutes had, as well as giving the crew a warming glimpse of Earth, allowed communication to take place between the ship and the company headquarters in Montana, and the reorientation kits were part of the result. Their contents – fired through in a ten-second information bleep – were intended to familiarize the returning starmen with the major changes that had taken place during their absence. This was Hobart's first voyage and as he glanced over the section headings on politics, world events, fashion, science, and sport, he tried to come to terms with the knowledge that in the past thirteen months of his own life the world and everybody in it had grown older by eighteen years. *I've done it*, he thought, bemusedly and proudly. *I've travelled in space, and I've travelled in time . . .*

'Before you delve in there and start checking on skirt lengths . . .' Stiebel paused long enough on his rounds to tap Hobart's shoulder, 'take a walk into George's office, will you? He wants to see you about some little thing.'

'George wants to see me?' Hobart looked up at Stiebel in open surprise. As the most junior officer in the entire ship's complement, he had been assigned a number of routine tasks, most of which were connected with monitoring erosion of the hull. There had been little enough actual work for him to do during the two acceleration phases of the voyage, and during retardation – when the ship was shielded against collisions with interstellar material by its own drive torch – there had been virtually no work at all. In any case, at no stage in the journey would Hobart have expected an individual summons from Captain George A. Mercier, commander of the *Langer Willow*.

'What do you think George wants?' he said to Stiebel. 'Did he say anything?'

For a reply, Stiebel stared at him with slightly raised eyebrows then passed on his way, performing a menial administrative duty with gusto and an air of importance, the picture of the corporate space traveller. Hoping the exchange had not been overheard, Hobart stood up and glanced around him. He was a tall man with silver-blond hair and exceptionally clear skin, and he had always found it difficult to do things without being noticed. Several of the ship's senior technical staff were watching him with amused expressions. There was no personal malice in their attitude, but he knew they were of a breed that firmly believed in the value of making life as irksome and embarrassing as possible for junior officers. Even if it were traditional at this stage of a trip for the captain to give a new man a drink and a clap on the back, nobody would have helped him by divulging the information in advance. Hobart nodded to the onlookers, left the rest room, and made his way along narrow corridors to the compartment Mercier used for office work and rare conferences. He tapped the door and immediately was told to enter.

'Sit down, Hobart,' Mercier said, indicating a chair opposite the desk at which he was seated.

'Thank you, sir.' Hobart lowered himself into the chair, noting as he did so that there was nobody else in attendance and that Mercier's desk was almost completely clear, as if the captain had come to the room for no reason other than the present interview. Hobart gazed at Mercier, wondering if such a thing could be possible. The captain was a strongly built man of about fifty, with conservative good looks which, had he been an actor, would have typecast him as a judge or an insurance company president. He examined Hobart with frankly puzzled blue eyes and then, unexpectedly and uncharacteristically, gave a deep sigh.

Hobart shifted in his seat. 'Sir?'

Mercier seemed to reach a decision. 'I contacted you through the day executive, rather than the general address system, because there's something going on here that I fail to understand, and I want to deal with it as discreetly as possible. Do you remember a junior technical officer called Craven? Wolf Craven?'

'Yes, sir.' Hobart suppressed his uneasiness. The sudden mention of Craven's name had aroused feelings of guilt, but they were associated with a personal matter, one which could hardly concern his professional life. 'I know him quite well.'

'Were you friendly with him?'

'I wouldn't put it as strongly as that – we just happened to be in the same intake at Langer Centre and went through our pre-ops course at the same time.'

Mercier looked dissatisfied, the overhead light accentuating ridges in his forehead. 'Have you ever been to any parties at Colonel Langer's house?'

'Yes, sir.'

'Was Craven at the same parties?'

'Yes, but . . .' Hobart developed a conviction that somehow, against all the odds, the private degradation he had experienced with Wolf Craven on that last night on Earth was leading to unforeseen consequences. 'Excuse me, sir – am I entitled to know what this is all about?'

'I never went to any functions at the Langer place,' Mercier said reflectively. 'Made a point of staying away from that sort of thing. Even in the old days.'

Hobart was reminded of the fact that, as a veteran starman, Captain Mercier had a memory which reached far back into the previous century. It was an incomplete memory, a thinly dotted line composed of months-long periods on Earth interspersed with decades in the relativistic limbo of the space traveller, but the span was there and it made Mercier *different*. Although the captain had lived some fifty years of body time, little more than twice as much as Hobart, he had a trick – possibly cultivated – of occasionally appearing to commune with eternity. In spite of his growing sense of alarm, Hobart was constrained to withhold his questions.

'I believe there was a party the night before this voyage began,' Mercier said at length. 'And that both you and Craven were present.'

'Yes, but lots of company personnel were there.' Hobart began to wonder if he was making a mistake in going on the defensive before any charge had been made against him, but he pressed on. 'We were leaving the next day, and the *Langer Rowan* – that's Wolf Craven's ship – was going out the day after that. It was' – he sought a form of words that might impress the captain – 'a fairly significant social occasion.'

'You didn't speak to Craven at all?'

'Well, I'm bound to have spoken to him at some time, at some stage.' Hobart tried to fend off an intrusive memory of Craven's dark and cleft-chinned face, the too-red lips lacquered with saliva, the eyes pleading and derisive at the same time. 'Sir, I'd like to know what's going on.'

'So would I, Hobart, so would I.' Mercier paused again, brooding. 'We entered the Solar System near the top end of our speed envelope, which is why we had to resume deceleration so soon after the confirmation report. There was only a minute or so, less the allowance for distance lag, for verbal communication – and I could have used that time in more productive ways than talking to the police.'

'The *police*?' Hobart was both surprised and reassured, knowing there were no criminal activities on his conscience. He made a show of relaxing visibly.

'Yes – the police. This is a serious matter, Hobart.'

'I can't think why the . . .'

'They seem to be of the opinion that Wolf Craven was murdered during your fairly significant social occasion.' Mercier paused again, giving Hobart's own phrase time to rebound on him. 'And, from what was said, you appear to be the chief suspect.'

Hobart suddenly became aware that the structure of the ship was alive, that stress patterns and subtle harmonics were coursing through the walls of the room, agitating the air which surrounded him. He could hear it whispering in his ears.

'That's ridiculous,' he said forcibly, then secondary implications came to his mind. 'Is Wolf Craven really dead?'

'I presume the police wouldn't be talking about murder otherwise.'

'But I know nothing about it.'

'You'd better not,' Mercier said gravely. 'You know my way of going by this time, Hobart – if you're innocent I'll back you all the way, and you'll get the same support I'd give to the most senior member of my crew, but if it turns out that you really are involved you'll find me a bigger enemy than the public prosecutor. The company can't afford this sort of thing.'

'The *company* can't afford it!' A lowering of the

captain's brow told Hobart he was failing to show proper deference, but such considerations no longer seemed important. 'Look, I'm entitled to know exactly what was said.'

'I've already told you more than I should,' Mercier replied, eyeing Hobart with fresh appraisal, as though suspecting that insolence in a junior officer could point to a capacity for more serious faults.

Hobart shook his head. 'Exactly what did the police say?'

'First they checked that you were still alive and on the ship's roster, then they requested me to put you in detention until we go into parking orbit.'

'Detention?' The atmospheric whispering in Hobart's ears grew louder and more malicious. 'Are you going to do it?'

'I'm obliged to.' Mercier pressed a call button on his desk. 'It will be done discreetly, of course. All I expect of you is that you will remain in your quarters until the parking manoeuvres are completed. I'm not proposing to put a guard on you.'

'Thank you, sir,' Hobart said bitterly. 'Will I be handcuffed to the shuttle?'

'You'll no longer be my responsibility at that stage.' The puzzled look returned to Mercier's eyes as he got to his feet, terminating the interview. 'I don't know what you've got yourself involved with, Hobart – but the police are going to the expense of sending up a transit vehicle just to take you off my hands.'

Investigator Charles Shimming was a medium-sized, fit-looking man with a long face and intelligent, worried eyes. During conversation he had a habit of lowering his chin on to his chest, as though suppressing a series of belches, but continuing to speak anyway. This had the effect of making every utterance sound weighty and deliberate, if somewhat disjointed. It also had the effect of irritating Hobart, who wanted his information delivered quickly and clearly.

'There are two ways we can handle this thing,' Shimming said in the privacy of Hobart's room. 'If you are reasonable and co-operative I won't even have to place you under arrest, and we can walk – or should I say float? – out of here like two friends going off somewhere to have a couple of beers. I think that would be the best way to do it, but if you didn't want to be reasonable and co-operative I could hit you with a spider, in which case . . .'

'Hit me with a *what*?' Hobart scrutinized the policeman's neat frame, looking for weapons.

'I forgot you've been away eighteen years.' Shimming opened his right hand, revealing what looked like a silver golf ball. 'This is a spider. If I threw it at you it would explode on contact and wrap you up in metal ribbons – same way some spiders truss up flies. It wouldn't hurt, but you'd have to be carried off the ship all done up like a Thanksgiving turkey, and it would be bloody undignified. It would be really embarrassing for you.'

'I see. Thanks for bringing me up to date.' Hobart pretended not to notice the threat which had been implicit in the description of the restraint system. 'I would have co-operated with you anyway.'

'That's good.' Shimming made no move to put the silver ball away. 'Shall we go?'

'Don't I get to hear what this is all about?'

'Not now, not in here – it wouldn't be considerate.'

'Considerate?'

'Yes. The ship has to remain officially sealed until I get you off, and it wouldn't be fair to all the others if we caused unnecessary delays. They must be pretty anxious to get their feet back on the ground after all this time.'

'Okay.' Unable to shake off a feeling he was being manipulated, Hobart detached his holdall from the spring clip which prevented it from drifting about the room. He glanced around the tiny compartment, scarcely able to believe he would not be spending the night in its familiar confines, and moved out into the corridor. It was a long time since he had walked in zero-gravity conditions with the aid of suction soles, and at first he swayed grotesquely as he made his way towards the transfer port. Shimming laboured along behind him, obviously ill at ease, allowing too much suction to build up under his shoes and having to struggle to lift his feet clear of the deck. His progress was punctuated by popping noises and occasional bursts of subdued swearing.

The pilot was already waiting in the blue-and-grey police transit vehicle, which looked strangely unreal against the background of powdery green that was the Langer Line's house colour. The vehicle was smaller than the company transits, too, making the cylindrical transfer port seem exceptionally roomy. Aware of the curious stares of the lock technicians in the control chamber, Hobart climbed aboard the shuttle and strapped himself into a deep chair in the midsection passenger compartment. When he looked out through the transparencies at his side he found he was now on a level with the lock crew, all of whom were gazing back at him with undisguised interest. Hobart's cheeks began to tingle. Suddenly angry, he turned to Shimming, who was hauling himself down into the next seat.

'This is an imposition,' he said. 'It's too much! I ought to have a lawyer here.'

Shimming frowned at the buckle on his seat belt. 'You're not being denied access to a lawyer – but think of the expense of bringing one up here. And the delay.'

'The company should take care of the expense – they're

supposed to look after contract officers. I should have spoken to Colonel Langer.'

Shimming looked up from the buckle, which he seemed to find as tricky as a Chinese puzzle, and an odd expression appeared briefly on his long face. 'How in hell do these things go together?'

'Like that.' Hobart slid the metal connectors home across the other man's stomach. He thought about the reaction his mention of Colonel Langer had produced, and it crossed his mind that he might benefit by showing he had friends in high places.

'Yes,' he said reflectively, striving for maximum effect, 'I should have spoken to the colonel. I'll call him as soon as we touch down.'

'You'll be wasting your time,' Shimming said. 'Colonel Langer died four years ago.'

'But that's im – ' Hobart broke off in the middle of the word, gagging on his first real taste of what space travellers called timeslip. As far as he was concerned, he had been away on a voyage lasting thirteen months – but during that period a total of eighteen years had elapsed on Earth, and the effect of those years was *real*. No longer was it an abstract idea in Hobart's mind, a textbook paradox to be marvelled at and dismissed from his thoughts. His world had run the gamut of eighteen winters, been warmed by eighteen summers, and there had been lots of time for old men to grow older still, and then to die . . .

'. . . how you guys do it,' Shimming was saying. 'Skipping ten or twenty years at a time would cut the feet out from under me – I'd be *lost*, if you know what I mean – but you just take it in your stride, calm as you like. Something I really admire, that.'

'How did the colonel die?'

'Some say it was bourbon, some say it was gin.'

'I'm sorry to hear about that,' Hobart said, deciding to pursue his original intent. 'He was a good friend.'

Shimming snorted. 'Some friend!'

'What do you mean?'

Shimming placed his finger tips together and lowered his chin to his chest a couple of times as a preliminary to speaking. 'It would be best for you, Dennis, if you didn't try to palm off some story about you and old man Langer belonging to the same social set, playing polo together, and that sort of thing. You were one of the bunch of young rams that Mrs Langer used to invite up to the house to keep her amused, and I doubt if the colonel ever did more than say hello and good-bye to you. Am I right?'

'Certainly not,' Hobart snapped, appalled. 'Colonel Langer invited me to his place personally, several times, and although we weren't all that close we had a good . . .'

'Dennis,' Shimming cut in, smiling apologetically, 'it was Langer who started this whole thing off. He was the one who said you killed Craven.'

Hobart was unable to prevent his jaw from sagging as a partial understanding of his predicament seared itself into his mind like a spark tracing a message on chemically treated paper. The colonel must have known what Wolf and I did, he thought in sudden panic. He must have seen us, or been told – and this is his revenge.

He became aware that Investigator Shimming was scanning his face with eyes as intent as those of a gambler watching the wheels of a chance machine shudder to a halt, and it came to him that he needed to protect himself. No doubt Shimming was highly skilled at reading expressions and interpreting instinctive verbal responses – so what was he to say in his own defence?

He composed his features with an effort and retreated into youthful pomposity. 'This is too ridiculous for words.'

'That's unfortunate, because words are the only tools I

can use,' Shimming replied. 'There's nothing . . .' He stopped speaking and glanced around him as the shuttle's doors sprang together with a pneumatic gasp. There was a diminishing hiss as the transfer dock was bled of air, and a few seconds later the outer door slid open to reveal the blackness of space. Because of the brightness within the dock the stars appeared sparse and dim. The shuttle wallowed slightly as the berthing clamps were released. Manoeuvring jets sounded faintly and the vehicle began to slide out into a boundless ocean of emptiness, forsaking the homely environment of beams, panels and pipe runs for one in which the mind was lost for visual anchors.

Shimming gave a wan smile, and Hobart realized the investigator was highly nervous. He repressed the sympathetic grimace with which he would normally have reassured anyone who was new to space and stared straight ahead, trying to assess the likelihood of his ending up in the death chamber. A chill descended over him as he considered the proposition that his life might terminate on Earth in a few months' time, in the year 2131, instead of at some vague and postponable date centuries ahead.

The transit vehicle was moving clear of the immense bulk of the *Langer Willow* now, and the sunlit Earth came into view, looking huge and mysterious as it curved away on all sides, comprising almost half of the visible universe. Powerful jets began to hammer up front, reducing the transit's orbital speed and putting it into a controlled fall. Hobart watched the milky blue immensities tilt and turn, dismayed at the contrast between actuality and his imagined homecoming at the end of his first voyage. The only crumb of comfort he could find was that Shimming was too overawed and wrapped up in space tyro's misgivings to continue the interrogation for the present. He had time to get his thoughts in order . . .

Colonel Langer's age and failing health had forced him

to give up active participation in space flight, but he had liked the company of junior officers who, because of their lowly positions, made an ideal captive audience for his reminiscing. For the most part he had kept himself occupied with his menagerie of frost animals, but there had been days when that pursuit had proved too passive and he had turned to other pastimes. One of them had been going into the strip of rough terrain at the rear of his estate to blast at snakes with antique firearms. Hobart, who had listed shooting as one of his interests, had been brought along mainly as gun-bearer on a number of the mini-expeditions.

The farewell party at the Langer house had been a rambling, multicentred affair which he had attended for a number of ill-defined reasons. He had been flattered at receiving the invitation from Colonel Langer, and inexperienced enough to entertain hopes that it could bode well for his future in the company; he had been lonely and scared on the eve of the departure for Sirius; and, underlying and colouring all other considerations, had been the possibility of sexual adventure.

The fables about Dorcie Langer had inflamed Hobart's imagination, filling him with a curious blend of contempt and yearning. He had scarcely dared meet her gaze during his previous visits to the house, and yet he had nourished a conviction – one he would not have voiced – that she had been specially aware of him, that she had singled him out as a prospect. For an unworldly and slightly repressed youngster of twenty-two, those ambiguous glances had been sufficient to trigger off lurid fantasies – none of which had correctly anticipated the event. Even after a lapse of thirteen months, he could remember the exact words with which Wolf Craven had greeted him in an upstairs corridor at the rear of the house.

'I don't know how you did it, young Denny, but you've connected with our good lady – she sent me to get you.'

The peremptory nature of the summons had shaken Hobart, as had the use of Craven as a messenger, but his initial shock had been swamped by the discovery of what Dorcie Langer had in mind for him.

'Come on, Denny,' Craven had pleaded, sinking his fingers into each of Hobart's biceps. 'I'm not going to let you blow this out on me, not after I've worked on her for weeks. What does it matter if she wants both of us at once? Don't be such a kid, for Christ's sake – it all adds to the fun.'

'Fun,' Hobart heard himself muttering as the shuttle began to sway, to come alive as it dipped into the tenuous upper layers of the Earth's atmosphere.

Shimming leaned closer. 'What was that?'

'Nothing,' Hobart said, shaking his head, wresting his mind away from the recurrent vision of three bodies twined together, straining, sweating, labouring; of the languorous opening and closing of the woman's mouth; of Craven's eyes, watchful and derisive. The subsequent events were what he had to think about and try to understand, because in them lay the source of his present danger. Hobart reviewed the rest of the fateful night and found he had nothing to work on, no memories of incidents which through hindsight had acquired new significance. The trouble was that he simply did not have enough information – while appearing to be friendly and communicative Investigator Shimming had, in fact, told him very little.

For the remainder of the brief flight Hobart forced himself to relax into his seat, trying to synthesize the feelings of pleasure and nostalgia he should have experienced on seeing familiar green horizons arise to enfold him.

It was early in the afternoon when the shuttle dropped

solidly on to a runway at Langer Field. Instead of rolling the vehicle into one of the company's operations bays, the pilot swung south and taxied into the section which the city of Corona Falls rented for use as an airport. They came to a halt beside a police car which was parked at a discreet distance from the passenger terminal and the doors swung open even before the turbines had growled into silence. Hobart had time for one glimpse of sharply etched snowy peaks far beyond a line of curved hangar roofs, then he was in the rear seat of the car beside Shimming, and the airport gates were looming ahead. The uniformed driver, without speaking or being spoken to, accelerated towards the city and in a few minutes they were entering the suburbs.

Hobart studied the procession of store fronts and small business premises, backed here and there by dwellings and tree-shaded streets, looking for signs of change. He had only a sketchy knowledge of Corona Falls, acquired during his period of training at the Langer Centre, and to him the lapse of eighteen years had created no striking differences in the place. Even the automobiles seemed very much as he remembered them, the designers having long ago surrendered to the dictates of aerodynamic efficiency. He strove to reorient himself as they neared the city centre, but the car abruptly swerved down a ramp and stopped in an underground parking area. Shimming escorted him from the car to an elevator, through a warren of corridors, and suddenly the two men were alone in a windowless office whose walls were painted the indeterminate green favoured by bureaucrats everywhere. The furniture consisted of a desk and four upright chairs. Hobart felt as though he had been cornered and driven into a pen.

'You'll have to advise me what to do next,' he said firmly. 'How do I contact a lawyer?'

Shimming sat down at the desk. 'I told you there's no need for that, Dennis. You're not under arrest.'

'It feels like it.'

'I hustled you down here in case there'd be any embarrassment with reporters.'

'Reporters?' Hobart selected a chair and sat down. 'I didn't think there'd be . . .'

'Local TV, radio, and the Corona Falls *Chronicle*,' Shimming said. 'The Langers have controlling interests in the lot. Old man Langer died about four years ago, but this is still very much his show.'

'But why did he start gunning for me?' Hobart examined his hands as he spoke, knowing the answer to his own question.

'That's what I want to find out. I've just had this case dumped in my lap, long after the whole thing has gone cold, but I'll sort it out even if I have to read microrecords in bed.' Shimming continued ducking his chin, suppressing belches.

'The Langer Line is the principal employer in this area, and the city couldn't get on very well without it, but I'm damned if I'm going to be used as an instrument for settling any of the Langers' personal grievances. Now, if it turned out that Dorcie Langer had given you a grapple or two . . . and that the colonel had found out . . . that would incline me to suspect his motives . . . and it would incline me to backpedal on this investigation.'

'There was nothing like that,' Hobart said heatedly. 'I hardly knew either of them.'

Shimming's lips twitched. 'At least we're getting that much straight. Eh, Dennis?'

Hobart met his gaze squarely. 'I demand to know why I'm here. For God's sake, I don't even know *how* Wolf Craven was killed.'

'That's just the point – neither do I.'

'But the body . . .'

'We haven't got a body.'

Hobart shifted in his chair and gave an incredulous laugh. 'Then what's going on? Why did you send a transit vehicle up specially for me?'

'That wasn't my idea. Somebody upstairs is putting on a bit of a show for the benefit of the Langer board.' Shimming put his elbows on the desk and leaned forward with a look of concern. 'Listen, Dennis, think it over carefully before you answer – are you *sure* there was nothing between you and Mrs Langer?'

Hobart thought about his career ending in a single blaze of sensationalism. 'Nothing. Nothing at all.'

'Okay, okay.' Shimming touched a button on the desk. 'I'm going to record the rest of this interview, for your benefit as well as mine. You'll be given a copy of the tape on request.'

'Suits me.' Hobart crossed his legs, making a show of relaxing. 'Perhaps now you'll tell me why I'm here.'

Shimming nodded. 'On the night of May 12, 2113, you – Dennis Hobart – were present at a party in Colonel Nolan Langer's house on Silverstream Heights. Also present was Wolf B. Craven, a junior engineering officer on a ship of the Langer Line. During the course of the party, at approximately midnight, you were seen by a number of witnesses having a heated argument with Craven, following which the two of you withdrew from the rest of the guests. Colonel Langer and other witnesses stated that you returned after approximately one hour, and that you were pale and uncommunicative, as though under mental stress.'

'That's wrong,' Hobart put in. 'That last bit is wrong – I talked to lots of people.'

'None of them remembers it. Anyway, do you admit to having an argument with Craven?'

'Yes, but it was nothing much. He was a bit drunk.'

'What was the argument about?'

'Well, he wanted me to go out to the freezer house at the back and look at Colonel Langer's collection of frost animals, and I didn't care for the idea.' Hobart heard the improvisation as though it were coming from a stranger and he felt a pang of unease. Lies, he sensed, should be kept simple and easy to manage.

'Were you afraid of the animals?'

'No – as far as I know they're harmless. It was just that I had seen them before and wasn't interested in seeing them again.'

'But you went with Craven anyway?'

'Only part of the way, to humour him. As soon as we got outside in the dark I slipped away from him.'

'What did you do then?'

'I walked in the gardens for about an hour – it was a fine night – then I returned to the house.'

'Was Wolf Craven there?'

'No. Not that I remember.'

'Did you ever see him again?'

'No.' It occurred to Hobart, for the first time, that it was strange that he had not seen Craven during the rest of that night. He had noticed Dorcie Langer more than once – drinking with friends, laughing a lot – but of Craven there had been no sign. Hobart experienced a momentary coldness, small but very real, like a single snowflake dissolving on his skin.

'You'll be interested to hear that two days after the party Colonel Langer visited the public prosecutor's office and made a deposition,' Shimming said carefully. 'In it he said that he went outside for a short time to check on his frost animals, at about thirty minutes after midnight, and that on his way to the freezer house he overheard you and Craven, still out in the garden, still arguing and apparently having a fist fight.'

'That's *wrong*,' Hobart countered, shocked. 'That's a lie.'

'Why would the colonel have lied?'

'I don't know.' A bizarre idea – in a way more disconcerting than anything that had yet cropped up – began to stir in the lower levels of Hobart's consciousness. 'Why did he wait two days before going to the police with his story?'

'I'm told he was ill – a touch of arthritis in his arms, something like that.' Shimming looked at Hobart with renewed interest, as though trying to tune in on his thought processes. 'Does the delay seem significant to you?'

'If he thought somebody had been killed . . .'

'That idea didn't get kicked around until it was discovered that Craven was missing – and by that time the *Langer Willow* had already departed, with you on board, and there's no way to communicate with a ship on drive.'

'Neat,' Hobart said, nodding, wondering if it would be possible to encourage a certain line of reasoning in Shimming's mind. 'Convenient.'

'Not for the police – we don't like the eighteen-year delays in our enquiries.'

'I didn't mean convenient for the police. It seems to me that . . .' Hobart stopped speaking as Shimming held up one hand in a theatrical gesture of warning and at the same time touched the control button of his unseen recorder. There was a moment of near silence dominated by the hum of the air conditioning and a fizzling noise from the light fitment on the ceiling.

'As you can see, I'm speaking off the record, as a friend,' Shimming said. 'It's to give you a piece of advice.'

'Which is . . . ?'

'Don't speculate on the record about who might have killed Wolf Craven.'

'What difference does it make when the colonel's dead?'

'He has an assortment of brothers, cousins, nieces, and nephews. Old Nolan was something of an embarrassment to the family, especially after he quit playing at exploring and settled down at home, but that only makes them more sensitive than ever about anything connected with him.'

'I see.' Hobart considered the notion that Investigator Shimming might actually be his friend. 'Does this mean you think I'm innocent?'

'It means I don't see how you could have disposed of the body in such a short time. You were on foot that night and you didn't make use of any of the other guests' cars. And we searched the whole area very thoroughly.'

'Craven just vanished off the face of the Earth?'

Shimming almost smiled. 'We considered that as a literal explanation. The *Langer Rowan* left the day after your ship, and for a long time we hoped there had been a foul-up in its papers. If Craven had got away to Alpha Centaurus on board it without being properly signed on – as has happened in the past – that would have solved everything. But the *Rowan* got back two years ago and we established that Craven had never reported for duty.'

The oppressive load began to lift from Hobart's mind. 'But you're not even sure that Craven is dead?'

'I don't think he ran away to sea, do you?'

'*Anything* could have happened to him,' Hobart said, gaining confidence. 'Why, he could have decided to quit the party and walk back to the Centre. A drunk driver could have zapped him and taken the body into the next state . . .'

'Clever theory, that. Not plausible – but clever.' Shimming brandished the index finger of his right hand to indicate he was about to start the recorder again. 'Just remember what I said about implicating Colonel Langer.'

He pressed the button. 'What were you going to say, Dennis? It seems to you that . . .'

'It seems to me that, even if you had proof that Wolf Craven had been killed, there's practically no case against me. Some people saw us arguing, which I admit and have explained. Colonel Langer says he *heard* me having a fight with Craven in the garden, which I deny. And that's it!'

'But why, out of twenty or so men who were present that night, did Colonel Langer think it was you he heard with Craven?'

'If he saw us arguing earlier he could have jumped to a wrong conclusion.'

'Thank you, Mr Hobart – I have no more questions for you for the present.' Shimming stopped the recorder once more and sat back, eyeing Hobart with moody satisfaction. 'I was scared up there today. Could you tell?'

'Most people are uneasy first time up,' Hobart said, wondering how soon he would be free to leave.

'I wasn't uneasy – I was scared stiff.' Shimming paused to make a ruminative movement with his chin. 'I could be psychologically marked for life, just so that the commissioner can make a political grandstand play. We could have picked you up at Langer Field and got the same useless piece of tape.'

'Useless?' Hobart spoke with a kind of pleasurable indignation. 'You can't call it useless if it clears up an eighteen-year-old case.'

'Who said the case was cleared up?'

'But you practically . . .'

Shimming shook his head. 'Craven was murdered, all right. I don't know who, how, or why – but I know he got himself snipped.'

'Look, when can I leave here?' Hobart said, his sense of unease returning in full force.

'Any time you like,' Shimming replied, getting to his

feet, 'but don't leave the city until you get clearance. And don't forget to let me know where you're staying.'

'I imagine I'll be at the junior officers' hostel at the Centre.'

'You imagine that, do you?' Shimming gave Hobart a wry look. 'I'll see you around, Dennis.'

The Langer Line personnel manager was called Toby Martyn. He was about thirty years old, but had adopted the dress and mannerisms of a middle-aged man, possibly with the intention of showing the staid and nepotic Langer board that he was director material. His eyes, behind gold-rimmed flakes of glass, were blue and unsympathetic as he selected various slips of paper from his desk and dropped them into an envelope bearing Hobart's name and citizen number.

'As you are no doubt aware,' he said primly, 'junior officers are assigned very few duties on their first interstellar voyage. Its main purpose is to determine how well they stand up to the psychological stresses of both the journey itself and the associated calendaric displacement.'

There's no such word as calendaric, you gasbrain, Hobart thought. He was shocked and angry, yet a detached part of his mind had noted a curious fact. With one round trip completed, he had seventeen years of timeslip under his belt and – although it was a paltry score compared to that of a veteran starman – it was already affecting his relationships with Earth-bound individuals. Martyn was about seven years his senior in actual body time, and therefore in experience, but Hobart had been born a decade *before* the other man, and on that account felt himself to be somehow the more complete of the two. He began to get an inkling of how he, as a junior officer, must have seemed to a man like Captain Mercier, and his yearning to bestride the centuries in a like manner suddenly intensified itself.

'I felt fine throughout the trip,' he said. 'I feel fine now.'

'That's not what it says on your psychometric profile,' Martyn replied, sealing the large envelope. 'Take my advice, Mr Hobart. You're a young man, with your whole life ahead of you – forget about space flying and take up some other occupation. With your engineering qualifications you should have no trouble getting into – '

'I'm not interested in other work,' Hobart interrupted. 'I'm doing the only thing I want to do.'

'Well . . . perhaps with some other line.'

'Some other line!' Hobart found he was almost shouting, but was past caring about propriety. 'That psych report was cooked up to prevent me working *anywhere*.'

Martyn's face underwent a subtle change. 'Careful what you're saying, Mr Hobart.'

'I'm saying my assessment was faked. Do you think I don't know the real reason I'm being booted out?'

Martyn slid the envelope across to the front of his desk. 'The references you have here will enable you to obtain another type of position. They contain no mention of the fact that you are suspected of having murdered a fellow officer, and that's something for which you should be grateful.'

Hobart drove forward and caught Martyn's wrist. Martyn flinched back, obviously afraid, but at the same time a look of furtive triumph appeared in his eyes, and it was that which enabled Hobart to regain his mental poise. A starship was an emotional pressure cooker, an autoclave in which certain kinds of character defect tended to trigger explosions, and no operator employed people with records of violence. The phrase 'physically assaulted a company executive' appearing on his sheet, regardless of the circumstances, would be an ironclad guarantee that he would never again serve on an interstellar vessel. Hobart released Martyn's wrist, drew his lips into a numb smile, and stood up, searching for words which would make him seem cool and dignified.

'You haven't heard the last of this,' he said, resorting to a formula he remembered from historical novels. Martyn adjusted his glasses and stared up at him without speaking. Hobart picked up his envelope, left the office, and made his way out of the building to the plaza, where late afternoon sunlight glowed on the alloy statues and islands of shrubbery. It was a perfect spring day, exactly the sort he had visualized for his homecoming, but that fact served only to aggravate the turmoil behind his eyes. He entered a dark-seeming side street and found an even darker bar. The place was empty, engulfed in a musty stillness which preceded the rush of customers at the end of the working day.

Hobart bought a glass of beer, carried it to a table which had a small peach-coloured light, and sat down to examine the contents of his envelope. The pay slip told him he had been credited with close to a hundred thousand dollars, a sum which at first seemed too much. Interstellar travel and its time anomalies had alarmed the world's bankers in the early years, and they had been quick to reach agreement that interest on any star traveller's funds should be computed on his body time and not according to Earth calendars. However, starship operators usually factorized crew salaries to compensate for inflation and timeslip, and when Hobart took that into account – along with tax refunds and severance pay – he found he had received no more than his due. He had no immediate money problems, but that was of little comfort when his career had been ruined, deliberately and with malice aforethought, by a man who had escaped into the grave after having . . .

The colonel murdered Wolf Craven! The thought, which had been swamped by other considerations, struck Hobart with sudden force, aweing him with its strangeness.

On that night, on that fairly significant social occasion, Nolan Langer – probably driven by jealousy or hurt pride – must have killed Craven and disposed of the body. And, being a man who never did things by halves, he had rounded out the act of revenge by shifting the blame on to Hobart, a move which would have increased his satisfaction and diverted the police investigation away from himself.

Hobart sipped his beer, reluctantly impressed. He could remember the colonel on the night of the party – tall, iron grey, limping, militarily correct – welcoming his guests, and . . . and . . . Hobart frowned as he realized he had no other recollections of the colonel on that night. Langer had absented himself at quite an early stage, which tied in with the theory that he was getting rid of cumbersome evidence, but there was an inconsistency somewhere. His memories of the party itself were all compatible, now that he understood what had been going on beneath the surface, so the discordant note must have originated during his talk with Investigator Shimming. Hobart stared into the peachy orb of the table lamp, unable to pin down the vagrant idea which was tantalizing him, then he recalled Shimming's promise that he could have a record of the interview. He pushed his beer glass away, crammed the envelope into an inner pocket of his tunic, and left the bar.

The street outside was more crowded now as the city's stores and offices began to close down for the day. Hobart walked one block south to the Lewis Hotel and checked into an expensive second-floor suite with a balcony overlooking colourful tulip beds. As soon as he was alone he went to the living room's infomat and put a call through to police headquarters, praying that Shimming would still be on duty. He relaxed somewhat as the investigator's long, serious face appeared on the screen.

'I'm glad I caught you,' he said.

Shimming nodded. 'No panic. I'm usually patched into the system – even in bed.'

'Oh! I'm staying at the Lewis, by the way.'

'Thanks for letting me know, Dennis.' Shimming lowered his chin, conducting one of his silent battles against internal pressures, but his eyes remained fixed on Hobart's. 'You decided against the Langer Centre?'

Hobart gave a rueful grimace. 'How did you know they were going to dump me?'

'It wasn't hard to figure out.'

'Well, I'm not leaving it like that. I'd like the tape you promised me earlier.'

'You want it now?'

'Yes.' Hobart checked to make sure there was a cassette of lateral-imprinting tape in the console's bulk information receiver and pressed the intake button. On the screen he saw Shimming looking down at his own terminal as he fired through an information bleep in which the entire interview was compressed into a signal lasting a fraction of a second. A green light appeared above the bulk receiver.

'Got it,' Hobart said. 'Thanks.'

'This sort of thing never works,' Shimming commented. 'Not in real life, anyway. Amateur investigators never turn up anything the police didn't know about all along.'

'Is that a fact?' Hobart suppressed an impulse to issue some kind of enigmatic challenge. 'You don't mind if I go over the tape a few times, do you?'

'Be my guest,' Shimming said, fading himself out. Hobart took the cassette out of the receiver and dropped it into a playback slot, all at once convinced that Shimming was right, that he was only play-acting. The idea which had seemed so close to the surface of his mind in the bar had retreated to deep tiers of consciousness populated only by unremembered dreams. Voices suddenly pervaded the room, his own the strangest of the two, and he began pacing the floor to work off his tensions. In that mood he had no expectation of success and consequently he was surprised to find his attention instantly caught by a single fragment.

'. . . the two of you withdrew from the rest of the guests. Colonel Langer and other witnesses stated that you returned after approximately one . . .'

And the point was that Langer had not been around when Hobart returned to the party. Hobart was certain of his ground because, with Dorcie Langer's perfume still in his nostrils, he had been supercharged with guilt, abnormally keyed up for the first encounter with the colonel. It had never occurred.

The fact was not very important in itself, but it could be used to prove to Shimming that Colonel Langer had lied when making his deposition – and if one part of his testimony was shown to be fake the remainder could perhaps be written off. Hobart strode to the infomat, but paused before making a call. As the matter stood, it was a case of his word against the sworn statement of a member of the city's most influential family – and he had an idea Shimming was likely to be unimpressed. After a few moments of thought, Hobart asked the machine for a communications code and put a call through to Joe Armitage, a dentist who did much of the contract work for the training centre. He had become friendly with Hobart when they found themselves attending the same concerts, and as youngsters with like interests they had seen each other at least once a week throughout Hobart's pre-ops course. The screen came to life almost immediately, showing a square-faced, ruddy-complexioned man in his forties against a background of antique books. Hobart stared at him in silence, filled with a curious timidity. I have travelled in space, and I have travelled in time . . .

'This is Joe Armitage,' the stranger said. 'My daughter isn't at home right now, if that's what . . .'

Hobart shook his head. 'Joe! This is Denny. Denny Hobart.'

Armitage frowned, his eyes taking in details of Hobart's tunic and service emblems. 'I'm afraid I . . . Wait a minute – you went off on the *Oak*, didn't you?'

'The *Langer Willow*.'

'That's right! I heard a ship had just come in, but I wasn't sure which one it was. I'm in private practice these days and I don't have much to do with the Langer organization.'

'Neither do I,' Hobart said. 'I was wondering . . .'

'I'm sorry I didn't recognize you,' Armitage cut in. 'I knew so many of the Langer boys in my old hell-raising days, and . . . It's a funny thing, but when people look the same as they did eighteen or twenty years ago you can't recognize them. I have no trouble with acquaintances who've been on Earth all along and who *have* changed. It's as if the old brain keeps a model of them and updates it year by year, putting in the sags and bags and wrinkles and so forth, so that when I see them I know who they are, even if they don't look much like they used to. Know what I mean?'

'I think so.' Hobart felt a pang of sadness at having been classed as an acquaintance rather than a friend, but he put it out of his mind. 'Listen, Joe, I'm sorry about springing this on you, but I'm in a bit of trouble with the police and I need somebody to back up my statement to them.'

Armitage looked interested. 'I'll help you all I can.'

'Thanks. It's about that party the night before I left. Colonel Langer walked out in the middle of it and didn't come back, but he swore that he did. All I need is somebody to . . .'

'Hold on,' Armitage protested, smiling. 'What party are you talking about? I don't think I was even there.'

'You were,' Hobart said, shocked.

'Sorry – I think you're wrong, Denny.'

'But . . .' Hobart searched his memory. 'Remember you spent most of the night playing poker with Mexy Gomez.'

'Did I? Gomez? Was that the character with the blue chin and all the muscles?'

'Yes. Do you remember now?'

'I'm trying.' Armitage gazed back at Hobart, his eyes slowly clouding, then he shook his head. 'I went to quite a few of the colonel's parties in the old days, but they've all run together in my mind. That was nearly twenty years ago, Denny.'

'I know,' Hobart said, learning something about timeslip and the nature of loneliness. He spoke to Armitage for another minute, fending off questions about his problems, and ended the call after making an insincere promise to get in touch again. The room seemed abnormally quiet when the screen went dead. He brooded for a moment, then took a pen from his pocket and made a list of twelve other men and women who had been guests at Colonel Langer's house on the crucial night. Seven of those were operations personnel and a series of enquiries revealed that they were all away on the Procyon run and would not be seen on Earth for another eight years or more. Of the remaining five, residents of Corona Falls, two had died of natural causes, and the others – far from being able to help – were unable even to remember knowing Hobart or having been in his company. After nearly an hour of awkwardness and embarrassment, he turned away from the infomat, went into the bedroom, and lay down.

It was growing dark outside, the sky turning a peacock

blue above the varicoloured glitter off the city beyond his balcony, and it came to him that by this time – had his dreams of homecoming materialized properly – he should have been bedding down with a woman. He had an intense yearning for the comfort and companionship of love. Hobart turned restlessly on the bed's pliant surface for a minute, then lay still, his eyes widening, as the idea which had lain dormant in his mind heaved upward and began to dominate all thought.

There was one person who had cause to remember the night of the party as clearly as he did, despite the passage of time, and as far as he knew there was nothing to prevent him from contacting Dorcie Langer without further delay.

Hobart was surprised to find that the big house was in comparative darkness. Subconsciously, having previously been there only when a party was in full swing or when the colonel was organizing a foray, he had it fixed in his mind as a place where such things were the norm, and the terse instruction from Mrs Langer's personal secretary had in an obscure way reinforced his preconceptions. As he parked his rented car in the driveway he admitted to himself that more than a year in the confines of the ship had disposed him towards a therapeutic blowout, garnished with excesses of every kind, and the insight was a disturbing one. His current troubles all stemmed from one shameful debauch, yet part of him had been ready to flirt with similar temptations and perhaps still was. The id, he suddenly realized, could be a dangerous encumbrance.

He slammed the car door and examined the house, wishing he were a smoker so that he could indulge in the ritual of lighting a cigarette. The two-storey building, with its stone mullions and complex roof, looked imposingly ancient. In the gardens at the rear he could see the outlines of the freezer house where Nolan Langer had kept his menagerie of frost animals, and he was further surprised to note a bluish glow from the windows, which indicated that the refrigeration system was still functioning. The enigmatic creatures, inhabitants of Sirius VII, were troublesome to support and he would have expected the colonel's widow – whose interests were more earthly – to have rid herself of the responsibility at the earliest possible moment.

Hobart walked to the house's main entrance and ascended the curving steps. A control system, responding to the identity code emitted by his citizenship tag, swung the door open for him and he went through into a dimly lit, spacious hall which seemed not to have altered since his last visit. The same pictures of extra-terrestrial scenes – souvenirs of the colonel's travels – hung on the walls, and the same photon-sculptures glowed in the corners and recesses. He was still getting his bearings when a door on the right opened and a woman he took to be Dorcie Langer's secretary appeared in a rectangle of pink light and beckoned to him. Hobart had almost reached her before he realized his mistake.

His talk with Armitage had alerted him to the effects of timeslip and he had steeled himself to find the young Dorcie Langer transformed into a woman in her forties, but other forces had been at work – and the person before him had an apparent age closer to sixty. She was dressed in salmon-coloured silks revealing a round-shouldered figure in which the torso had plumped out while the legs had grown thin, giving her an odd sparrow-like aspect. Her face, in the flattering light, was much as he remembered it, except for a waxy, unnatural sheen. Hobart, in spite of his naïvety in such matters, sensed that a cosmetician had all but erased the real face and used it as a canvas upon which to paint the woman who had used to be. His stride faltered.

'Hello, Denny,' she said in a burry voice. 'Don't stand there gawking. Come in!'

'Of course.' Hobart entered the room behind her and closed the door. 'Hello, Mrs Langer.'

'Mrs Langer he says! You don't need to be formal with *me*, Denny.' She threw him a brilliant smile as she went towards a liquor cabinet. 'What are you drinking?'

'Ah . . . anything.'

'Good for you. Still game for anything, eh?' She splashed two glasses of clear liquid from a decanter, came back and handed one to him. She looked closely into his face as their fingers touched, and her smile vanished. 'Just as a matter of interest – what age are you?'

'Twenty-three,' Hobart replied, too nonplussed to avoid a direct answer which carried a whiff of danger.

'My God,' Dorcie said, walking around him as though inspecting a statue. 'My *God*! It isn't fair – you're still just a kid. How can you still be just a kid?'

Hobart strove to be diplomatic. 'Age isn't important.'

'Not important!' Dorcie drained her glass, wetting the side of her chin in the process. 'Not important, he says. Of *course* it isn't important for somebody who doesn't change in eighteen years.'

'For me it's only been one year,' Hobart said soothingly. 'The time dilation effect – '

'Don't give me any of that scientific crap,' she shouted, chilling Hobart with the abrupt contortion of her face into a mask of fury. 'Time is time, for God's sake! It's the same everywhere. Nobody will ever convince me . . .' She stopped speaking, glanced around like someone who had just heard a stealthy footfall, and her smile returned in full force. 'Let's have another drink.'

Hobart held up his still brimming glass. 'I suppose you can guess why I came to see you.'

'I can guess, all right – you young spacers are all the

same,' Dorcie said coquettishly, appalling Hobart even further. She refilled her glass and sat down on a low-backed couch. 'Don't stand around, Denny – we're old friends, aren't we?'

'Yes, indeed.' Hobart sat down near her and sipped his drink, which proved to be a cloying almond-flavoured liqueur. 'Look, Dorcie, you don't believe I killed Wolf Craven, do you?'

'You? That's hardly your style.'

'Have you any idea why Colonel Langer told the police I did it?'

'I know exactly why.' Dorcie gave a sharp laugh. 'Don't you know? It's because he was a bastard. Through and through. He tried to keep me shut up as if I was a goddamn Sister of Mercy or something – but it didn't work.'

'That's not what I'm getting at.'

'Funny thing is, he was able to do it better after he was dead. I'm not allowed to give up the house, you know. I'm tied to this mausoleum and that damned ice box out in back, otherwise I lose three fourths of my lousy income.'

Hobart shook his head impatiently. 'Do you remember the party the night before I left?'

'Do I?' Dorcie rolled her eyes, put a hand on his knee, and leaned closer. 'Are you trying to get me going?'

'In his deposition to the police,' Hobart said steadily, repressing the urge to shrink away, 'the colonel said he rejoined the party soon after midnight, but you must remember that he didn't. Nobody saw him for the rest of the – '

'I don't want to talk about that old goat,' Dorcie cut in, setting her glass aside. 'All right, Denny – let's go upstairs.'

Hobart's mouth went dry. 'Upstairs?'

'Don't act so innocent.' She slid her hand along his

thigh. 'You've been stripping me with your eyes ever since you came in here.'

Hobart disengaged by jumping to his feet. 'You're the only one who can help me. Think back, *please*. Can you remember exactly what the colonel did that night?'

Dorcie made as if to come after him, then a slow smile appeared on her face and she settled back on the couch, spreading her legs a little. 'I probably could remember – given the right sort of encouragement.'

'He was missing for the rest of the night, wasn't he?'

'Down on your knees,' she commanded, eyes bleak and threatening. 'Down on your knees, boy.'

Hobart backed away, shaking his head. 'You're sick,' he whispered. 'Crazy.'

'Crazy?' Dorcie Langer seemed to savour the word while she kneaded the flesh of her thighs. 'Perhaps I am. I could be crazy enough to remember anything I wanted – good or bad. It's up to you, Denny, my love.'

Hobart turned and fled the room, running with the leaden-footed ponderousness that characterizes nightmares.

Later that night Hobart experienced a real nightmare. He dreamed it was the night of the party again, the location in time and space convincingly established by a shifting montage of images and impressions – large rooms with minimal lighting; a sense of imminence – the dreadful starship waiting; trays of drinks, tables of food; intermingled wisps of music and distant laughter; the choking press of bodies in slithering nakedness . . . Suddenly Hobart was in a silver room – it was the freezer house – watching in mute terror as the tall figure of Colonel Langer stood over Wolf Craven and methodically destroyed him with an ice pick. Craven was lying on the floor, twitching and flinching under the blows each of which added to and elaborated the pattern of blood-red, dark, centred flowers covering his body from neck to groin. His mouth was open, but the horror of the scene was increased by the fact that he did not scream. Instead, there came from his lips a thin, sad keening, a plaintive note like the beat of insect wings in summer pastures . . .

Hobart awoke with the sound ringing in his ears and sat up immediately, unwilling to risk falling asleep again and sinking back into the same nightmare. He checked the time, saw that it was almost six in the morning, and decided to get up. While taking a hot shower he pondered over the dream, marvelling at the ways of the subconscious mind. He had a nodding acquaintance with the Faraday theory, which stated that the overt content of dreams – which psychologists had once dismissed as mere 'day residue' – was more significant than the Freudian and post-Freudian interpretation of symbols and could be treated as genuine attempts at communication between different levels of the mind. But what might his subconscious be trying to say? He had already deduced that Langer had killed Craven, probably in or around the freezer house, so that part was no help to him – and the strange whining sound seemed no more than a grotesque incidental detail. Was the message simply that Craven's body was hidden in the refrigerated building, where it would be immune from decay?

Hobart considered the idea later while eating breakfast in his room and decided it was of little merit. Investigator Shimming had told him the entire area had been searched by the police, and the freezer house and associated workshop were among the first places anybody would think of checking. He was pouring a third cup of coffee when the infomat buzzed to announce a call and Shimming's long face appeared on the screen, looking professionally impassive while he waited for two-way communication. Hobart pressed a button to accept the call.

'I was wrong about you, Dennis,' the investigator said without preamble. 'I had an idea you'd go up to Silverstream last night, and I expected that you'd be totally ineffective – but I was way off the beam. You really managed to churn things up.'

'Really?' Hobart kept his voice level. 'In what way?'

'One of Mrs Langer's tame lawyers spoke to the commissioner this morning. It appears that she too remembers your having a fist fight with Wolf Craven in her garden on the night he disappeared.'

Hobart shook his head emphatically. 'The woman's insane. You might have warned me about that.'

'Rich people don't go insane, Dennis – at most they become eccentric. In any case, we now have a second statement corroborating what Colonel Langer told us, and that makes things worse for you.'

'You're not going to take it seriously, are you?' Hobart was unable to read Shimming's eyes. 'I mean, why did she wait eighteen years before coming out with this?'

'The line they're taking is that she saw no point in getting involved until you were back on Earth, that nothing could be done until now.'

'Garbage,' Hobart snapped. 'Specious garbage, at that.'

'Nevertheless,' Shimming said, dipping his chin, 'it increases the pressure on me within the department. What did you do up there last night, anyway?'

'It was what I wouldn't do,' Hobart muttered, and was instantly sorry he had spoken.

'Oh? Gone off her, have you?'

'I was never . . . Look, we've been through all that already.' Hobart sought a way to wrest the conversation on to a new track. 'When you were searching for Wolf Craven's body did you go through the freezer house?'

'Me? I was in my second year in the police academy in 2113.'

'You know what I mean,' Hobart said, refusing to think about timeslip. 'Did they check the freezer house?'

'Naturally.' Shimming glanced down at something on his desk. 'It's all here in the report. The investigating officers – with Colonel Langer's full co-operation, by the way – went all through the workshop and the cold area itself. They looked under the refrigeration machinery housings, behind all movable wall, ceiling, and floor panels, underneath the salt storage unit . . .'

'What storage unit?'

Shimming inspected his records again. 'It seems that those things the colonel brought back from Sirius way, the frost animals, need trays of mineral salts to keep them alive.'

'I know that – but when I was in the freezer house those trays just sat around on the floor.' As a synaesthetic background to his own voice, Hobart heard the curious sound from his nightmare, and memories began to stir.

'So what?' Shimming gave an elaborate shrug. 'It wouldn't have been too tidy that way, so Colonel Langer had a special unit built.'

'Correction! He built it himself.'

'All right – he built it himself. I'm told he liked doing things like that.'

'You don't understand,' Hobart said quickly, above the pounding in his chest. 'I was in that freezer house only three days, or it might have been two, before the party – and at that time the trays of salts were still sitting around on the floor.'

Shimming pulled on his chin and looked puzzled. 'What do you think you're getting at?'

'He built it the night of the party. *During* the party.'

'You haven't any proof of that. It could have been . . .'

'I do have proof,' Hobart put in, telling the lie which

might not have been a lie had his conscious memory been perfect. 'I remember going near the back of the house two or three hours after midnight and hearing somebody outside using a valency saw. You know that weird droning noise they make – you can't mistake it.'

'It doesn't matter exactly when the unit was built,' Shimming said through a silent gulp, showing his disapproval of Hobart's excitement. 'The point is that the officers looked at it after Craven disappeared.'

'They didn't look well enough,' Hobart asserted. 'That's where Craven's body has to be.'

Shimming turned his gaze towards the ceiling for a few seconds, then gave Hobart a wry smile. 'It says in your file that you were born way back in 2091, and that makes me forget you're just a kid.'

'Kid nothing,' Hobart said angrily. 'I'm able to think.'

'Yes, but you think the way a kid does. You think a team of trained police officers could search a room and fail to find an object as large as a human body; you think crimes are solved by a Great Detective sucking on a pipe and making deductions – but that's not the way it is, sonny. The police success rate is very high these days, but it's because we get information. There are too many systems for acquiring data, and storing it, and processing it. That's what gives us the edge.'

'What about the information I've just given you?' Hobart demanded. 'Aren't you even going to . . . ?' He broke off as someone knocked heavily on the door leading out to the corridor.

'That'll be my men,' Shimming said. 'The way the situation has developed, I have to bring you in. I'm sorry about this.'

'I'm sorry, too.' Hobart allowed his shoulders to droop as the pounding on the door grew more insistent. 'I'll let them in.' He left the infomat, walked straight out to the balcony and – praying the flower beds were no further down than he remembered – vaulted over the railing.

It was growing dark when Hobart left the cover of the timber plantation and approached Silverstream Heights from the west, picking his way through the swathe of gullies and sheared ground that helped protect the big houses against intruders.

His main concern throughout the day had been that of keeping well away from store entrance scanners and any other devices which could read the signals from his citizenship tag. He might have thrown the tag away altogether, but many commercial security systems could sense the nearness of a human body and when it was not accompanied by appropriately coded radiation they tended to react loudly. Less embarrassing, but more dangerous from his point of view, was the type that remained silent and sent a microwave call to the nearest police station. Hobart's strategy had been to leave the city on foot and go into hiding at the first good opportunity, and although his day-long wait in the sanctuary of the trees had been uncomfortable and boring he had successfully retained his freedom.

He followed a track up to the fence which marked the western edge of the Langer estate and, his progress now hampered by darkness, located the gate the colonel had installed to facilitate his snake hunts. Its rails were covered with spirals of barbed wire and, predictably, it was locked. Hobart took off his tunic, wrapped it around the top bar and managed to climb over without incurring any injury. He began to retrieve the garment and then, recalling that he might need to make a rapid exit, changed his mind and knotted the jacket in place by the sleeves. An ivory-coloured moon, horizontally striped with cloud, was lifting clear of the distant hills, but its luminance was weak and Hobart had to move cautiously as he went towards the house. After five minutes the exterior lamps came into view, interfering with his night vision and creating the illusion that he was nearing the edge of a black and dangerous pit. He continued to feel his way forward and it was with a considerable sense of gratitude that he reached the smooth turf of the gardens and was able to pick out the sloping roof of the freezer house and workshop. A blue glow from the square high-set windows told him the environment necessary for the survival of the frost animals was still being maintained.

Hobart felt strangely uneasy and uncertain as he approached the freezer house door. The notion of taking direct action to solve a murder mystery had seemed both logical and attractive during the day, but the reality – involving illegal night entry and, for all he knew, a risk of getting himself shot – was a different matter. He looked up at the dark bulk of the house, wondering if Dorcie Langer was in it at that very moment, and he was gripped by a desire to complete his mission as quickly as possible and slip away before his situation deteriorated in some unforeseen manner. Moving with self-conscious stealth, he opened the door, stepped inside, and stood for a moment in the small, square lobby. On his left was the insulated door of the refrigerated area, with its single viewing aperture; on the right was the workshop, with a cone of yellow light illuminating one of the workbenches. Did that mean he had been unlucky and that a maintenance engineer was actually on the premises?

He cleared his throat loudly and strode into the workshop, his mind working on a passable cover story, and found it deserted. Aware of the need for haste, he gathered up several types of screwdrivers and a hammer and carried them out to the lobby. He slid back the bolt on the insulated door and went through it into the menagerie itself. The door closed behind him with a pneumatic sigh. For a brief moment, while his clothing retained a protective layer of air, he had the impression the temperature in the room was quite moderate – then the coldness closed with him, grappling and clawing like an invisible enemy. Pain flared in his nostrils and throat.

Hobart looked around, breathing in shallow gasps, and saw one of the captive animals on the wall at his side. It resembled a beautifully symmetrical array of frost ferns, almost a metre in diameter. As he watched, its crystalline patterns began to alter – a seething of diamonds – and the flower shape grew smaller. In the space of a few seconds the creature had vanished altogether. Hobart turned nervously and saw that the alien had re-formed on the wall behind him. At the edge of his vision he saw others blossoming or shrinking on every flat surface, like glassy lichens.

Reminding himself that the frost creatures had never been known to settle on a human, he went further into the room, past the refrigerator housing, and immediately saw the fabricated unit of which Shimming had spoken. Basically, it was a squat pyramid fringed with silver laminate-covered shelves on which sat trays of the mineral salts commonly found in the deserts of Sirius VII. The structure was screwed to the floor, and Hobart's pulse quickened as he noted that the central pyramid was large enough to contain two or three bodies if required. Wishing he had retained his tunic to help ward off the cold, he began lifting the wide trays from the shelves and placing them on the floor. It seemed to him as he did so that the migratory activity of the frost animals increased slightly, but he dismissed the idea. Xenologists had been studying the creatures for some years and still had not managed to classify them or produce any behavioural responses, so it would have been fanciful for him to suppose they were reacting to his presence.

When he had disposed of the trays he lifted the heavy shelves off their brackets, stood them against a wall, and began taking up the screws which secured the pyramid to the floor. By this time he was shivering so violently that he had to use both hands to guide the screwdriver into the slots, and he realized he could remain in sub-zero environment for only a few more minutes. He removed the last screw with trembling hands, slid the screwdriver under the base of the pyramid, and tilted the structure on to its side.

The interior was completely empty.

Unable to accept the evidence of his eyes, Hobart sank to his knees and tapped the laminated boards, looking for dimensional or angular discrepancies which would have betrayed a hidden compartment. Cracks of light glimmering between the boards told him the quest was hopeless – even a master magician would have found it impossible to conceal a rabbit within the simple structure. Hobart, sick with disappointment, sank back on to his heels and pressed a hand to his jaw to dampen its vibrations. He looked around the featureless walls of the room, heedless now of the transient flat rosettes of the frost animals, and cursed himself for the senseless egotism that had led him to go against a professional like Shimming. The best thing he could do now was to put things back as he had found them, in the hope his trespass would remain undetected, then go back into the city and give himself up to the police.

He got to his feet and was trying for a good grip on the toppled pyramid when there was a sharp metallic sound from the direction of the door.

Hobart froze in the act of lifting, certain he was about to be apprehended. He remained in the same attitude for a few seconds – then a more disquieting idea entered his mind.

Letting the pyramid fall, he ran to the door – seeing a

pale face flicker and vanish in the dark rectangle of the viewing aperture – and tugged on the handle. As his premonition had told him it would, the metal-sheathed door refused to move.

'Dorcie!' he shouted. 'It's Denny. Don't do this. *Let me out!*' There was total, black-velvet silence.

He turned away from the door and cast about wildly, his breath pluming in the gelid air. The hammer he had taken from the workshop was lying on the floor. He picked it up in stiffened hands, went to the nearest window, and struck it with all his force. The head of the hammer rebounded from the toughened glass without marking it in any way. Hobart tried again and this time the hammer spun from his grasp and fell behind him. He dropped to his knees and was going after the tool that represented his hope of salvation when a silent voice – perhaps that of his super-ego, perhaps of the wise, worldly, and dispassionate Denny Hobart he had always hoped to become – spoke to him, commanding his attention. He listened for a moment and rose to his feet, smiling apologetically with one hand on his forehead, then gathered up the screwdrivers and went to the true source of his peril – the flanged and louvred mass of the refrigeration plant.

The main side panel was held in place by six spring-loaded screws requiring only a half-turn each. Using his two-handed technique, Hobart was able to remove the screws in a matter of seconds and to lift the sheet of metal out of his way, exposing the machinery itself. The type and its operating principle were unfamiliar to him, but he had no difficulty in identifying a thermostat which had a slide control on a scale running from −40° to +30° Centigrade, which meant the system could double up as a heater. Grunting with relief, he reached for the control, then jerked his hand back as the entire thermostat housing became enveloped in a thick coating of frost. The white crystalline layer continued to thicken and exhibit patterns, diamond petals furling out on diamond petals with bewildering rapidity, until quite suddenly the thermostat was locked inside a shell of ice.

Hobart gaped at it, dumbfounded, then raised his head to look around the room. Most of the elaborate, jewelled rosettes of the frost animals had disappeared from the walls and ceiling. He looked back at the refrigeration machinery and saw that no part of it had been affected by the encrustation except the control he had been about to operate. Hugging himself to ease the growing pain in his chest, Hobart rocked backward and forward as he tried to make sense of what was happening. The only conclusion he could reach was that somehow, by some process he could not even begin to understand, the alien beings had divined his intention. Switching off the refrigeration would save his life, but as a consequence the frost animals would be destroyed – the temperature in the room had never been allowed to rise above −20° Centigrade in the decades of its existence – and it appeared they had taken preventive action.

Questions began to clamour in his mind. Had he, Denny Hobart, accidentally made the first intellectual contact with an extra-terrestrial race? Had no xenologist researcher thought of testing for motivation by threatening a frost animal with death? Or, unknown to him, had progress been made in that field during his eighteen years of absence in space?

The stabbing sensation in his lungs grew worse and he realized that, at this stage, questions and answers were without relevance. His very life was at stake – and there were more ways than one of stopping a machine. He turned to reach for the fallen hammer and in that moment became aware of another phenomenon, one of silent but flurried movement. The shelves he had removed from the storage unit were still leaning against the nearest wall, and all over their sloping surfaces a number of frost animals were forming, fading away to nothingness and re-forming in a kind of regimented dance, creating fantastic, shifting, geometrical designs.

Wondering why he was squandering the short time left to him, Hobart rose painfully to his feet and approached the shelves. The activity of the beautiful enigmatic beings reached a frenzied climax, dazzling his eyes.

I can learn from you, he thought, numbly, as though his brain cells were turning to ice. The same lesson that old man Langer learned. Rigid bodies make rigid minds make rigid thinking . . .

He watched his hands reach out like servomechanisms, the blue-knuckled fingers crooking in preparation, and in that moment the frost animals vanished from the shelf he was about to touch. Hobart dug his nails under the top edge of the plank's silvery laminate and slowly peeled it downward, revealing the core material, which appeared to be a red semitransparent plastic, variegated here and there by whitish spots and areas of blue and black and brown.

Thunderous seconds passed before his mind came to grips with the mosaic of lines and charnel-house colours, imposing a pattern on them, letting him know he was looking at a longitudinal section cut through a human body. He turned away, retching, and went back to the refrigeration plant.

'I'm sorry,' he said aloud. 'You've given me what I wanted, but I'm not going to die. Not in this century. Not in the next . . .'

He knelt at the machine, grasped a slim feed pipe, and tugged on it with what remained of his strength. The pipe began to bend, but in that instant his breath was cut off. He fell sideways to the floor in the grip of a searing coldness unlike anything he could have imagined as the frost animals attacked, suffocating him beneath a mask of sparkling ice.

Investigator Shimming paused for a moment, nuzzling his chin down on to his chest. He remained in that attitude for a short time – perhaps coping with gastric explosions, perhaps ordering his thoughts – then activated the recorder in his desk.

'It is now obvious,' he said, settling back in his chair, 'that having unlawfully killed Wolf Craven, Colonel Langer placed the body of the deceased in an oblong box, filled the box up with water and put it in the refrigerated room he used as an extra-terrestrial menagerie. Forensic reports will reveal whether or not he added any chemicals to the water to accelerate the freezing process. As soon as the contents of the box had frozen solid he took a cutting implement – almost certainly a valency saw, which is quick in operation and generates no heat – and sliced the resultant block into longitudinal planks about three centimetres in thickness. An engineering consultant from the University of Montana has already confirmed that ordinary ice has quite good structural properties below a certain temperature, and in this case we are talking about ice which was reinforced with bone and strips of clothing.

'Colonel Langer then covered the planks with metallic laminate, to disguise their nature, and used them to build the shelf unit I referred to earlier in this report. Evidence suggests that this work was begun on the night of 12 May, 2113, while the party was still in progress, and was completed late the following day – by which time Dennis Hobart had already departed on the *Langer Willow*. Having disposed of Craven's body in a manner he was confident would escape detection, Colonel Langer went to the office of the public prosecutor and made a deposition in which he attached the blame for Craven's death to Hobart.

'I have not been able to establish any motive for his desire to incriminate Hobart, and am of the opinion that Hobart was chosen fortuitously, simply because he had been seen arguing with the deceased. That concludes my interim report on this case.'

Shimming switched off the recorder, surveyed the drab green walls of his office, then allowed his gaze to settle on Hobart, who was sitting opposite him. 'As you'll have gathered, I'm letting you off the hook,' he said. 'You know, I don't think I've ever met anybody so lucky.'

'*Lucky!*' Pain caused Hobart's face to twist spasmodically beneath the surgical dressings and he fell silent, wishing he had not reacted so violently.

'That's what I said. You're alive when you ought to be dead, and you're getting your job back. The Langers didn't have to reinstate you.'

'Didn't they? Can you think of a better way to remove an embarrassment?'

'Perhaps not.' Shimming took a roll of white tablets from a drawer and began to suck one, rolling it about his mouth as though tasting a rare wine. 'All the same, Dorcie Langer could have blackballed you.'

'She ought to be put away for trying to kill me.'

'We have no proof of that, Dennis. She says she locked the door on an intruder, which is what any normal woman might have done in the same circumstances.'

'Normal?' Hobart winced and gingerly pressed both palms to his cheeks. 'The frost animals are more normal than she is.'

'Could be. Have you thought about how we must appear to them? Perhaps we're the real frost animals.'

Hobart nodded, waiting for the pain in his face to subside. The creatures from Sirius VII no longer seemed quite so enigmatic since it had been established that they were life-oriented, reacting as positively as they could against any form of killing. It was due to that facet of their nature that he was still alive – because eighteen years earlier they had attacked Nolan Langer. Nobody would ever know the precise details of what had happened that night, but it seemed that Langer had lured Craven into the freezer house to kill him, and that the frost animals had attacked their owner during the crime. The colonel had not been forestalled – he was good at killing – but he had been obliged to seek medical treatment for frostbite.

And it had been Shimming's belated discovery of this fact, hidden in a computerized medical report, which had set him wondering about the veracity of the long-dead colonel's deposition. It chastened Hobart to realize he had been allowed to get away from his hotel, and that he had actually been under long-range surveillance right up to the moment he entered the freezer house, even though the final outcome had been in his favour.

'I ought to thank you,' he said, getting to his feet. 'If it hadn't been for you . . .'

'Forget it.' Shimming extended his hand. 'I've had the pleasure of putting a couple of department politicians in their places. Come back and see me any time.'

'Thanks.' Hobart shook hands and paused awkwardly. 'I'd like to come back, but they've assigned me to the *Langer Maple* – on the Sigma Draconis run – which means . . .'

'A three- or four-year round trip for you, but forty years for me on Earth. I'll most likely be dead when you get back.'

'I wasn't going to put it like that.'

'Don't worry about it.' Shimming laughed, almost brutally, and for an instant his eyes resembled those of

Dorcie Langer – suspicious, resentful, hostile. 'If I'm not worried about it, why should you be?'

Hobart nodded, his sense of alienation complete, then turned and left the office, already wondering how he was going to get through the month that lay ahead before he could rejoin his own kind and take flight among the stars.

ALSO BY BOB SHAW IN PANTHER SCIENCE FICTION

THE CERES SOLUTION

'Powerful, subtle . . . his best novel so far'
The Times

Embittered and cynical, Denny Hargate is doomed to spend his days in a wheelchair. But one day he sees a beautiful young woman make a strange and elaborate sign in the air – and vanish!

He is Terran. She is Gretana ty Iltha, an observer from the distant world of Mollan. They were not supposed to meet.

When they do, the resulting culture shock cuts both ways . . . with explosive results!

'After Ballard himself, Bob Shaw is the nearest we've got to a home-grown Great'
The Observer

'SF whose glow not only illuminates the mind but warms the heart'
The Times

'Outstanding: unusually well-written, well-paced, economically and stylishly constructed . . . Shaw creates a new viewpoint from which to reflect upon the human, or rather, more particularly, Terran condition'
Times Literary Supplement

£1.50